THE
DRAGON
IN THE
WHITES

A LIAM TRYGGVISON ADVENTURE - BOOK I
A NOVEL BY

TIM BAIRD

The Dragon in the Whites is a work of fiction. Names, places, and incidents are either products of the author's imagination or are used fictitiously.

Book cover design and layout by Ellie Bockert Augsburger of Creative Digital Studioswww.CreativeDigitalStudios.com

Edited by Tom Willkens

Author photograph by Samantha Melanson
www.samanthamelanson.com
Used with permission. All rights reserved.

PART ONE
IN THE LAND OF FIRE AND ICE

Chapter One
The Camp

It was a day like any other in Iceland: cold and wet, with a strong breeze coming in from the sea. A young boy named Tryggvi Brynjarson was exploring the tiny island of Vestmannaeyjar with his father and the other men. His father, Brynjar, was one of Ingolfr Arnarson's finest warriors. Brynjar had brought his family along when Ingolfr had decided to settle on the southwest coast of the newly claimed land. While arduous and dangerous at times, the explorers eventually settled in a natural inlet of the island and established the village of Reykjavik.

It had taken several days of sailing, but the group arrived at Vestmannaeyjar with the help of a strong, healthy wind. They came in search of new plants, animals, and anything else useful. The Norsemen were curious as to what may lie on this volcano laden chunk of rock sitting off in the ocean. By choosing to settle in a remote location such as Iceland, the Vikings had to give up the small luxuries available to them back home and be content with scavenging the land and compromising their tastes.

However, Tryggvi was not thinking about what types of fauna and flora may be found on this desolate expanse of earth. While mature for his age, he was still a young kid whose attention was easily diverted by fun and excitement. He had just received his first real weapon from his father, a well-worn and hard-used, but reliable feeling, short sword. It was only about a foot and a half long, but it was very sharp. The blade had been in his family for many generations, and the sides of the blades featured a string of runes depicting the many brave men who had once carried it. It had been Brynjar's first sword when he was growing up, and now it would be Tryggvi's. The grip felt smooth and proper in his hand, wound tightly with reindeer leather and worn smooth from years of use. A small hilt protected the wielder's hand from an opponent's blade, something that could save you in the right moment.

Running madly through the tall grass in the field near the shore, Tryggvi hacked and slashed at illusory foes and mythical beasts which made the mistake of crossing paths with him. Dragons, minotaurs, evil knights, centaurs, and countless champions of evil fell before his mighty attacks. He had often watched the older men of the village practice their swordplay and would lie awake at night replaying their moves in his head. He now swooped low at the base of the plants, struck high towards the spikelet and seed heads, and roll beneath imaginary counter-attacks. His father had said that he was too young to fight for real, but promised to help him practice with his newly gifted sword when the time was right. In the meantime, these tall blades of grass would have to do.

A shout from the distance roused Tryggvi from his play. "Tryggvi! Tryggvi, my son, where have you wondered off to now? Come back to camp and grab some food while the meat is still hot."

Tryggvi had completely lost track of time and was almost out of breath from swinging the steel blade around for so long. He would have to practice more and build a strong body to wield it. He looked down at the blade and found it to be covered in green chlorophyll and plant matter from all of the foes that he had vanquished. He carefully wiped the blade clean on the end of his cloak before sliding into the sheath on his belt. Looking happily upon the mess that he had made, Tryggvi smiled to himself, turned, and ran in the direction of his father and his awaiting supper.

As he approached the camp, his nose perked up at the hearty scent of roasting meat and some form of root-based stew hanging over the roaring fire. Before entering the circle of men seated around the roaring fire, he stopped to take in the scene in front of him. Several of the men were squabbling over whose spoils were the grandest, while several were standing up and demonstrating fighting techniques and told stories of battles long ago. While Tryggvi didn't understand much of the context behind the stories, he did enjoy the lively acting and jovial storytelling.

Sitting down beside his father, he launched into a string of questions about the hunt: What had they seen? Where did they go? What did they get? His father, amused by the boy's enthusiasm, chuckled and began to count off the more exciting details of their exploration: three goats, two small birds called "puffins," and a collection of tough roots. The goat now rotated around a makeshift spit above the fire, while the puffin and roots were boiling in a kettle for a stew to be eaten later. His father handed him part of a goat leg, which Tryggvi graciously accepted and began to devour.

The trip from the mainland had been long and cold, and food was not always guaranteed to be around in this cold land that they had decided to settle. The Saxons and Celts, whom his father had fought in many battles, were not rugged enough to handle this land. But they were Vikings: tough, stubborn, and adaptable to anything. For Tryggvi, the hot and delicious goat meat had almost made this trip bearable.

As the group enjoyed their meal for the evening, Brynjar recounted the day's exploits. The men had rowed around most of the small island, which took the better part of a couple of hours, even for its minute size. They observed birds settling in nests on the cliff walls, nestled close as they braved the harsh and unrelenting weather. They observed several caves worn into the rock by countless years of erosion by the brutal wind and pounding waves. Several of the men within the group even claimed to have seen orcas surfacing near their boats as the animals hunted in groups close to the shoreline.

Tryggvi was entranced. Each man around the fire had his moment in the forefront of the storytelling and would captivate every ear in the circle until he was done. Tryggvi couldn't wait until he was older and stronger and could go off on missions such as these. For now, however, his father urged him to enjoy his childhood while he could. Playing, learning, and growing strong were his only responsibilities for the near future.

After the men had cleaned up the mess from their dinner, Tryggvi went into their shelter to lie down, but was having trouble falling asleep. Despite a long day of playing around the campsite, he was still too excited about his new sword and thoughts of adventure. In addition, in this part of the world, it was almost the summer solstice, and the sun remained in the sky for most of the day. With the solstice only a day away, you could possibly miss the sunset if you blink as it dipped below the horizon. Lying under his deerskin blanket inside the shelter his father had erected, Tryggvi stared up into the sky above through an opening in the flap, dreaming of future adventures, battles, and tales that had yet to be written. While he eventually fell asleep, it was not before several hours of thinking, wondering, and pondering the great unknown.

The next morning came and went as the past few mornings had on this trip. The men would dig some meat out of the salt barrels and cook it over the fire for breakfast. As the warm, savory scent filled the air, the stragglers would make their way towards the central fire. It was hard to remain asleep once the intoxicating aromas of yesterday's kills began to tickle the senses in your nose. After everyone had eaten their fill and warmed up their muscles from the cold sleep during the night, they would venture out into the wild again in search of food, sod, timber (which was very scarce), and anything else of interest that they may stumble upon. While these trips offered the promise of interesting and tale-worthy adventures, most of the trips were often somewhat boring.

Tryggvi, being the youngest out of the group at only ten years old, was tasked with staying behind in the camp and keeping the fire going while the men were gone. With the ever-present chill on the wind, it was important to have a warm fire ready upon their return to cook the meat and stave off the chill. Although it was summer, the island was still extremely cold due to the pummeling North Atlantic winds. Tryggvi, unlike most children his age, felt honored by his duty. While tedious at times, he knew that tending to the fire helped to keep his people alive and safe. As the day passed, the men wandered back into camp one or two at a time. Each man, at his eager request, stopped to show Tryggvi their finds from the day. Many were now preparing the carcasses and food for dinner around the fire, anxious to fill their bellies and warm their spirits.

One of the men regaled the group with the tale of a tremendous view he had seen from the top of the crater ridge on the west side of the camp. Rising above their camp, as they had settled within its protective walls, was a massive semi-circular mountain side. The ridge appeared to be the blown out remains of a massive volcanic explosion that must have happened eons ago after the island's birth in the middle of the Atlantic Ocean. The highest point soared up several hundred feet into the sky. Everyone around the fire listened with uninterrupted attention.

Tryggvi had climbed mountains, hills, and glaciers back at home, but he had always been with his father or another some older member of his adventurous family. He had not yet, however, had the opportunity to venture out on his own during this trip. His father worried that he would get hurt or into trouble on his own and requested that he stay close to the camp to "look after things" as he was told. He knew what that really meant.

The men, at least, continued to share their colorful narratives. He heard about the families of goats roaming the hillside, huge breeding grounds of puffins burrowed into the side of the hills, and the vast, endless expanse of ocean on the other side. From what they had said, you could see the mainland on one side, but then absolutely nothing but ocean and horizon on the other. The seas stretched out into the distant nothingness, begging to be explored.

During the storytelling, Brynjar had returned and sat near his son while his friends were describing something that they had seen on their travels that day. While settling himself in on a large, flat stone, the elder Viking listened to a detailed description of a small beach at the bottom of a hill. They said that while exploring the top of the ridge above the camp, they had worked their way around the curve of the volcanic ridge to look for signs of approaching weather, available food to hunt or forage, and any signs of other humans. While scanning the ocean, one of the men spotted a long stretch of gravel heading down the hill. It had created a trail of sorts and was surrounded by the small holes in which the puffins burrowed. At the base was a small beach enclosed by rocky walls, where the air was quiet and the water was calm.

Tryggvi was half-listening and half-daydreaming about climbing the volcano's remains and exploring the beach. Unable to wait another second, he asked his father in a whisper if he could go explore it.

"Perhaps next time, my son. I am sorry, but it is already growing late, and we must leave early in the morning if we are to make it to shore before the next nightfall," Brynjar said. "There will be plenty of time for adventures in the future, just you wait and see," he added with a wink. Brynjar was the leader, and his men saw him as strong and unyielding. But he secretly found it hard to say "no" to his daring and ambitious son.

"Brynjar," one of the men said from across the roaring fire, "do you think that we'll see another one of your dragons on this trip?"

As a barely perceptible smirk crept across the hardened features of the leader's face, the elder man gave him a quick wink. "Magnus, I don't know. They typically only appear to the bravest and mightiest of warriors."

Hearing the word "dragons" alone made the young boy perk up, but picking up on the implication of his words, Tryggvi immediately spoke up. "Dragons? Here, on this island? Dad, do you think that I'll get to see a dragon?!"

"I'm not sure, son. Dragons come to those who are brave, strong, pure of heart, and in need of their help... or, they appear before the evil of heart and seek to extinguish their dark taint from this world. If you find yourself upon a dragon, you best hope that you are among the former."

"I am a good boy, honest!" shouted the young Tryggvi, to the laughter of the men in the circle. Jumping up from his seat at the

CHAPTER TWO
THE DISCOVERY

With a confused look on his face, Tryggvi curiously watched his father walk away from the shelter and towards the other men. While he firmly believed that his dad had just given him indirect permission to leave the camp and explore during the night, he was still skeptical. Brynjar very rarely broke his position of prim and proper authority when the other men were around, so it could be a trick. However, that cheerful wink made Tryggvi believe the offer was sincere.

As the minutes slowly passed by, Tryggvi decided to take the risk and explore the island on his last night here. The fire was dying down as the men drank their ale, exchanging stories of battles, mead hall fights, and hunting trips. One man even claimed to have seen a sea monsters while sailing. In between obviously exaggerated tall tales, the group planned their return trip back to the mainland. The men had had their fill of this island and were anxious to sleep in their own beds back home.

Tryggvi, meanwhile, could barely contain his excitement over his recent gift. His very own horn! He now had both a ram's horn and a short sword. Slowly but surely, he was becoming a man. One day, he would join the ranks of warriors and explorers. With the gift of the signaling horn, Brynjar obviously wanted him to go exploring before they sailed for home. A chance like this was something that Tryggvi was not going to pass up.

It was the night of the summer Solstice and the Sun would just barely dip below the horizon in the western sky at midnight. All his life, Tryggvi had watched the sun set at night and rise hours later in the morning. To see the sun rise back up in a matter of seconds was an event that he could not miss! He could explore the volcano crater all night long without the need for a torch and see his way as clearly as if he were walking in the afternoon sunshine. The risk of getting into trouble, at least from his father, which he highly doubted at this point in time, was well worth this once-in-a-lifetime chance.

Quietly gathering his cloak, sword, and horn, he crouched low in the doorway of the shelter. Seeing none of the adults glancing his way, he stealthily snuck out and crept away from the encampment. Remaining low to the ground, he made sure to keep their shelter between him and the campfire as he slinked off into the distance.

Looking around to get his bearings straight, he began his adventure by heading towards the base of the crater. The walls were massive, and seeing the crater from afar was entirely different than looking around from inside. He could have fit his entire village within this geological monstrosity. The unimaginably destructive volcanic explosion that had torn the mountain apart must have been tremendous to remove that much of the earth and rock. Not wanting to waste time, he decided to continue his sightseeing from up on top.

Moving soundlessly towards the genesis of the incline up the crater, and away from the prying eyes of the men back at the camp, Tryggvi made his way to the goat trails. Creeping up the trails and staying low in the rocks and grasses, so as not to be seen, he began his ascent towards the peak.

As he soon found out, it was much higher than it appeared from far away. Perspective is a funny thing, and it can easily trick a young, curious mind. Although in good shape for a boy of his age, his small legs still had a hard time navigating the rocky terrain. Large rocks, deep berms, and tall grasses littered his path, forcing him to take many detours and circumnavigate the unpredictable geological features. It took an hour to reach the summit ridge, and he was feeling quite winded by the end of the climb.

Upon reaching the pinnacle, Tryggvi took in the view with amazement. Endless miles of ocean stretched out before him into the unknown western expanse. Turning to the south, he saw nothing but water, waves, birds, and the faraway horizon. From what he had been told, no Viking had ever been out that far. Seeing these things for the first time stirred up feelings of fear, excitement, and anticipation. There were talks within the village of someday traveling out past the horizon to see if more land existed beyond Iceland, but there were no concrete plans in place, just yet.

The tenderfoot dreamed that once the new village was settled more permanently, and his people itched for further adventuring and exploring, that he would be old enough to join them and do his part. He was shaken from his daydream by a ferocious gust of wind blowing in off of the water. From where he stood, there was nothing blocking him from the open water and the fierce wind that whipped up off of it. Despite being a hardy lad and conditioned by years of exposure to the cold, he shivered a little bit, albeit briefly. He grinned at the thought and speculated how cold it must be to have elicited that feeling.

Looking down to the bottom of the slope and the rocky beach where the water lapped at the rocks and sand, he could see icebergs floating further out in the water below him. Having spent most of his life so far in southern Norway, he hadn't seen many icebergs, but was not surprised at all by how much colder it was at this higher latitude. While the icebergs would often melt as they drifted further south, they roamed freely up here in the northern waters. They followed the ocean currents as they continued their slow journey throughout the ocean.

Hearing some noise and rustling nearby, Tryggvi crouched down behind the nearby tall grasses and peered around. A few feet away, in the grass and rocks around him, a family of wild goats was walking the rocky paths from one grazing area to another, perhaps in search of a cave or outcropping to hide from the cold wind. He watched them for several minutes until they spotted him and, startled, fled in the opposite direction.

Gazing down near the shore at the crashing waves and rocky terrain, Tryggvi soon spotted the hidden cove that the older warrior had described earlier at the fire. Down below him to the left, a wall of rock jutted up from the dark blue water to create a natural shelter which blocked off a small area of sandy beach and a calm pool of water from the ocean outside. Within this tiny cove, the water was still and relaxed, and its surface reflected the surrounding hillside like a mirror. Providing nature protection, it attracted a variety of birds, fish, and seals, which occasionally disturbed its glasslike appearance as they played in the water. There was a good chance that none of these animals had ever encountered a human being before, and he wondered if they would even fear his approach.

This adventure was exactly what his blossoming and inquisitive mind had hoped for on this trip. He was eager to reach the cove and imagined all the fun he would have before heading back home. Realizing that he had lost track of time, and the fact that part of this trip was to witness the rise and fall of the non-setting Sun later in the evening, he looked back to the west to see the position of the celestial entity. Given the position of the Sun on the horizon now, it looked like it was already back on the rise. "I missed it!" Tryggvi muttered to himself. While he may have blundered this portion of the expedition, it was still impressive to watch it rising at such a late hour in the night. Based on its angle in the sky and what he understood of astronomy, he estimated that it was around two o'clock in the morning. If that were true, then the adults back in the camp would wake in a matter of hours. It was time to get to the cove.

Looking for a clear path to the bottom of the slope, he was surprised to find that there was no easy way down. A colony of puffin holes extended down to his right for several hundred feet. He could tell by the small holes pocketing the hillside and the swarms of small black flies hovering a few feet above the grass. He had investigated a few of the peculiar bird's nest tunnels the other day near the camp and was familiar with their tell-tale signs. Off to his left, however, was a slide of gray-white gravel that stretched almost the entire length of the hill to the far end of the cove.

Deciding that this was a substantially quicker way down to his goal, Tryggvi set off through the grass to the top of the rock slide.

Upon reaching the top of the rock slide, he quickly came to terms that it was much higher up than it had looked from the top of the crater's ridge. The rock slide appeared to go down all the way to the beach cove, meaning that he would be doing a combination of walking and sliding down an almost one-thousand foot declination. The rocky terrain to either side of the slide meant that he either carefully and slowly made his way to the bottom, or he risked his neck on a dangerous but faster option. The former was safer, but would take far too long. If he wanted to pull this off without getting in trouble, he would have to take the fast way down.

Taking a deep breath and building up his courage, Tryggvi stepped forward onto the gravel and began his journey down the slope. Things were going well for the first few minutes of his experimental run. He took careful, measured steps and tried to limit how much he let each foot slip in the flowing stream of rocks. He smiled as he continued, happy to see that his risk was paying off. That was, of course, until the gravel started to move around him more rapidly. More importantly, he noticed that the rocks and sand were sliding down behind him and a larger volume of the slippery rock surface was pouring down around his feet while he tried to walk. Trying to walk soon turned into trying to not fall down, slide down on his backside, nor become buried in dirt and rock. As the gravel gave way and slid faster down the hill, Tryggvi soon found himself out of control and unable to maintain his balance. He began tumbling down through the sand and rocks; feet-first in the beginning, rolling sideways after a few seconds, and soon he was flying head-over-heels as his tumble turned into a full-blown cartwheel down the hill.

Throughout all of this, he valiantly tried to maintain control over his body, especially his head, and his array of new equipment. Despite the scrapes, cuts, and bruises that he was conscious of acquiring as he rapidly descended down the slide, he was cognizant of the fact that this could destroy his new horn. Additionally, he was not used to having a weapon strapped to his hip, and feared that he might kill himself on his sword alone. He wasn't about to break his newly acquired horn in this unfortunately graceless debacle, nor was he interested in impaling himself upon his own blade. If he kept this up for any longer, though, he might not have a choice in the matter as either or both options became more relevant.

Realizing that doom may very well be a tumble or two away, Tryggvi decided to put an end to it. Seeing a whirling blur of green and brown color getting closer and closer to him with each passing revolution, he recognized that he was rapidly approaching a small bush down to his right. Reaching out desperately, he managed to grasp the base of the plant and hold on with all of his might. The sudden stop was not without trouble, however, as the instantaneous stop jerked his arm upward and put immediate and violent strain on the bush, its roots, and the ligaments in his shoulder and elbow. As the hillside was covered in an extremely thin layer of soil and moss, he instantly ripped the bush's roots from the earth and thin covering of organic matter. The jerky motion whipped him up into the air, and he spun around before and crashing into the sand below. His vision blurry, he found himself to be very tired all of a sudden, and darkness overtook the world around him.

After what felt like hours, Tryggvi awoke. He was staring up at the hill that he had just fallen down. From his new vantage point, the hill appeared much taller than he previously believed. The sky was also much brighter. He counted the puffy clouds drifting by overhead, and he suddenly remembered where he was and what he was supposed to be doing. Still holding the small bush in his hand, he looked up at the divot where he had ripped it out of the ground. The bush had saved him from falling straight down to the bottom and slowed him down just enough to only get bruised and a little banged-up on the landing.

Thankfully, the fall had only injured his pride, and he was very glad that there were no witnesses to this exploit. If any of his friends back home had seen this plunge of his, he'd have been the brunt of their jokes for a while. He would be sore for a few days but he had at least made it down in one piece.

After a few more minutes of rest, Tryggvi stretched out his muscles and built up the strength, and dignity, to try to stand up again and get back on his feet. Looking around, he took in the beauty of his hidden sanctuary. The sand here was packed firmly from the lapping waves that rose to this level during high tide. The untrodden ground was smooth and pristine.

The rocks rose high above, at least three times his height, and the sun shone brightly down inside. Despite the vast ocean on the other side of the rocks, he could barely hear the waves or howling wind. Grasses grew in the sunny spots, and birds flocked to feast on fish and bugs in the placid water. This was the most relaxing place he had been since leaving his native land. It was a shame that he had to head back so soon.

Not wanting to waste another minute, Tryggvi began to walk around the cove and observed the plant and animal life as he explored. There were various small flowers and bushes growing, several species of grasses, a collection of small sea birds and puffins, as well as a mixture of fish schooling in the shallow water gently lapping the shore. In the water, he could see an assemblage of igneous rocks formed from spewing molten lava during the volcanic creation of this island. The strange beauty of the volcanic rocks never ceased to amaze him. Each one was unique and a wonder to behold. All in all, this was a neat area and he was glad to have stumbled upon it, even if it had hurt a little in the process.

Glancing up to the sky above, he noticed that the sun had risen even higher over the horizon, meaning that the morning hours were approaching quickly and his exploration time was rapidly coming to an end. The men would soon rise to restart the fires and make breakfast. He should start heading back soon if he wanted to see anything else on this part of the island and still make it back in time to not be noticed.

As he turned to walk back towards the hill, he noticed an indentation in the rock face off to the side that looked curiously out of place. Walking a little closer, it appeared to be not just an indentation, but possibly the entrance to a small cave. Inquiring as to what might be in there, he quietly approached and almost stuck his head into the area. Brave as he might be, he was wary of unknown spaces and decided to draw his blade for the first time. Firmly gripping his fingers around the leather-wrapped handle, he extracted the weapon from its sheath. He cringed at the light scraping sound it made on the way out, as part of the steel had contacted one of the small rivets holding the leather together.

Gathering his courage, he extended his sword beyond the edge of the mouth of the cave and slowly rounded the corner to peer inside. As his eyes passed the edge of the mouth of the cave, his eyes quickly gathered in all of the information and relayed it to his brain to process. The opening was about five feet deep, four feet tall, and just wide enough for him to walk through without bumping his elbows. From what he could tell, it was empty aside from a few rocks and pebbles on the floor. Laughing to himself, Tryggvi slid the sword back into the sheath and allowed himself to relax.

Looking more closely around the bottom of the cave, one of the stones immediately captured his attention. He noticed that this stone appeared to be very different from the others nearby. It was ovular in shape, as wide as his waist, and too thick for him to fully wrap both hands around it. Its speckled surface had an alluring blue-green tint. Intrigued, he picked the stone up and found it surprisingly lightweight given its size. He walked it back to the water's edge to wash off the sand, algae, and debris that had accumulated on it over time. Once clean, the stony surface shone brilliantly and glowed in the early morning sun. He decided to keep it as a souvenir.

Turning back towards the hill, Tryggvi pondered how to best climb back up to the top of the ridge. It was clear that he couldn't go back up the way that he had come down. The steep rockslide was unforgiving and would not be an easy, nor productive, ascent. To the right of the slide was a nearly sheer rise of rock and would have to be climbed by hand and feet together. As he was still tired from the beginning of this adventure and now had the rock to carry, he ruled this option out immediately. However, to the left of the rockslide there was a hill that rose steadily up to the top, the one that he had seen before with the puffin holes. While he had concerns about potentially damaging some of these burrows of the funny little birds, it was his best way back up. Taking a deep breath, he began his long climb upward.

Several minutes into this hike, he began to regret bringing the stone. It was light enough to carry for a boy his size, but heavy enough to drain his energy reserves as the trip progressed. The journey was made more difficult by the constant bombardment of tiny flies that buzzed angrily around the colony. Attracted to the carbon dioxide in his breath, the innumerous pests attacked him from all angles as he struggled to climb the steep incline of grass and moss. They got in his eyes, his nose, and some even found their way into his mouth. He swatted at the ones that he could with his free hand, but still many others advanced and dove towards his face. Several times, he had to spit to clear his mouth of the aerial vermin. He cursed them under his breath as he picked up the pace. Dodging flies and trying not to step on puffin holes, he was glad to reach the top of the ridge within an hour since leaving the cove below.

Looking down at his clothes, he found himself to be covered with squashed flies and spots of blood. The flies must have been busy this morning, as he was now covered in their stolen meals from the animals on the hillside. He'd need to clean up later before anyone saw his clothes and asked too many questions. Scanning the horizon once more, he took in the awesome views of the land and boundless miles of ocean stretching out before him. With one last glance, he headed back down the ridge towards the camp below.

His descent was uneventful. The goats from before had scurried out of sight, and he passed only a few startled-looking puffins as he ran down the path. Once at the base of the hill, he swiftly snuck back towards the shelters of the sleeping men. He heard some random grumblings and sounds of movement from some of them, but he had managed to get back in time before anyone was outside to spot him. Heading towards the shelter that he shared with his father, he found a pocket in one of their packs with enough room to hide the stone. After stowing it away and securing the flap so that it wouldn't be seen, Tryggvi stealthily crept back inside the shelter, changed his shirt, and lay down to sleep. His father stirred briefly as he ruffled the animal hides upon entering, but for the most part, his secret adventure appeared to have gone unnoticed and was a success. Exhausted from the long trek and midnight hike, he quickly slipped into a deep, albeit short, sleep.

In no time at all, his father was already waking him up for breakfast. It seemed as if he had just fallen asleep, but the sun was a little higher in the sky than he had remembered from before, so he must have gotten at least a few hours of sleep. The other men were finishing their meals and preparing their packs for the journey back to the boats. While chewing on leftover grains and reheated puffin meat from last night, he glanced over to see his father looking into the top of the pack where he had stashed the stone. Brynjar peeked inside, saw the stone, and smiled. He looked back over at Tryggvi with a curious, but knowing, look on his face and gave him a nod. He didn't know what exactly his son had been up to since speaking with him last, but he knew that Tryggvi had at least gotten a chance to stretch his legs and explore on his own. As a natural explorer himself, few things gave Brynjar more pride than sharing such experiences like this with Tryggvi. Not having more time to spend with his son one-on-one, as he was the leader of his men and had many duties, was his only regret in life.

After breakfast was done, everyone joined in to clean up the camp and disassemble the shelters. The gear was securely packed onto their carts, and the men made their way back to the boats on the far side of the small island. The journey only took about an hour, given the light weight of the loads that they carried and the small diameter of the islet, and they were on their way soon afterwards.

As they sailed back to the mainland, Tryggvi's heart swelled with happiness from the fun times that he had had on this exploration with his father. He would soon become a man, and he longed to join his father on bigger and more dangerous trips. As the ships plowed through the waves and the wind pushed their sails, the young boy's thoughts drifted back to the stone. Staring over the side of the ship into the deep blue water below, he wondered what type of rock it was and where it had come from. It would be something to look into later during his studies when he had a chance someday.

Chapter Three
The Mission

Tryggvi looked around at the assembled boats in the harbor with renewed vigor. It had been ten long years since that trip to the Vestmannaeyjar Islands, and he was now a fully grown man and a prominent member of his village. As he had grown older, stronger, and more mature, he accepted new responsibilities within the village and served as his father's page in their most recent explorations in and around Iceland. As the years had passed, he had continuously studied, practiced, trained, and developed superior sword handling and horsemanship skills. He was several years ahead of the other boys of Reykjavik in terms of experience and education and was beginning to find his place among the older men.

Now, the men and women were preparing for another expedition, this one bigger and bolder than anything that he had participated in thus far, let alone heard of others doing before him. While Tryggvi had been on plenty of voyages around the coast of Iceland to discover new harbors, lands to try to grow on, and mountains to explore, he was going on his first trip to a newly discovered land. He had traveled last summer with his father to Greenland, but only for a short time. The land there was cold and barren, and they had opted to return home instead of remaining behind with some of the volunteer settlers. While Greenland was interesting and unusual, it never felt like home while he was there.

However, new rumors were rapidly spreading around the village. Ever since the boats of his kinsmen had recently scraped back into the gravel shoreline earlier that spring, a new land had been on the lips and ears of everyone in the settlement. The adventurers had just returned from a great voyage and were eager to share their stories. According to tales whispered in the mead hall late at night, some of these travelers had immediately decided to keep going west as they had not been content with the cold, icy land. They sailed for many days under full sail and oar and found a large expanse of undiscovered land. They followed its coast to the south and kept on going. They found no foreseeable end to this coastline, and the temperatures only grew warmer as they traveled onward.

By the accounts that Tryggvi had heard, one of the boat captains deemed this discovery important enough to turn around. They delivered their findings to the settlement on Greenland, and now, in turn, back to Reykjavik. From there, the stories had naturally spread like wildfire.

Everyone in the village spoke of new trees, plants, animals, metals, gems, nuts, berries, and other wonderful foodstuffs sounding increasingly more appetizing than the fish and sheep that they typically lived on in their frigid environment. Rumors of the untamed lands grew more exaggerated as they spread. Depending on how late into the night it was (and how much mead had been poured from the barrels), the stories grew more outlandish by the hour. Throughout all of this, though, two things were certainly true: the new land was warm, and there would be more than enough food for everyone. For these reasons, the village prepared for travel.

It took many months of hard work that summer by everyone in the village, even those who did not intend on travelling. By the arrival of autumn, when the days grew dark and the air never quite seemed to warm up regardless of how hot the sun burned in the sky, a new fleet had gathered in the harbor. While some of the ships came from neighboring villages, many were custom built specifically for this journey. Tryggvi and his father helped build and test a number of boats designed for the challenges that they anticipated encountering. These boats had longer and wider hulls to carry more crew and supplies, deeper keels for staying upright in rough waves, and collapsible roofs to provide shelter at night.

The roofs would be closed easily each night to help hold in the body heat of the sleeping crew, as well as provide extra protection during stormy weather. After countless hours of labor, the crafts were finished and safely stored for the upcoming voyage in the spring.

As winter set in, the men, women, and children alike of Reykjavik either busied themselves with cooking and preserving food for the travels, packing their families and belongings together if they were leaving, or manufacturing tools, weapons, and other gear needed by the expedition and its participants. While not all would leave on the trip, the mission became their common goal for the betterment of their own lives, and those of their descendants. The success of the village was the success of everyone, and new lands and resources would improve all of their lives in one shape or form.

As his mother had passed away several winters ago during an especially harsh storm, and he had yet to court and marry a wife of his own, it was only Tryggvi and his father in their house now. Despite their strong wills and fearlessness in battle, it was too quiet and lonesome for either man to bear. Moving on to a strange, new land appealed to them both. For Brynjar, it was a chance to put bad memories behind him and move on to a fresh chapter in his life. For Tryggvi, it was a chance to test his strength, will, and determination, and to prove to himself and his people that he was ready to join the ranks of the warriors in his clan. The completion of the voyage would mark the first step in his passage into manhood. His father was happy to help his son through these new experiences and yearned to see his boy become a man of the clan. Both were ready to leave Iceland behind and build new memories together.

As the winter melted away with the spring, the new boats were placed back into the water for retesting and final preparations.

With their water-tightness and overall functionality proven to be robust and reliable enough for their journey, the voyagers filled them with supplies and gear that had been painstakingly fabricated and assembled over the past year. The village had sacrificed much and wanted to see the travelers succeed in their quest. While these hardened Vikings thrived in the Icelandic cold, the prospect of a better life in warmer and easier climates with more easily obtainable food and building materials gave them renewed hope. Those who were leaving said their goodbyes to the others and gave away what they couldn't bring along.

Tryggvi had almost everything packed. All that remained were his clothes, weapons, and tools which he needed on a regular basis. He and his father were leaving their home and furniture to a cousin who was remaining behind. Their house was much like the others, dug into the side of a hill with rock walls, covered with timber joists, and layered with sod. The earth kept the men warm in the winter and cool in the summer, and the front door and two windows allowed for air to flow. It was a simple home for a simple life, but it provided the men with easy living and little maintenance. While some of the travelers were bringing their wood and hide huts along with them, the father and son had decided to build a new home from scratch upon their arrival wherever they decided to settle. If the rumors were true, there would be plenty of timber with which to construct a proper dwelling.

Looking through the items of his trunk, Tryggvi was pulling out the remaining clothes and blankets that he would be bringing on the voyage. He was leaving some of it behind as it was not needed and his cousin could probably find a better use for it. While some of it was important and would be hard to replace, a maximum of fifty pounds of equipment, gear, and clothing were allowed per person on the ships. The new boats, while spacious by seafaring standards, were still cramped, and storage was at a premium. Sacrifices had to be made to fit everyone safely and comfortably.

As he pulled out an old goat-hide blanket that he had made many years before, he noticed that there was an odd shape to the blanket and it weighed substantially more than he had expected it to. While the blanket was normally bulky from the patchwork of fur and hide, it seemed especially heavy in his hands. Placing the blanket onto his bed, he unrolled it and was astonished to find a surprise hidden inside. The stone! The stone that he had discovered in Vestmannaeyjar! It had been nestled inside the hide for who knew how long. "Woah! I completely forgot that I even had this!" he thought. Picking the stone up and feeling its heft in his hands, he remarked at how much lighter it felt now compared to his memory. Granted, it still had some good heft to it, but years of hard labor, training, and fighting had given the still blossoming young man strong muscles and a toned physique.

He was about to put the stone back down into the trunk, but he remembered the excitement he had felt upon discovering it all those years ago. He also noticed something unusual. It had been ten years since he last held the stone, but it seemed larger now, and the colors were a little different. While it had once been primarily blue and green, the stone's surface now had a reddish tint to it. And, crazy as it seemed, the stone almost felt warm to the touch. He did not know why, but he didn't want to leave it behind.

Knowing that his father would probably laugh at him for imagining such things, he decided to keep the discovery to himself. As it would be deemed imprudent to bring the stone along on this dangerous voyage, he decided to hide it amongst his belongings. As he was already approaching his maximum allowable weight and volume for cargo, he would have to be careful about how much else he brought and who saw him with it. He was becoming a leader amongst his people and needed to set a good example. But he was still young at heart. The stone was coming on the trip.

A month later, the boats were finally packed and ready to journey across the vast open ocean. It had taken a long time to load and test the vessels to ensure their soundness, but it was all worth it. The time had finally come for this bold group of explorers to start the next chapter of their lives.

The voyagers finished stowing away their belongings in the lower holds and getting themselves and their children ready for the journey. Farewells were shouted, gifts and mementos were exchanged, and hugs and embraces were shared aplenty. The unpredictable Icelandic weather was remarkably clear that day. The skies were bright, the sun's rays warmed all that they touched, and the waves gently lapped against the hulls and shoreline. With the boats loaded and the crew prepared to row out to where the sails could be efficiently employed, the group departed the shores of Reykjavik and headed west into the unknown.

As Brynjar was already seated and settled in with the men sharing their boat, Tryggvi spared a long moment and looked around the village one last time. He had made many memories here with his mother and father, but it was time to move on to somewhere else. With a heavy sigh, he firmly gripped the short rope ladder, climbed aboard the vessel, and shouted the order to start rowing. Within minutes, the boats were up to speed and disappearing into the distance.

CHAPTER FOUR
THE VOYAGE

It was cold. Bitterly cold. The spray of the icy water on his face chilled Tryggvi to his very bones. With each oncoming wave and gust of wind, the ships and their occupants were repeatedly pummeled from all directions. Flexing his hands occasionally, one at a time in between strokes of his oar, he noted that he could barely move his individual fingers anymore, let alone feel them. And to make matters worse, he was fairly certain that he had frostbite on his nose.

They had been on the open water for several days now, but each and every one of those days had been very long. The men and women took turns rowing to keep up their strength and speed. When they were lucky, the wind filled their sails and propelled them through the crests and troughs of the humongous waves. However, that very same wind also chilled the air and sapped the travelers of their heat.

Normal humans would have turned around by now and returned home. The safety of their cottages, the warmth of their fireplaces, and comfort of their beds would have had too much allure to make them quit this harsh experience. However, these were not normal humans. These were Viking men and women, and their children who were as strong-willed as the parents who brought them into this world.

They had passed beyond the point of no return on this journey and there would be no going back now. From what the previous explorers had said, it was about a week's sail from the western shores of Iceland to the eastern shores of Greenland. They hoped to see the coast sometime before the sun set tomorrow and get a chance to rest their muscles and restock fresh supplies.

"Shift change! Let's give these rowers a well-deserved break," Brynjar called out. While he admired their tenacity, he did not want anyone to burn themselves out in the middle of the ocean. His crew had been at it for hours and needed rest and nourishment if they were to remain productive. There were too few people on each boat to afford to lose any man or woman for too long due to fatigue or injury.

Tryggvi took his spot at his oar. Sitting down on the bench, he smiled at the fact that it was still warm to the touch from how long the last man had sat there. A little gross, perhaps, but comforting nonetheless as he settled his cold body into position. He repositioned his oar to better suit his body size and posture, set a good grip on the well-worn wooden handle, and began rowing in time with the others.

It only took a few strokes before the new team was in sync with each other and performing as one. The boat accelerated through the water and quickly built up velocity as they resumed their normal rhythm. Before long, they were back at their cruising speed and were well on their way to completing the first leg of the trip.

As night began to fall on the water, the boats came within view of the coastline. Despite their exhaustion, the welcome sight of dry land gave them the motivation that they needed to carry on. Following the light of the village fires, the navigator of each ship kept his or her crew on course. Within several hours, the last of the ships scraped into the shoreline with a satisfying crunch and came to a stop. Every man and women currently on shift jumped out, breathed a collective sigh of relief, and congratulated each other on a successful voyage. Several jumped off of their boats and knelt down on the ground to start kissing the soil. While these Vikings were naturally skilled at sailing the high seas, not all enjoyed such prolonged trips away from land.

In the excitement of reaching the shoreline, most of the children were awoken from the shouting and grinding sounds coming through the hull. Running to the edges of their boats and climbing over, some with the help of an adult, they started running around the beach, laughing and playing. Tryggvi and Brynjar, still catching their breaths, joyfully watched the children play. At the end of the day, this trip was all about them and their futures. If the adults of this expedition could pull this expedition off, it would provide the next generation and countless others to come with easier lives.

While they still had a long way to go before their journey was over, they had covered a considerable distance without losing a single sailor. Not that they hoped for that kind of loss, but it was to be expected from time to time in this way of life. Nor had they ran into any troubling weather, aside from some rough waves and the occasional rain shower. All in all, it had been very smooth sailing. Tryggvi looked to the stars above and thanked his ancestors for watching over him and his crew. It was dangerous to venture out into the unknown ocean like this, and he counted his blessings with every nautical mile that they travelled.

Glancing up and to his right, he spotted the North Star and admired how brightly it glowed tonight. He would often look up at it and think of his mother, as if she herself were the star and its bright, guiding light. As he stared at it a while longer, a troubling feeling nagged at the back of his mind. This trip had been easy... almost too easy. While he prayed for their good luck to continue, he feared that this was just the beginning and that the adventurers were about to have their resolve tested on the next leg of the trip.

The next several days went by uneventfully. After making their landing on that first night, the leaders of the expedition spoke with the members of the camp who were still awake at that point and spent the night catching up, sharing stories, and passing letters back and forth from family and friends on each side of the ocean. While most slept on the boats that first night, the next day was spent setting up a temporary camp further up the beach from where they first landed. In council that second night, the elders of the party decided to stay for several nights while everyone rested and regained their strength. They foraged what they could find on the nearby shore before venturing inland briefly, gathering what plant life they could. They didn't want to dig into their rations on the boats if it wasn't necessary, and they certainly didn't want to take away food and provisions from the settlers who were struggling to survive in this relatively new village.

Some of the men set out to do some hunting and see what kind of wildlife lived in this new land. In an impressive display of skill, and hunger, they slew and brought back the meat and hides of several seals, walruses, and reindeer. They were overjoyed with their success and relished the prospect of eating something other than fish and salted meats from back home.

The few days that they spent resting in their make-shift camp was exactly what the people needed. They hunted, gathered, played, swam (albeit briefly and accompanied by shrieks and shouts from the children as their parents tried to bathe them), and slept. They had pushed their bodies hard for over a week on the open ocean, and it was good to have some downtime.

Once the crew had rejuvenated themselves, they decided to move onward without further delay. They dismantled the shelters, packed the boats to the brim with more food and gear, and bade farewell to the villagers in the Greenland settlement. From that point on, they rose early each morning, sailed along the coastline as far as they could until sundown, and then set up camp again. It was slow going compared to sailing on the open water, but they wanted to ease back into the effort while charting and mapping the geological features and topography of this land. Any information gathered along the way would be beneficial not only to them, but to future travelers, as well.

Greenland, which most of the party had never seen before, was covered in steep mountain ridges rising out of the water, deep fjords cutting deeply into the mainland, and massive glaciers carving their way down from the mountains to meet the salt water at the coast. Colossal icebergs littered the waterways and crept out into the open expanse of the ocean. The crew had to carefully navigate around the icy behemoths as they navigated around the lower end of the island.

After a week, the shoreline moved progressively northward. After checking the stars with his astrolabe and consulting the adventurers from the first mission, Brynjar decided that they had gone as far west as was possible along the coast. While the sight of dry land was comforting to the people and allowed their cartographers to enhance the details and measurements of their charts, it was time to get back to exploring. Any further coastal navigation at this point would only take them further away from their goal. It was time to brave the open water again and seek out their destiny.

The crews spent one final night on the island to rest and plan the next leg of the trip. From what the other explorers had described, the next span of water was almost the same distance as they had traveled previously from Iceland to Greenland. Settling in for the night, the Vikings made themselves as comfortable as possible and prepared themselves, mentally and physically, for another hard week of sailing and arduous rowing. While it was hard to leave behind the inherent safety and comfort of having the sight of the nearby shore within their telescope lens, the prospect of charting new land and starting the next chapter of their lives was motivation enough to continue.

The following morning, the crews finished loading the boats once last time, secured their gear and provisions, and set out on the open ocean once more. Using the rising sun as their guide, they pointed their boats towards the southwest and took the wind as strongly as it would carry them. Setting the sails to full and rowing when needed to maintain a swift gait, the boats traveled at maximum speed to shorten the trip as much as possible.

All were anxious to find this newly discovered land and explore its riches, wonders, and new opportunities. The unanimous enthusiasm gave them the strength and fortitude to continue rowing at a furious pace. Tryggvi and Brynjar kept reminding the crews to slow down and pace themselves for the long voyage ahead, but it was hard not to share in their zeal. Now more than halfway to their destination, everyone was eager to see the trees and plant life, new animals to hunt and feast upon, and new mountains, lakes, and rivers to explore. A new life awaited every man, woman, and child in these boats, and they were ready to experience them.

The sun had risen and set five times now over the water. In both directions, the crew only saw endless expanses of dark blue ocean. However, they were making progress and their continued success was promising. If his astrolabe readings were correct, Brynjar was confident that they were heading in the right direction and making good time, considering the rough water and disagreeable wind that they were experiencing. While the rowing had slowed down from the feverish pace of the first day of this leg, the crews were still optimistic and rowing with great vigor. The air and water, although slow to detect, felt warmer and more alive as they pushed further south. This was the lowest latitude that most of these people had ever been, and they bristled with excitement.

Tryggvi had just gotten off of his most recent shift and laid face down on the side of the ship. Hanging his arm over the side, he allowed his hand to run in the rapidly passing water below the edge of the boat. The cool waters felt good on his heavily callused hands and helped to restore some moisture to his dry, chapped skin. While he had spent most of his life using tools and weapons, he was no stranger to having his palms covered in an impressive collection of calluses. However, this trip made his previous hands feel dainty and soft. He was pretty sure that he could grab one of the spiny sturgeons that they were sometimes catching with his bare hands and not even feel it. While seemingly childish in nature, this little act of reverie always cheered him up after a long and brutal stint at the oars. The calming water flowing quickly underneath and passing around and below his hands made him think back to simpler times as a young boy. He would do this on his father's ship as a young boy, back before he was counted on to row and help the crew. While he was a grown adult now, he had never lost his innocent youthfulness or enthusiastic sense of adventure.

Swinging his legs back around, he stood up on the main deck and dried his hands off on his cloak. Making his way to the stern, he checked on the food stores. They were running dangerously low on provisions and would need to make land within a few days to keep going. Based on their calculations, they should only have another day or so to go before making landfall. If the crew maintained their current pace and were fortunate enough to find favorable winds at their backs, they would reach their destination with food to spare.

Tryggvi reminded himself that landfall would not be the end of this adventure. The group would need to establish a new village. Food will need to be grown and hunted, and there would be no easy handouts from the village pantry. If they ran out of supplies too early and were not prepared to start producing their own, the people would quickly starve and make this whole trip pointless.

As the day slowly turned into night, the crews called it quits for the day and decided to conserve their energy for the next morning. They pulled in their oars and settled into the nightly ritual of cleaning up and securing the ship for another long, cold night. As it was too dangerous to navigate in the dark, each boat took down its sails and drifted in the current. This would sometimes set them a few miles off course in any random direction, but it was far safer than sailing blindly into the black morass of the North Atlantic night. Ropes were thrown from boat to boat so that they would remain connected during the downtime and prevent one or more of the small fleet from becoming separated from the group.

Wooden braces were set over each hull with hides pulled taut overhead, creating a roof over the deck on each craft. This provided the crews with shelter from the cold winds and held in some heat during the cold hours adrift. This was not the greatest way to sleep each night, but it was good enough for these hardened people. One crewmember of each ship kept watch over the area in two-hour shifts. This ensured that the rest could sleep through the night without fear. As each person settled in and huddled together under their blankets, the night enveloped them and all soon passed into slumber.

Well, most people quickly fell asleep. Amongst the crew, two of the members had difficulty falling asleep that night. More specifically, one did, and the other loved him too much to ignore his late night questioning.

"Dad, are you still awake?"

"Yes, son. Are you okay?"

"I think so," started the young man, "but I feel like something is wrong. Something that I cannot see in front of me, yet is there, looming in the background, ready to strike. It is as if a shadow is looming over our expedition, yet I cannot see what is causing that shadow."

"Are you telling me that you're a mystic now, my boy? Did you have some kind of premonition?"

"No! Not at all. I am a warrior, like you. I protect my people through bravery and strength, not by hiding in some cave breathing incense and smoke."

Chuckling quietly, the older man responded, "Now, I did not mean any offense. I was merely asking because I have had similar feelings in the past, especially before great battles or momentous events in our village's history. Call it a premonition, intuition, or something else. It could just be a pessimistic outlook on the situation coupled with a strong urge to be prepared for any and all outcomes."

In an unusual move for the younger man, Tryggvi was quiet for several minutes. Just as the father thought that his son had fallen asleep, he spoke up again. "Did you feel like this when you saw the dragon?"

"Ah, you remember that, do you? I had figured that you'd forgotten about the conversation."

"Forgotten? Heck no. I've been waiting for the day that you'd tell me. I just knew that you'd bring it up again when you thought that I was ready."

"You really are a remarkable young man, you know that?" replied the father, beaming. "Well, as it's quite late and I don't want to wake up the others, let me give you the abridged version then."

"It was about twenty years ago now, just before you were born. We were back home in Norway and under attack from a band of Germanic raiders. It had been a bitterly long winter, and they had come to steal our food and supplies to bring back to their village across the sea. While we probably would have tried to share had they asked nicely, they did not, and we answered their raid in kind."

"We had been holed up within the barricades encircling the village for several days when their attacks became more brazen. Instead of simply yelling and throwing things at the wooden walls, they began trying to light the wood on fire and shoot arrows through cracks in the embrasure. Mind you, our fortifications were rather simple back then, and not the sturdy structures that we build today."

"So what happened?! Where does the dragon fall into all of this?"

"I'm getting there, young one." chided the father, but with a smile on his face.

"After a day or two of them pressing their attacks more aggressively, we knew that we needed to take action or it would be the end of us. Several men had been killed, and a few arrows had come far too close to our personal homes in the center for anyone to appreciate. Additionally, we were running low on water."

"In between one of these attacks, we charged through the gate and rushed their encampment just over the hill from our village. Catching them by surprise, we clashed with their warriors and filled the air with the sound of steel on steel and the cries of the fallen. It was a glorious battle and many of our men went on to Valhalla that day in honorable combat. What we didn't know, however, was that the enemy had broken their troops into two separate camps. While we attacked the first one, the second group circled around us and closed in from behind."

"So what did you do?" asked Tryggvi, eyes wide in surprise at this previously untold bit of information.

"We did the only thing that we could do. We fought hard. And we fought bravely. Pushing towards the enemy group between us and our village, we fought our way towards the shelter of our walls and the reinforcements that were surely waiting for our signal to come out. But as we attempted to push onward, we were cornered into a small gulley where the stream ran through and found ourselves trapped between two clusters of angry enemy warriors."

"I watched as several of my closest friends fell to the attacks of the Germanic invaders. As I held my shield up to ward off an incoming volley of arrows, I looked up to the heavens and called to the Aesir. Pleading to Odin, I asked for his assistance. I prayed for him to save us, or at least the men around me. I would have gladly given my life that day if it meant that my brothers in arms would make it out alive."

"As I finished my prayer and looked back up over my shield, the enemies surged forward for what would surely be our final stand. As I braced myself for their onslaught, a great roar was heard all around us and a giant shadow loomed over the battlefield. Warriors on both sides froze in place and looked up and around to see what was happening. Confusion set in amongst the men as nobody could tell what had made the sound or blocked the light out during that last pass."

"So what was it?"

"It was a thing of beauty, my son. Pure beauty embodying pure rage. As we looked to the shadow passing high above the clouds, the source of the roaring plunged through the clouds and descended towards our group. It was a mighty dragon, as big as a house with a head full of teeth. The creature dove towards our battle and leveled out just above the enemies. As we were fearing that our time had come, the angel of death opened its jaws and belched stream after stream of fire upon the invaders. Those who were not instantly consumed by the flames were scattered in all directions as they fled their demise. The creature laid out a ring of fire encircling our band and drove off any further attacks on our position."

"And as quickly as the creature had arrived, it simply disappeared back into the sky. We never saw the dragon again, and we certainly never saw the invaders on our shores again. Ever since that day, their raids have hit villages up and down the coastline from that area, but never in that same spot."

"So do you know where the dragon came from? Where it went to? How did the dragon know to come to you, and why did it save just our people?"

"I do not know, son. We are not meant to know everything. I have always shown loyalty to the gods in combat, and they have shown their loyalty to me. Trust in the Aesir, my boy, and they will look after you. As for the dragon... I'm not sure of its connection to the gods. Is it a tool of their will, an ally to their cause, a god in itself, we may never know. What I do know, is that if you find yourself in the presence of a dragon, you best be on your best behavior and hope that it's friendly.

"Now, it is very late, my boy. Let's get some rest before the night is over. I have a feeling that tomorrow is going to be a very long day indeed."

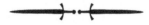

Tryggvi awoke with a start as he felt the boat shudder and grind to a violent halt. The boat pitched up on a slight angle, and several sleeping people near him rolled towards the back of the craft. Curious about what the hell had just happened out there, he pulled open the flap at the end of their makeshift quarters and exposed his eyes to the chilly night air.

It was bitterly cold, but sea was bathed in bright white moonlight. Looking over the side of the upraised boat, Tryggvi could see that they had run aground a massive sheet of ice. Apparently, they had drifted into an ice field during the night and were now surrounded by giant icebergs drifting in the cold sea around the entire fleet.

"Sir! It is all my fault!" shouted Gunnar, the man who was currently on-watch for Tryggvi's boat. "I was at the end of my shift and dreadfully tired. I must have fallen asleep and never saw the ice coming!"

"'Tis all right, Gunnar," replied Tryggvi, with an understanding tone. "The moonlight can play tricks on your eyes when you're tired. Besides, out of the whole fleet, nobody else noticed them either. Just get these people stable, and let's get the boat back in the water!"

Tryggvi found that nobody had been seriously injured. A few bumps and bruises were reported, mainly from the children who couldn't hold on as tightly during the crash. Overall, thankfully, they were safe. Just as he was breathing a sigh of relief for the good fortunate shown to his people, a chorus of panicked shouts of distress resounded from the vessels around them.

Out of the fleet of twenty boats, eight of them, in one manner or another, had run into ice. The other twelve now maneuvered through the black water to the aide of those in danger. Two of the former group were pitched up against the ice, while another two had run aground onto flat sheets and could easily be pushed off. However, the other four boats did not fare nearly as well.

In the dark distance, Tryggvi could see that one of the boats had capsized and showed no signs of movement from its occupants. Two others were sinking as their passengers and precious cargo spilled into the dark, freezing water. Men, women, and children clambered to hold onto anything around them that would float and keep them from submerging into the deadly cold sea.

Feeling helpless as he watched his people in the distance, Tryggvi rallied his crew together and organized a hasty, but sound, plan of action. Half of the crew jumped onto the ice and started pushing the boat while the other half steadied the craft with the oars. As the ship began to move, everyone jumped back inside and rowed with due haste in the direction of the screams. The water, at this time of night, was cold enough to kill a submerged person within minutes. If Tryggvi did not reach them in time, many friends and kinsmen would be lost.

It took careful navigating, but Tryggvi and his crew managed to get to the closest of the submerged crafts. Not wanting to get wet himself or endanger his crew members, he cast out ropes, extra wooden boards, and the ends of the oars into all directions. Anything that wasn't tied down suddenly became a rescue tool and was projected outward with the hopes of getting it into the hands of someone in danger. The moment that they saw someone struggling to stay afloat, something safe to grab onto was immediately offered.

They managed to pull everyone on board who had fallen from the first damaged boat. Unfortunately, though, all of the supplies were lost as they sank to the bottom. With his ship beyond safe capacity, Tryggvi called over other nearby boats to take some people and better distribute the weight. With the rescue of this vessel mostly in order, Tryggvi gazed around to see who else needed help. With a heavy heart, he noticed many people strewn about in the water several minutes of hard rowing away. Most of them appeared dead and lifeless in the dim light. He feared that their souls may have already been lost to the water before his crew had even begun to row towards them.

Shouting to the men and women on his oars, Tryggvi got them synced up and moving. Rowing as hard as they could with the extra weight on board, the ship soon approached the mass of wreckage, debris, and floating bodies. From what Tryggvi could tell, two separate blocks of ice had floated towards each other, trapping the unfortunate boat in between. The weight and momentum of the two icebergs smashed and shattered the boat's hull and decking. Splinters and shards of precious timber, harvested and worked by hand just months earlier, were scattered in the frigid sea around them. Many on the boat must have died in their sleep. This was a great loss for their village.

With great dismay, Tryggvi realized there was nobody left to rescue. Some people appeared to have died in the initial impact, while others had succumbed to freezing and drowning in the following minutes. Despite the gory scene playing out in front of him, he had to still think of the remaining people in his crew. Ordering anyone who was free to pull everything out of the water that they could salvage, he hoped to at least save some food and tools out of this to help the survivors.

Tryggvi scanned the area around them to see how the others were doing. Another group of ships had managed to pull everyone out and were passing goods around to even out the weight. With a glazed look in his eyes, he watched as several bodies began to sink below the surface of the water, passing beyond the point of rescue and forever lost.

One appeared to be an older boy, perhaps just a few years younger than Tryggvi. It was a stark shame to see such a young life lost in such a fruitless manner. This young man could have had long and prosperous life in their new community. He might have become a powerful warrior, a skilled craftsman, or a great hunter. To have his life cut so short, so close to their destination, seemed utterly pointless.

As Tryggvi contemplated what to do next, he swore that he heard coughing in the distance. He asked the crew to remain quiet, and, gazing around the boat, he heard it again. Asking one of his men to pass over a lamp, he shined the light out over the water. As the firelight played over the waves, he strained to look for any break in the water. To his surprise, the boy that he had just seen floating was now struggling to cough the water out of his lungs. He grabbed onto an overturned portion of the cracked shell of the boat. Without needing to be told, the crew quickly moved the boat into position and threw a rope out for the boy to catch. Grabbing on with strength beyond his age and physical condition, the boy began to climb onto the boat. He strained his muscles and clawed his way up the outer hull of the craft, but began to slip. With no time for hesitation, Tryggvi threw himself over the edge to grab onto the boy. Several crew members, sensing his intentions, swiftly advanced forward and grabbed onto his belt and legs as he shot out over the edge. Working together, the team plucked the boy from the water and brought him onto the deck of the boat.

Looking down at the shivering adolescent, Tryggvi removed his own cloak and wrapped it around his smaller body to stay warm. The boy looked up into Tryggvi's eyes with gratitude, grabbed hold of him, and passed out from exhaustion. Despite the heavy losses they had all suffered, the boy's rescue was enough to put a smile on Tryggvi's face and make him forget about all that had happened, even if only for a second.

Several hours later, the crew finished pulling everyone onboard the ships and were ferrying people and gear across the remaining vessels. The fleet was down four ships after the incident, so they'd need to carefully stow everything aboard the surviving ships to travel safely onward. Many who had dived into the water during the rescue efforts now tried to warm themselves up in the radiance of the rising sun. The group was glad to feel the warm rays kiss their skin, and their spirits immediately brightened.

With solar energy heating the crisp air around them, the crew continued to search for survivors and salvageable gear. As they were heading into the unknown, it was imperative to save any resources that they could. It was a grim job but necessary for survival.

After watching his people work tirelessly throughout the night and into the early morning, Brynjar had never been prouder to call himself a member of this community. While they had no houses yet to call their own, this was *his* village, and he beamed with pride despite the current circumstances. After scanning the waters around him for more icebergs, he drew his boat closer to the damaged vessels to inspect them for wood, nails, rope, and anything else of value. As the men and women worked nearby to haul everything in, he found himself to be absent mindedly gazing off to southwest. Without looking for anything in particular, he spotted an unusual sight in the distance.

The edge of the water had a green and brownish hue, and he swore that he heard the caw of birds in the far distance. Jumping from the edge of the boat that he was on, he leapt over to the one adjacent, his boat. Clambering over the oars and benches, he retrieved his bag. Grabbing his scope from its protective pouch, he raised the brass device to his eye and swung his attention back to the previous spot. Staring out at the horizon, he realized that he was staring at land.

"Land," he muttered to himself in disbelief. "Everyone!" he shouted. "Look to the southwest! We have found our destination. Our new home lies at the horizon!"

Every man, woman, and child jumped to their feet and grabbed onto the edge of the boats. Upon seeing the distant shoreline for themselves and confirming their leader's good news, an eruption of cheers and cries of joy rose throughout the fleet as everyone hugged and rejoiced. News traveled quickly to those below in the lower holds, who joined the others in celebration. While they were not entirely safe just yet, the end was within sight and their pending victory hung palpably in the air. The morning's disaster and loss of life had taken a heavy toll on many of the crew, and this was the discovery that they needed to keep going.

Allowing the crews to enjoy the moment and celebrate as one, Brynjar looked over at his son and smiled. After the cheering had finally died down, the leader ordered them to finish packing and get ready to move out. The sails were raised, the oars extended, and the fleet was back in motion within a few minutes. Never before had the crew rowed with such coordinated vigor. By the end of that day, all sixteen surviving ships slid safely onto the rocky beaches of the long-awaited new land.

With a satisfying toss of his rope line to one of his men, Tryggvi's boat was secured, and he looked to his father in the boat next to him with a large grin on his face. The two men beamed at each other as the weight of their achievement sank in. Unwilling to waste any time, and wanting to keep up their momentum, Brynjar issued orders to get the gear out and the crew to safety on dry land. It had been a long journey, but they were now safe and ready to begin their new lives.

PART TWO
A NEWFOUND GLORY

CHAPTER FIVE
THE SETTLEMENT

Five short years have passed since that dangerous voyage across the open sea from Iceland to the new world. After the first landing, the crew started exploring the land around them. After finding a suitable patch of forest near a small body of fresh water, a temporary village was hastily erected using the wood and other materials from all but two of the boats, as the original fleet was not needed anymore. While not intended to be permanent, these shelters would keep the people warm and dry while they explored the land for a final village location.

Unlike their icy homeland, this region provided everything that the villagers needed to establish a new life. Trees of innumerable species grew abundantly and rose higher than they could ever have imagined. The lush forest generously provided them with building materials, fuel for cooking and heating fires, and natural protection from the cool climate, which was nonetheless much warmer than they were used to. Animals thrived in this land and gave the people all the meat and hides that they could desire.

While starting fresh was difficult, it was a welcome challenge. The chance to build and shape a new settlement in their vision was exhilarating. They set down their own rules, laws, and customs. The people finally had a home of their own where they could flourish happily.

Björg, the older boy whom Tryggvi had rescued, had lost his parents to the icy waters on that fateful night five years in the past. Afterwards, Brynjar formally offered to adopt the lad. As Björg had no other family still alive on this expedition, and given his admiration and appreciation for his rescue to both Tryggvi and Brynjar, the teen graciously accepted. Brynjar, accustomed to caring for the independent and self-sufficient Tryggvi, was nervous about taking on the responsibility of a second son. Despite this, Brynjar treated Björg like his own flesh and blood and didn't differentiate between him and Tryggvi regarding their status within the family or village. Tryggvi, being an only child, relished the addition to their family. He had always wanted a sibling with which to share his adventures and fun.

The two boys bonded rapidly. Björg, saddened by the sudden loss of his parents, looked to Tryggvi for guidance, protection, and brotherly love. While not very young, he still needed a strong father figure in his life. With the help of Tryggvi and Brynjar, Björg could live a normal life as he grew into manhood.

However, it was difficult for him at first. Very difficult. For a time, young Björg, still suffering from his loss, closed himself off to the rest of the world. He ate very little, rarely smiled (only for Tryggvi's corny jokes), and mostly kept to himself.

It was equally rough on Tryggvi. He remembered what it was like to lose his mother just eight years earlier. He tried to relate to the boy and gave his new brother what he would have wanted at that time. He offered counsel, wisdom, and a shoulder to cry on, but also gave him his space and made sure that he knew that his privacy was respected. Tryggvi did everything that he could to see that the boy had whatever he needed to be healthy and happy.

It took a while, but Björg ultimately opened up to them, and especially took interest in Tryggvi. While nothing could replace his lost parents, he knew that they would take care of him and teach him how to become a man in this strange, exciting land. Björg couldn't do it alone, and he needed help from somebody.

And so, this is how their lives began in this new world across the sea. When they had first approached the region, the explorers found themselves at the mouth of a large river that headed south-west into the dense wilderness. Following it deeper into the wild, they eventually settled on a quiet side of the river. The site was surrounded by large expanses of open fields and lush forests.

By felling the great trees of the forest, the villagers could build larger, more complex homes than they could in sparse Iceland. This meant warmer and healthier lifestyles, which led to longer lifespans. With more wild game and produce, fewer people were tasked with finding food. A communal pantry was established to store food for everyone to share. Others devoted their time to building strong walls, watchtowers, common buildings, and an armory. People, who once clung to existence in a cold, barren land, had built a thriving community with a bright future.

Much like the rest of the group, Brynjar, Tryggvi, and Björg built a home out of logs and chinked the cracks with mud and grasses from the banks of a nearby stream. They used thinly stretched animal hides, shaved thinly and oiled, to create window panes for the home. While not transparent like glass, they allowed light to come in while keeping the bugs at bay. They framed the roof with strong timbers and created a dense thatched covering to repel the wind and water.

It was a great start to new lives for the three men, and they enjoyed every day that they had together.

While their lives were better than on the cold, windy shores of Reykjavik, the new world still had its own dangers. The winters consisted of blizzards, freezing rain, and heavy snowfall. Waterways turned to icy plains which were deceptively fragile and could easily shatter beneath one's feet.

Additionally, there were occasional run-ins with the native populations, who had already lived there for hundreds of years prior to the Vikings' arrival. While trade and commerce began soon after their first encounters, some tribes were suspicious of the newcomers. The Vikings were doing their best to appease everyone around them, and it was starting to form a mutually beneficial relationship for all involved.

However, one of the biggest risks facing the men and women of the Viking village was the wildlife. While they had established a modern village with food, shelter, and protective defenses to help ensure their safety, they were still in the middle of a densely forested region inhabited by a large array of wild animals. There were several species of large deer, elk, moose, wolves, coyote, bear, and mountain lions roaming freely around the woods, often at the very gates of their encampment. Even the small, but fierce, bobcat posed a threat to the very young and old. Each Viking who set off into trip into the wilderness risked being hunted by some hungry creature.

On a cold winter morning, the men of the village went out to hunt game in the surrounding forest to gather more meat and hides to replace their dwindling reserves. Each hunting team would typically consist of two to five people heading off in different directions from the other teams. It often worked out so that the teams would track and kill whatever crossed their paths, or they would scare the animal into the direction of another hunting party. Depending on the area and amount of hunters available, they would sometimes have one team walk through a region making a lot of noise to drive the animals into the waiting ambush of a second team. Over time, the villagers became more familiar with the traits and habits of the local animal population and honed their hunting skills to the point of perfection.

On this day, Brynjar, Tryggvi, and Björg settled into their typical hunting trio and began tracking what appeared to be a smaller adult black bear. While Brynjar was the leader of the village, it was Björg who was their de facto leader while out in the woods. The young man had a natural, instinctive ability to sense small changes in the environment, discover imperceptible pieces of evidence, and follow the paths of anyone or anything that moved through his domain. While on hunting trips, it was Björg who directed where they should go and how to find their prey.

Along their trek, the trio would stop every once in a while for Björg to inspect broken twigs, scuffed patches of dirt, or tufts of fur caught on a branch. Small details which would go unnoticed by a normal person were like clues to a puzzle for the young tracker. By tapping into his years of experience and intuition, he could piece together what he found, analyze it instantly in his head, and deduce the direction of travel for the target. He was also known, from time to time, to simply walk through the forest and observe different animals in their natural habitat. Learning how they lived and moved gave Björg invaluable knowledge and wisdom.

As they traversed several miles of rough terrain in pursuit of this elusive black bear, Björg became noticeably more excited as the group progressed. The tracks were getting fresher, and he sensed that their target was only a few minutes away. As they rounded a large outcropping of rocks, they spotted a dark blur ducking behind a group of bushes. Dropping low to the ground, the three men silently approached, keeping their eyes pinned to the source of some rustling in the far edge of the cluster.

Sensing their approach, the bear burst from the bushes and tore through the undergrowth towards several trees looming over a small stream. The bear, which was noticeably smaller than they had anticipated, dropped low over the embankment and disappeared from sight. Not wanting to lose their prey, which they had spent the better part of a day searching for, the three men took off after the fleeing creature in hopes of catching up with it before they lost all trace of its existence. As they made it to the edge of the embankment and looked down into the stream bed, they stopped abruptly at what they saw.

The young bear was not just a young bear, but rather a fairly large cub. And the cub was not only running away from the men, but running towards its very large mother. The mother bear now sidestepped in front of the frightened cub. Another cub, perhaps the sibling of the first, was already crouching behind her.

Sensing danger and solely interested in protecting her kin, the mother bear let out a low, deep throaty growl. Watching and waiting intently, the men remained still. She followed with a voluminous, harsh roar, in hopes of sending the men fleeing into the forest. Standing up on her hind legs, the bear reached an impressive eight feet tall and snarled before crashing back down to her huge front paws.

The three men looked at each other, and all had the same thought. "Not today, lads," Brynjar said softly. "This mother bear is far too mad for my liking, and we've already lost the element of surprise. There are other game to be found in this forest."

Keeping their eyes locked on the bear, they slowly backed away from the three animals and started putting some distance between the two parties. However, after walking only a few feet, Tryggvi's boot came down onto a dry stick laying in the dirt. The weight of his step instantly broke it in twain, and it let out a loud crack.

Startled by the noise, the mother bear thought it was an attack. She reacted instinctively. Roaring again, she leapt forward in a powerful stride and raced towards the source of the noise.

The men, ready for anything, spread themselves out side-by-side, hoping to confuse the angry bear with more options and to minimize the potential injury to each individual man. Digging their feet into the soft earth, they braced for the impending attack. As the bear swiftly closed the gap between her cubs and the awaiting humans, she launched herself into a brutal campaign of offensive attacks. Targeting Tryggvi first, she pounced at his chest, but he jumped sideways and dodged the near deadly assault.

Sensing she had overshot her mark, the bear twisted her head to the left and gnashed her deadly teeth at his head while passing. Foreseeing the attack on his son, Brynjar rushed forward and shoved his boy out of the way with all his might. The bear's impressively strong jaws and collection of razor-sharp teeth connected and sank deeply into the older man's right shoulder. Thick, red blood gushed down the length of her lower jaw, and Brynjar grunted as he felt his bones being crushed. The thrashing bear pinned Brynjar's right arm in place, rendering it useless.

Coming to the rescue of his adopted brother and father, Björg crossed the ten feet in the blink of an eye and jumped onto the back of the bear. Holding onto the ferocious beast's thick fur with all his might, he raised his hunting knife in his free hand and prepared to drive the blade down into the bear's skull. As he was about to deliver the death blow, she whipped her head up and around to counter his attack. Launching the human backwards into the air, the bear turned again and tossed the injured Brynjar at the young man. Brynjar soared through the air and landed with thump on top of the winded and startled Björg.

The two men watched grimly as the bear stood on her hind legs and swung a massive paw at Tryggvi, batting him to the side. A dull crack could be heard as the paw connected and broke several of the man's ribs on impact. He dove away from the bear with the force of the hit in an attempt to lessen the force and managed to roll away from the infuriated apex hunter. Coming to a stop on the ground a few feet away, he lifted his head and desperately tried to raise himself off of the ground. As his eyes sought out the location of the bear and found his objective, he was met with the vision of the rushing bruin covering the distance in a single leap and pouncing on his legs. The impact knocked him down again, and he hit his head hard against the ground.

Sensing that this human was no longer a problem, the bear turned her attention to the two men on the other side of the clearing. While the attack on Tryggvi was going on, however, the men had planned their counterattack. They circled around the bear in opposite directions, readying themselves for the right moment. The bear saw the massive amount of blood oozing from the older, injured man. Sensing weakness, she charged after him in an attempt to take him out of the fight to lower the number of attackers.

Not anticipating the speed of the attack, Brynjar barely had time to duck out of the way and raise his sword to strike. Unused to wielding a weapon with his left arm in combat, however, his hold was awkward and lacked the strength of a normal attack with his right arm. Wincing through the pain in his shoulder, he struck at the bear as Björg rushed in from behind. The younger man, having learned from his previous failure, drove his blade into the neck of the bear as Brynjar stabbed at the heart. Strong as the mother bear was, she could not sustain an attack of this magnitude. Quickly losing all strength from the dual onslaught, she dropped to the ground in a loud crash and laid still.

A cloud of dust hung in the air, kicked up by the body of the fallen animal. The two men watched in nervous anticipation, waiting for the bear to rise and make a last stand. But, it never came. The fight was over.

Björg leaned down and rested his palms against his kneecaps, slowly catching his breath as his heart hammered inside of his ribcage. After a moment of recuperation, he ambled over to where Tryggvi lay dazed on the ground. Shaking his head to drive away the confusion, Tryggvi grabbed his brother's proffered hand and pulled himself up.

It was at this moment that both men looked over at the two bodies on the ground. Leaning against a tree next to the body of the mother bear, Brynjar was struggling to keep himself upright, and sadly, conscious. The wound from the vicious bite was deep, but not bad enough to have killed him instantly. Unfortunately, though, the flow of blood was heavy. Time was running out.

Tryggvi and Björg sharing a stygian grimace between each other, walked over to the tree and slumped to the ground beside their wounded father. Björg looked to Tryggvi for guidance, but Tryggvi could do nothing but stare at his father. His knowledge of battle medicine was primitive at best, and they didn't have any fresh supplies to deal with such an injury this far out into the forest.

Brynjar, sensing the distress in his two boys, broke the silence. "Accept it, lads. I am dying. I have lived a good, long life. I'm proud of the men that you have become," he said. "Do not weep for me. Instead, let us spend my final moments resting together under this tree and remembering our adventures."

The three men, slowly at first, spent the next half an hour recalling the favorite tales of their lives. Each one took their turn going around and around, with many smiles and laughs being shared amongst the trio. With each painful chuckle from Brynjar, the two other men winced in sympathy. While they couldn't fully understand what he was experiencing, they could very well imagine how he felt. From the injuries that he sustained, even laughing must have hurt dearly for him right now.

After telling his final story, Brynjar relaxed and leaned more heavily into the tree at his back. He closed his eyes and listened. Tryggvi told Björg about a particularly interesting scouting mission on a glacier one time back in Iceland, when he had killed his first reindeer. The story went on and on, with all three men enjoying their time together. Brynjar slowly opened his eyes once more. He took in the sights of the forest, the mountains, and his boys one last time. Without interrupting the story, he quietly slipped away.

The two boys, who had become so completely engrossed in the tale, then looked down and realized that Brynjar was gone. Tryggvi, the strong Viking man that he was, did not cry, as tradition warranted. It was not for lack of desire, though. He wanted nothing more than to embrace his father one more time and never let go of the man who had been his father, guide, mentor, advisor, and best friend. He wanted to tell him all the things he had never had a chance to say. He wanted to keep talking with him, plan new adventures, and live out the rest of his life with his father at his side.

However, what we want and what we are given are two different things. His father was gone now, and he must learn to accept it and continue on with his life. He silently vowed to live on in his father's memory and do all he could to continue his legacy. After a shared moment between each other over the body of their fallen elder, Tryggvi froze and glanced sideways in both directions. He noticed that Björg was doing likewise. For, it was at this moment that the two men remembered that they weren't alone.

On the other side of the clearing, lying down beside their dead mother, were the two bear cubs. Tryggvi and Björg both slowly looked at each other, imploring the other to tell him what to do next. Björg had never hunted bear before today, let alone gotten this close to one, and Tryggvi had only hunted bears with the intent of killing them for food.

These bears, however, were just babies. For the first time, these young cubs were without their mother. An odd thought dawned on Tryggvi. All four of them were now in the exact same situation. An overwhelming sense of compassion washed over him as he stared down at the frightened creatures.

These two bears, much like the young men, were now alone. While they had each other, they had no parents to help them in their lives. There would be no more killing today, Tryggvi decided.

Firstly, Tryggvi needed to carry his father back home through the woods. His duty was to ensure his father received a proper funeral and interment for his father amongst his people. While Brynjar had died bravely fighting in combat, his spirit still needed to be sent off respectfully. Taking his axe, Tryggvi trimmed two long, straight, and strong branches from a nearby tree. Weaving a rough net using the rope in his pack, he carefully built a gurney for carrying his father on his last journey.

Björg offered to help, but this was something that Tryggvi needed to do on his own. It had been his responsibility to look out for his father, and he had let him down. Now it was his duty to see him home. Björg, remembering how he had felt after losing his own parents, gave Tryggvi the distance that he needed and would help only if and when he asked for it.

In the meantime, Björg had a plan of his own. After gathering the weapons that had been strewn about in battle with the mother bear, he wandered into the forest adjacent to the clearing. Searching the area's bushes and trees, he gathered a large handful of berries and nuts. Glancing back, he noticed that the two cubs were still hiding behind the mother's body; hiding from the humans who had just killed her.

Slowly and purposefully, he approached the bears. The two cubs paid careful attention to every motion that he made, fearing that he would finish what he had started with their mother. Taking small, careful steps, Björg got within ten feet, looked both cubs in the eyes, and lowered his hands toward a flat rock on the ground. He placed the berries onto the rock, took a step back, and watched for their reactions.

After a few minutes of patiently waiting, when none came forward to inspect his peace offering, he slowly reached forward, grabbed a few of the berries, and put one of them into his mouth. As the sweet juice ran down his throat, a smile crept across his face, which the bears seemed to notice. Sensing that his mission was accomplished, Björg slowly stood up and backed away. Once he was at least another ten feet away, the bear cubs slowly moved towards the pile of berries, sniffed them, and started to nibble. Accepting that they were safe to consume, the two bear cubs cautiously ate the food over the next few minutes.

While this was going on, Tryggvi and Björg finished the sled and carefully loaded Brynjar's body onto it.

"Do you want help carrying him, Tryggvi?" asked Björg.

"No, but thank you," replied Tryggvi. "This is something that I must do myself."

"What do you want to do about the bear's body?" Björg inquired. "That's a lot of meat and good hide that we need for the coming winter."

"I am not in the mood to deal with it now," replied the mournful Tryggvi. "We are already too overburdened to bring it back now anyways. Besides, I have not the heart to approach the still-warm corpse while those cubs are watching. I will ask the men to come back and retrieve the body when we return to camp."

With that said the two finished packing their things, pulled on their packs, and commenced their long journey back to their home. Heading the way that they had come, the two men solemnly walked back over three sets of footprints left in the earth.

As they walked, Björg looked back and noticed something unusual. "They're following us," he whispered.

Struggling under the weight of his father and his own hunting gear, Tryggvi grunted. "Who's following us? We were the only ones out here."

"The bear cubs," Björg whispered again.

Not wanting to stop and seem suspicious, Tryggvi stole a glance over his right shoulder as he continued walking and pulling the gurney. Sure enough, about 100 feet behind them, were the creeping cubs. They darted behind some trees upon realizing that they were being watched, but cautiously emerged whenever the two humans looked away. This little game of follow-the-leader continued on throughout most of the several mile trek, all the way back to the village.

CHAPTER SIX
BEARS

Another ten years had passed since that fateful day in the woods. The two young men had sadly told the others about the fight with the protective mother bear and how their leader had fallen. Tryggvi mourned the passing of his father. Björg, who had looked up to Brynjar as his father, had a hard time dealing with all of this, himself. In a few short years, he had lost not only one, but two men whom he had called "father." However, the young men were not alone in their sorrow and could rely on the support of the village. The other villagers came to Tryggvi's aid and helped him with the preparation and burial rites for Brynjar.

It was a traditional Viking funeral for the people of this time. Brynjar was clad in his finest clothes, with his axe across his chest. Together, Tryggvi and Björg built a raft, covered it with lamp oil, and laid the elder man down on top of it. Working together, they pushed the raft out into the current of the river and watched it lazily drift away. Soon it caught the pull of the passing current and moved with the flow of the water.

They both drew an arrow from their quivers and used a torch to light the tips on fire. Taking careful aim with their bows, they fired a fiery pair of flaming arrows onto the deck of the craft. The raft, continuing to move downstream, burst into a wash of glorious flames.

It was difficult to watch, but it was an important moment for both of the men. Their culture allowed no time to mourn the passing of their elders. There was much work to be done, and a strong man must focus on the living people around him. Later that night, the village elders voted in council and decided that Tryggvi should take up the mantle of Village Leader in his father's stead.

Brynjar was the greatest leader that his people had ever known. Who would be better suited to continue leading them than the young man personally trained by the former leader? Tryggvi, honored and humbled by the decision, accepted the title and quickly fell into his new role.

In the subsequent years, the village prospered in almost every quantifiable manner possible. The physical boundaries of the village more than doubled, trade with the natives increased, and the population continued to swell at a healthy pace. Under Tryggvi's leadership, the village went from several dozen inhabitants to almost one-thousand people in only a decade. Many of the couples had children, raising them to be strong members of the community. Many newcomers sailed over from Iceland, Greenland, and even Norway. The area was finally named Newfoundland by a consensus of the elders of the conglomerated villages in the region.

Tryggvi, now almost thirty-six years old, was at the peak of his physical prime and made frequent productive use of it throughout his daily chores and duties. His arms and legs bulged with powerful muscles, and his furs stretched tightly across his body. Years of hard work, heavy lifting, and fighting had crafted his body into a fearsome weapon in and of itself.

It was with both his body and mind that Tryggvi kept his people safe and fed. Whether leading his people on explorations around the area for new food to gather or game to hunt, or defending themselves from attacks by animals, hostile tribes, or even internal problems, he was always at the forefront of command and led by example. This was how his father had led his people, and he would continue to do so in his honor.

This morning was no different. As Tryggvi finished his morning meal, he walked to the door of his home and whistled loudly into the woods. Off in the distance, a tree rustled. He heard the sound of claws dragging on bark, followed by a loud thump. Every small tree and bush shook as the sound finally came to the edge of the high grass. A large black bear burst into view and jumped through the air towards the lone Viking warrior. Tryggvi widened his stance, dug the balls of his feet into the soft earth below, and braced for the inevitable impact.

The bear, relying on instinct and years of muscle memory, moved quickly and had his front paws on the man's shoulders in the blink of an eye. However, rather than throwing him backwards with crushing force, the bear lightly pushed Tryggvi to the ground. Some slobber dripped onto the man's formerly clean shift. The mighty beast playfully pinned him in place and excitedly licked his face.

A roaring laugh erupted from Tryggvi's lungs. "Hah! Good morning to you, too, my friend!" Tryggvi managed to say as he brushed himself off and caught his breath. "Come inside, Baldur. There is still some food left for you."

Baldur, one of the orphan cubs, had bonded with Tryggvi soon after the devastating event. Their tough spirits and shared loss created a tight knit link that could not be broken. With the loss of its mother, and not fully understanding the role that this human had in killing her, the young cub latched onto the closest form of protection and friendship that it could find.

In the beginning, Tryggvi had feared that the bears would retaliate against him and Björg for causing her death. But, after ten long years, his fears had yet to be realized. It was safe to say that the bears held no animosity towards the two humans. Their friendship was sincere, albeit odd and unusual.

Though he lived in the forest, Baldur came to Tryggvi's house each morning so that they could begin their adventures for the day. The two spent most days together, working, hunting, and playfully exploring wherever they went.. The bear hunted on its own in the wilderness, but Tryggvi still brought him snacks and scraps of his own food whenever he saw him.

As he reached into his pocket for a handful of berries, he nuzzled the adolescent bear behind the ears. Baldur, knowing what was coming next, got excited and stood up on its hind legs. With a mighty roar and playful swat of its front paws, the bear crashed back to the earth and excitedly jumped up and down in front of him with a pleading, hungry look in its eyes. Tryggvi tossed the berries up into the air one by one and marveled as the massive bear nimbly caught them. While the young bears had once been tiny, Baldur was now easily up to three hundred pounds of solid muscle and claws. With the berries depleted, the two made their way next door to where their two brothers lived.

The other cub, Hallbjörn, had likewise bonded with Björg for similar reasons. Björg, however, babied the bear more than Tryggvi and had built it a cave-like enclosure into the side of the hill behind his house to allow it to live close by. The young man had felt much sadness following Brynjar's death during that hunt ten years ago and gladly welcomed the companionship of the young cub. Watching the two bear brothers grow up together had been joyful and rewarding for the young men.

Hearing his brother coming nearby, Hallbjörn growled happily and bounded out of the cave to greet Baldur. The two bears jumped at each other and playfully bit at each other's fur as they swatted back and forth with their paws. Not intending to hurt the other, both bears avoided using their claws and teeth. As the roughhousing came to an end, Björg exited his home and joined the gang in the yard.

"Well, I see that the boys are already at it," Björg said to Tryggvi. "What's on the agenda for today?"

"We're going to walk to that ridge a few miles north and cut around the backside. One of our hunting parties found a large pond there being fed by several streams. It could be good, easy fishing," Tryggvi replied.

As the population of their village continuously expanded, they needed to find more sustainable sources of food and supplies. Having more hands in the group to work and fight was always welcome. But Tryggvi, as their leader, had to ensure that they were also fed, healthy, and happy. Fearing that they might deplete their resources close to home, he encouraged his hunting and gathering parties to venture further from home and seek out new options.

Björg squinted his eyes against the bright morning sun in an attempt to see the ridge that Tryggvi had indicated. Finally catching sight of it, the younger man said, "You mean that one over there? With the tall peak and the rock slide coming down the side?" It was more than a "few miles away." "That's easily a two-day hike away!" exclaimed Björg.

"Ah, you know me. I'm getting older, and my eyesight's not what it used to be," quipped Tryggvi. "The sooner that you stop whining about it, the sooner that we can get going. Go kiss your wife goodbye, and grab your gear."

Over the years, Björg had learned that there were some situations when he could fight with Tryggvi, while others were a lost cause. Shrugging his shoulders and letting out a defeated, yet comically exaggerated, sigh, Björg walked back to his home and disappeared for a few minutes.

Tryggvi turned back to the bears and let out a hearty chuckle. Apparently getting bored by the conversation of the two humans, the bears had spread out on their backs in the grass and were laying belly up to the warm sun. Hallbjörn was currently twisting side to side to scratch his back in the warm grass as Baldur snored. It always amazed Tryggvi how these large, dangerous animals could still be so playful and childlike.

Moments like these, watching the young bear cubs grow into adolescents sadly reminded him of how he had no children of his own. His leadership duties had been hard on his social life. However, he had loved every moment that he had had over the past twenty-plus years of living with his neighbors, his younger brother Björg, and now the cubs. Doing all this while leading his people to the point that they've reached was accomplishment enough.

Walking back to his own home, Tryggvi went to grab his pack and weapons. On trips like these, he always brought his bow, arrows, several knives, and his short blade. The same short sword Brynjar had given him as a young boy, while diminutive compared to his current combat sword, was easy to pack and conceal. It gave him good protection while trekking through unknown lands. While a larger sword duel another man on the battlefield, a small blade was often more useful in the thick undergrowth of uncharted woodlands.

He quickly finished packing his gear, tucked some bread and dried meat into his bag and checked that the coals in the fire were extinguished. Giving his home a quick look around, he walked through the door and firmly pulled it shut it behind him. There was no need for locks in this village. Tryggvi ran a tight ship, and the villagers protected each other against danger and crime. If you wanted to live here, you played by the rules and pulled your weight.

Outside of his door, Baldur anxiously awaited the return of his human friend. Bouncing from foot to foot, the bear excitedly jumped up on his hind legs as Tryggvi exited the house and waved his paws in the air. Tryggvi, pretending to box with his woodland friend, went in for a few playful swats at the bear's stomach and paws. The bears had learned over the years how to safely play with their fragile human companions.

Leaning in, the bear gently, but still forcefully enough to let him know how strong he was, pushed the Tryggvi to the ground with a mild 'humph' escaping the man's lungs. Jumping up on top of him, Baldur sloppily licked his face and let out the closest imitation that a bear could make of a human laugh. Laughing himself, Tryggvi pushed his furry friend off of his chest and rose to his feet. Jumping up and ready for action, the bear and human dusted themselves off and made their way next door to Björg's home.

The younger man stepped out a moment later, shouldering a large rucksack. He turned to kiss his wife on the cheek. Giving her one last smile, he walked over to meet with his assembled friends.

"Are you able to carry that pack all by yourself, young Björg?" teased Tryggvi. "Perhaps I should have Anna carry it for you. I'm pretty sure that she's stronger than you by now, with all of the cleaning up that she does after you."

"Har, har, har, old man," retorted Björg. "Let's get this show on the road. The sooner we get moving, the sooner we'll reach new hunting grounds. I could really go for some freshly cooked deer venison tonight."

After Tryggvi had worked the jokes out of his system, and Björg had successfully deflected the abuse, the three companions made their way north.

After trekking through a variety of terrain, mostly forested hillsides and shaded valleys, the party of four found themselves at the top of a tall ridge overlooking a beautiful expanse of land. The low-lying mountains and hills surrounded them on all sides and limited their views to twenty miles or so. Inside this bowl, green colors of every shade enveloped the landscape and created a soothing sight for the eyes to behold. In the distance, the fading horizon turned to purple and dark blue.

Far down below them, the two men took in the sight of a long, winding river coming in from the east. The river culminated in a large, deep lake that sat at the base of the ridge. The two bears, not at all interested in the sights which fascinated the humans, were carefully walking along the edge, sniffing the ground and plants for any signs of food or other creatures.

"How high up do you think that we are?" asked Björg, staring down at the water far, far below. He wasn't necessarily afraid of heights, but this ridge was tall enough to perturb even the mightiest of warriors.

Looking down, Tryggvi said, "Hmm, I'm not sure. Let's find out." Tryggvi gave a rock by his foot a forceful kick and sent it sailing out horizontally away from the ridge. Creeping closer, he carefully peeked over the edge of the rock face as the stone plummeted down to the water below.

"One Valhalla, two Valhalla—" started the older man.

"What in Odin's good name are you counting for?" questioned Björg.

"Shh!" he hissed. While unfamiliar with physics or complex mathematics, Tryggvi had decades of experience in the natural world. Based on his previous encounters with falling objects and childhood experiments while hiking, he could intuitively guess the rough distance that the stone would fall. "Three Valhalla—ah! Four Valhallas," he said. "I'd venture a guess and say that the stone fell about 150 feet to the water below."

"Well, regardless, I'd rather we keep our distance before one of us falls to our death," said the younger man.

"Agreed," stated Tryggvi. "Let's find some shelter for the night. We can explore some more tomorrow morning."

After pitching their tents and setting up camp, the two men rested their tired bodies after the long day of hiking. Following a simple breakfast, they set off on what would turn into several days of exploration. They hiked, fished, hunted, and took in the beauty of the natural landscape. Not once did they see any evidence of other inhabitants living or hunting within the region. They agreed that future expeditions to this land should commence immediately.

On the third night, the two men decided to retire earlier than usual and rest up before they headed back to the village. After walking for two days straight to get here, and many miles of adventuring, it was time to relax and rest their muscles.

Finishing their meal and washing it down with some freezing cold water from the nearby stream, the men decided to call it a night. Tryggvi rose from his spot beside the smoldering fire and poured the rest of his water over the coals. Turning to avoid the rise of hot steam and ashes propelled towards the heavens, he paused a moment, and looked back satisfactorily to see that all traces of the fire had gone from the embers.

He walked back to their tent and looked down at the two sleeping piles of fur outside of the flaps. He grinned. Even in their full-grown bodies, the two bears were still as cute and cuddly, to him at least, as they were had been as when they first found the boys as cubs. Sneaking past them and crawling into the tent, he settled into his blankets, closed his eyes, and quickly fell into a deep sleep.

"Quick, Tryggvi, get up. GET UP!" pleaded the younger man.

"Huh? What is the matter?" Tryggvi muttered. The last that he knew, he was in a deep slumber and dreaming of heroic adventures. He had fallen asleep some time ago. A minute? An hour? He did not know given the darkness around him. However, he could hear what sounded like a brawl happening outside of the tent. Grabbing his sword, he nodded at Björg, and the two rushed out side by side and ready to fight.

Tryggvi was surprised to discover that the attackers were not fellow men, but hunters from the wild. Look around in the dim light, he counted six vicious wolves surrounding the camp and ready to strike.

From what he could see, the fight had already begun. Several of the wolves had bloody slashes down their sides, and Baldur and Hallbjörn both sported bloodied claws and paws. The bears, unfortunately, had not escaped injury. The two strong bodies were riddled with bite marks. It was clear that Tryggvi's boys were in great pain from the ordeal.

One wolf alone was not a great threat, but six wolves together formed a powerful pack. They refused to back down from the two bears. The alpha male noticed the two humans joining the fray and let out a string of angry barks at the defending party, followed by a short series of commands to his pack. Moving as one, the wolves crept closer. Keeping their shoulders high and their heads low, the wolves kept as small of a profile as possible. Looking from one another, the pack members conveyed to the alpha that they were ready for a coordinated strike.

On his command, a quick, harsh bark, the pack converged on the adventurers. Identifying the two black bears as their primary targets of interest, four wolves leapt forward, two for each one of the bears. The others circled around to attack the still sleepy humans. While they were on the defensive, the Vikings and their furry friends would fight to the end.

Baldur rushed the wolf coming in on his right, furiously swiping with his left paw where he estimated that the wolf's head would be at the end of its leap. Not holding back, as he did during his play fighting, Baldur slashed the air with all of his might. As anticipated, his massive paw connected with the wolf's lower jaw in midair. A terrible crunch was heard as its jaw separated from its skull and hung limply by skin and muscle. A stream of blood soared through the air and sprayed his brother Hallbjörn's fur. Having suffered a hammering concussion, the wolf crumpled to the grass and remained motionless.

Baldur's victory, unfortunately, was not without cost. The second wolf took advantage of the distraction and positioned itself to strike at the bear's side. Seizing the opportunity, the battle-hardened wolf leapt onto Baldur's shoulder and bit into his neck. Skills honed from many hunts throughout its lifetime and aided by the distraction of the bear, the wolf sunk its sharp fangs deeply into fur, skin, and muscle. Connecting with Baldur's primary arteries, the attack was too much for the overwhelmed bear. Still recovering from the first attack, the bear could do little to defend itself against the life-draining bite. Stumbling towards his human companions, both to close the gap between them and to protect his friends one last time, Baldur let out a pained roar and fell to the ground in a defeated heap.

Meanwhile, Hallbjörn had his paws full as two wolves attacked him from opposite sides as one. Unable to completely defend himself from both attacks at once, the bear was receiving an increasing amount of minor cuts and bites from the two wolves while batting aside their primary attacks. These wolves, unlike their counterparts from the attack on Baldur, were more cautious and tested the defensive capabilities of their prey. Swinging and snapping his jaws, Hallbjörn managed to deliver several blows to the wolves as he fought to keep them further away from his brother and the two humans. Raising his right paw, Hallbjörn was about to deliver a killing blow to the head of one of the wolves when he saw his brother fall to the ground.

With an anguished roar, Hallbjörn unleashed a series of blows at the wolves within reach. Knocking his attackers aside, the bear turned to see the two other wolves circling his human friends. Putting all matters of self-preservation aside, he bravely lunged towards his friends to help in their battle.

As he swung his sword back and forth at the annoyingly probing wolf on his right, Björg finally managed to land a slash on the face and front left leg of one of the wolves trying to attack Hallbjörn. As he went in for a strike against a second attacker, the wolf fighting the remaining bear was suddenly, and powerfully, thrown into his path by the vengeful arms of Hallbjörn. Quickly sidestepping the fallen foe, he barely dodged the onslaught and made his way back into the fray.

With two dead and another few badly hurt, the wolves now acted more cautiously. Seeing that the first bear was no longer moving, the four wolves slowly closed in on their foes. Hallbjörn, limping in pain, backed up to protect the two men. The three surviving members of the expedition huddled together and prepared to defend each other to the end from the next round of attacks.

While each was of stout heart and strong in spirit, they physically had their limits. As the battle wore on, their strength and energy waned. One error at this point in the fight could mean the very end for them all.

One wolf, playing the role of decoy, leapt in halfway to draw the attention of their enemies. As one, the three heroes braced to meet the false attack of the predator. Lashing out, they quickly struck down the sacrificial wolf, but this left them open on the sides. With their attention distracted, two of the wolves concurrently ran and pounced on Tryggvi from the back and the side. Seeing the attack coming, Björg pivoted backwards to aide in his friend's defense. The ruse was successful; however, as the final wolf jumped from the shadows, slashed at Hallbjörn's head, and buried its teeth into the shoulder and upper arm of the younger Viking.

Regaining his balance and seeing his moment to strike, Tryggvi ducked below the pouncing attack and stabbed out towards the lone wolf. Surprised by the sheer speed with which the older warrior moved, the wolf was unable to respond in time. Tryggvi buried his sword to the hilt into its furry chest. As the tip of the sword emerged from the wolf's back, a spray of blood soared into the night sky.

Bracing his foot against the chest of the dead wolf, Tryggvi pulled the bloodied weapon from the body of the dead creature. Swinging around with his sword, he moved to fend off the beast still latched onto Björg. Catching his injured friend with his other arm, he slashed at the biting wolf and sent part of its skull flying off into the nearby bushes. Literally losing its mind, the wolf instantly lost control of itself and fell from the younger man's bleeding body.

The remaining wolf, the calculating alpha of the pack, saw the fates of his pack mates. Grasping the complete loss of initiative and surprise, it snarled, backed away, and sped off into the undergrowth surrounding the clearing. The battle was over. Tryggvi screamed with all his might and slashed his sword after the fleeing wolf. Watching the dark silhouette disappear into the black night, he turned to tend to his friends.

What he saw, however, was dismal. Baldur lay motionless on the ground, and Hallbjörn labored heavily just to breathe. Tryggvi rested a gentle hand on the bear's body and tried to comfort him, in some fashion, while examining Björg. Looking over into the man's pained eyes, Tryggvi knew then that his friend was lost. Björg had already lost a lot of blood from the vicious attack, and

Tryggvi had no means of helping him out here. No healing magic could replace the blood lost by the noble warrior. All Tryggvi could do was to stay until the very end and comfort his dying companion. Resting against a nearby tree, Tryggvi pulled his brother towards him and laid him gingerly on his lap. Firmly grasping his hand, he stared down at Björg with pleading eyes.

"I'm sorry, my friend," he said. "What can I do to help you?"

"Nothing, Tryggvi. Nothing at all. You saved me all of those years ago when I was left to die in the open sea," stated Björg. "I could never thank you enough if I tried. Every day since that fateful night has been a blessing. All that I ask now is for you to return safely and live your life to the fullest. While I never had a brother growing up, you were the best brother I could have ever asked for. I thank you for that."

Björg closed his eyes and tried to relax despite the pain radiating from the multiple mortal wounds along his body. Watching him intently, Tryggvi felt his friend's grip on his hand loosen, and then ultimately slip away. Looking to the side, he noted that Hallbjörn had stopped breathing as well.

Tryggvi was alone. For the very first time, he was utterly and truly alone. Exhausted and in dreadful pain from the battle, he suddenly realized how tired he really was. Leaning back against the tree trunk, and not overly concerned with what happened to him at this point, he rested his weight against the tree and closed his eyes. With his friend and the dead bears at his side, Tryggvi slipped into a deep sleep.

Waking at some point mid-morning, Tryggvi found that Björg's body was still lying in his lap. Awful memories of the night before flooded his mind as he relived some of the more terrible moments. After coming to his senses, he carefully slid out from under his friend's body, stumbled to the nearby stream and crawled into the slowly flowing water.

Letting it flow over and around him, the cold water helped to cleanse both his physical and emotional wounds from the night before. Parts of his body stung badly as water swirled past the scrapes, gouges, and bites. After several minutes of trying to relax, he washed his face, drank deeply from the cool, clear water, and dried himself off on the bank.

He buried the two bears and his dear friend in shallow graves along the bank, up above the flood line. Piling stones from the stream on top, he gave them the most honorable burial he possible given the tools and materials at his disposal. Afterwards, he stood solemnly over their bodies for a long time, speaking to the spirit of each one, saying his final words.

With his gear packed, including some of Björg's personal items, he made his way out of the camp and headed home. It was slow going on the return trip, but he made it back to the village without any further troubles. Lacking motivation, and fearing the conversation that he'd have with Anna regarding her now-deceased beloved, he spent the next three long days returning home instead of the fast paced two that the group had covered on the way out.

Upon his arrival, he went to Anna's home first. He didn't want her to hear about Björg through anyone else. Sitting her down, he told her of how Björg had fought bravely in the skirmish and how he had saved his life. The words helped to take the sting out of the news, but just barely. All Vikings knew that they may lose a loved one at any given time, but it was never easy to face the truth. Promising to return soon, Tryggvi made his way into the village and called for a general assembly.

Later that night, he told all the villagers about the scouting trip. He revealed what they had found, and what they had lost. The people mourned the loss of Björg for many days. Even the two bears would be missed, as they had become unofficial members of the community during their years with Björg and Tryggvi. They did, however, find comfort in the prospect of new food sources and the promise of an easier life for their people.

Tryggvi retired to his home and didn't come out for a long while.

CHAPTER SEVEN
FORGOTTEN

Five years had passed since the battle with the wolves. While Tryggvi was a strong-willed man, the loss of his best friend hurt him deeply. Watching his friend and their bears die in his arms after trying to fight off a wild force of nature was gut wrenching for the Viking man.

It took a while, but Tryggvi finally came around. While he had lost everything dear to him personally, his sense of duty and honor to his people had managed to pull him back from the brink. He could not allow his loss to affect all those who relied upon him. An entire town looked up to him, and it was his responsibility to carry on for their sakes.

True to his word, Tryggvi looked after Björg's widow. Tryggvi and Anna had been friends for many years, and he enjoyed spending time with her. He always made sure to bring her game meat and provided her with fresh skins from various animals. This allowed her to continue living her life in the village without having to worry about hunting in her husband's absence.

Not to say, however, that she couldn't take care of herself. Like all Viking women, Anna was thick-skinned and tough. She could hold her own with weaponry and was well accustomed to wielding a bow out in the field. She had often gone hunting with Björg in their younger years, but gradually pulled back from the hunts as she focused more on her craft.

Anna's role in the community was that of a carpenter. Her father had taught her the basic skills of woodworking at a very young age. She enjoyed making little projects more and more throughout the years. On any given day, she would be somewhere helping to build a new hut or protective wall. Many tables, chairs, and beds in the village had been built by her hand. She often worked alongside the blacksmith and glassblowers to create unique and innovative weapons and functional items.

As the years passed, and the pain from Björg's loss began to ease, Tryggvi and Anna grew closer to one another than their original friendship would have warranted. Over time, their friendship turned to one of a romantic nature, they fell in love, and eventually, they married. As neither had previously bore children and both yearned for companionship to replace that which they had lost, their union brought each of them great comfort.

Tryggvi worried at first about betraying the honor of his friend by even contemplating such a venture. But love is a mysterious thing, and it is hard to fight off when two people feel that way for each other.

Their marriage ceremony was a simple service, held in the village's church and attended only by a small gathering of their friends. Tryggvi and Anna decided afterwards to live together in Tryggvi's home. The larger and more sturdy of the two, it was the better option. Anna gave her house to another pair of newlyweds who needed help starting out in the world together.

Anna was amazed at the amount of available space at her disposal. Tryggvi lived a simple, Spartan lifestyle and kept very few personal items. He had a basic kitchen table for preparing and eating meals and a chest in the corner for extra blankets and clothing. There were cabinets on the wall above the table for storing cooking tools and dinnerware, and a few shelves around the cabin for candles and random trinkets. The one exception, she noted, was the beautiful stone he kept on a shelf above his bed. It was the only item in the home without a distinct function other than its aesthetic qualities. She was amused that a man such as

Tryggvi would have such an impractical, but lovely, possession in his home.

While eating dinner on their first night living together as husband and wife, she mentioned how much she admired the beautiful object. Puzzled, Tryggvi turned around and looked over to the other side of the room.

"Oh, that stone?" he stated, questioningly. "I found that as a young boy before we left Iceland for the new world. I picked it up on one of my first big expeditions with my father. It was on this tiny island and I found it sitting within this sheltered cove. I thought then that it was the most intriguing thing I had ever seen, but I had practically forgotten about it."

"Do you want me to build you a new shelf?" asked Anna. "It looks ready to collapse under the weight of the stone. I can make you one tomorrow over at my shop."

"That is very kind of you, dear Anna, thank you. But it is fine," replied Tryggvi. "That stone has been sitting upon that shelf for many years. If it hasn't fallen yet, it will probably stay up there until the end of time."

They both chuckled and returned to eating their dinner. They spent the rest of the meal updating each other on their day's activities, and simply enjoying their time together.

Another few years had passed. Tryggvi, now forty-three years of age, and Anna, at forty-one, had happily settled into their new lives together. Things were peaceful in the land. The Icelandic travelers had forged strong alliances with the native inhabitants of the land and a flourishing trade system was established. They created tools, weapons, and other wood-worked products, which were traded for skins, meat, and new species of plants to grow. By now, the villagers have fully adapted to the land in which they dwelled and developed a harmonious relationship with the environment and animals around them. While the Vikings still followed their traditions of the past, they enjoyed the warm weather, better growing conditions, and overall easier way of life.

At Anna's request, and with respectful acceptance by Tryggvi, the couple made a trek out to the ridge where her husband, and his best friend, had died. While other members of the community had traveled out that way for hunting and fishing trips, neither Anna nor Tryggvi had previously wanted to go. Anna had conflicted feelings about her fallen first love, and Tryggvi felt guilty for his death even after all these years.

It took three days to reach the burial site. While both wanted to go, neither was necessarily in a rush to get there. They leisurely walked along the paths and camped when they grew tired.

Obviously nervous about the trip, Tryggvi slept very little and stayed up late each night to guard over his sleeping wife. The memory of the wolves haunted him, and he remained on watchful alert. When he did manage to sleep, it was light, short, and dominated by nightmares.

When they finally reached that clearing by the stream, both Tryggvi and Anna sat in solemn silence for what seemed like hours. Anna recalled joyous memories of her first husband, Björg, and how their union had been prematurely ruined by the appetite of wild monstrosities. Tryggvi, unable to hold back, wept as the scenes played out in his mind's eye. Seeing the clearing again immediately brought terrible memories to the forefront of his mind and wouldn't leave his head. But seeing the three mounds of stones piled up, with the hand-carved wooden markers which he had labeled each burial mound with, was almost too much for the man to handle. Anna put her arm around his waist and leaned in closely. Pressing her face to his muscled left bicep, she dried a tear against his sleeve.

"Thank you," she whispered, looking up at his saddened face.

"For what, my dear?" asked Tryggvi.

"For taking me here. For taking me to see where Björg fought and fell to the wolves," she replied. "And for all of this," she said, motioning with her hand. "Despite your injuries and distraught state, you took the time to carefully and respectfully bury my former husband and those two beloved bears of yours. I never understood how or why you managed to befriend wild bears and keep them as companions. But they loved you and fought with you side by side. To lose everything in one short moment, yet still carry on, is commendable. For that, and for all that you continue to do for me, I thank you."

Tryggvi, in a rare occurrence, was completely speechless. Looking down at her beautiful face, he simply smiled and put his arms around her. Holding her closely, they remained lovingly embraced for a long, long time.

The two made the journey home shortly afterwards. They never again returned to that clearing. The events that transpired there and the friends buried within the ground were part of their past lives. For now, Anna and Tryggvi had each other. They would do all that they could to protect one another from harm.

Another year passed, and the couple had splendiferous news to share. After consulting with the village doctor, and the fact that Anna could not physically hide it any longer, the leader and his wife announced that they were expecting a child. This was a joyous occasion and delighted everyone that they knew.

As the village was still comparatively small and many of the residents were beyond child-rearing age, a new birth brought hope to all. Not only did a child mean more love for the family, it also helped grow the community. While that meant more required resources, it also meant that there would be one more person, eventually, to help with protecting the village, growing and hunting for food, and synergistically contributing to the overall health and wellness of the community.

As it was late summer, the couple estimated that they would be expecting the arrival of their son or daughter in either late January or early February of the following year. Anna and Tryggvi spent the cold winter months preparing their home and getting things ready for the baby's arrival. Anna rested as much as she could, while Tryggvi tried to pick up the extra slack for the care of his wife. It would be a big change for them, but they looked forward to new experiences for their growing family.

Several months later, late in the evening on a cold February night, Anna went into labor. After summoning the doctor, the team of three brought forth a healthy, smiling baby boy. Lying in bed, trying to relax from the hard labor that both went through, Anna and the young child snuggled together for the first time. Having sent the doctor home already, Tryggvi sat on a small stool next to their bed and quietly admired his family.

Looking at his glowing wife, he smiled. "What shall we call the young lad? Tryggvi inquired. "I know that you were unsure on a name before. But now that we know he is a boy, have you decided upon a name?"

Beaming, Anna looked up at her husband and said, "Tryggvi, I would like you to meet your son, Skùli."

"Skùli? Skùli. I like it," he replied. Picking his son up, he grinned. "Skùli, The Protector. He shall inherit the world with which we leave him, and possibly govern this village someday. May he protect them and keep them strong, as my father did before me, and I shall do for him."

Tryggvi had wanted to become a father all his life. He could hardly believe that his dream had finally come true. He had waited many years, and he feared that it would never happen for him. While most of his friends had had children much earlier in their lives, Tryggvi had instead spent his adult years overseeing the exploration and development of his people, their lands, and their culture. He spent very little time selfishly seeing to his own desires, but was glad now to have gotten a little selfish. Looking down at the face of his sleeping son, he held him a little more firmly. The new father would not allow anything happen to his little buddy. and could not wait to see where their lives would take them.

Ten years later, during an especially harsh winter, Tryggvi was out hiking through an unexplored area looking for deer. While not old by modern standards, he was nearing sixty years of age and was considerably old given his choice of lifestyle and dangerous habits in those days. You didn't see many older adventurers back then, unless they were very good or very lucky. The long, hard years had sapped him of his strength. Trips like this were much harder than they had once been.

Standing still for a moment to catch his breath, Tryggvi scanned the area for tracks and any other signs of animal activity. He found this clearing quite strange. Long and thin, it snaked through the woods in a most unusual fashion. He decided to return here in the spring when the snow and ice had melted to investigate. Taking a few more steps, he found the ground to be especially slippery. "There must be some ice packed under the snow right here. I should be careful," thought the Viking. With his next step, a sharp crack reverberated through the ice. A low thud echoed from underneath as air pockets shifted around. All too late, he finally realized what he was standing upon.

With a final snap, he fell through the surface of the ice and rapidly sank until his feet touched the bottom of the river bed. Soaked up to the chest in icy water, he could already feel his body temperature dropping. His head hurt, and he felt dizzy, but his years of experience kicked in. He gently grabbed the edge of the ice, eased himself onto the lip, and rolled sideways away from the broken hole.

Looking to his right, he noticed a trail of blood leading from the hole. He must have hit his head hard enough to draw blood, which would explain the massive pain and throbbing coming from behind his eyes. He rapidly pulled off his wet clothing and put on clean, dry garments from his pack, which thankfully stayed dry enough in the short dunk under water.

Even with his swift recovery, he still found himself in a dangerous predicament. He had already lost more blood than he'd care to admit, and it was still seeping out. Ripping off one of the sleeves from his soaked shirt, he tied it tightly around his head. Compressing his head tightly, he hoped to stave off the flow of blood leaving his wound to buy him some additional time to get to safety.

Still shivering, he looked around for any source of dry fuel to burn. But it had recently rained and everything around him was covered in heavy snow. Not one to easily give up hope, he gathered up a pile of twigs and cloth. He showered the pile with sparks from his flint and steel, but it failed to catch fire. He went so far as to rip off more sections of his clothing to get the fire started. He would have gladly traded his cloak then for a burning fire in this state of desperation in which he found himself. Alas, even when he could get some of the cloth to smoke, he didn't have enough dry kindling to keep the flame alive.

He now faced a harsh reality. He couldn't fully dry off without getting into some shelter and removing all of his wet clothing. He needed fire to warm his freezing body, and he also needed food to keep his strength up. Worst of all, he had none of those things here and wouldn't anytime soon. Between his lack of supplies and his still bleeding head wound, he would need to head home immediately before it was too late.

Unfortunately, home was another day's hike away, and he was already bitterly cold, even with some new clothes on. Not wanting to waste time with the extra weight, he threw his soaking wet clothes aside and set off as fast as his tired body would allow.

For the next day, he traveled harder and faster than ever before. Hey may not be a doctor, but he knew enough about human physiology and battlefield healing to know that he was in trouble if he didn't get home soon enough. Stopping only to drink water and correspondingly relieve himself, he stubbornly pushed on until he reached the village.

By the time he had arrived home to the cabin, several of his fingers, toes on his right foot, and most of his whole left foot were deeply frost-bitten. He burst through the door to find Anna carving a figurine at the table. A pot of hearty stew boiled over the fire.

"Tryggvi! My love, what happened?" exclaimed his startled wife.

"I was out hunting... ugh! And I broke through ice and fell into the water," he managed to mutter out. "I think that I have frostbite in several places, and I injured my head. I just need to get warm and lay down."

With the help of his wife, he stripped out of his cold, wet clothes, dried off, and climbed into bed. Anna grabbed some stones from the hearth, wrapped them in cloth, and put them under the blankets. She climbed into the bed with him and hugged him closely, hoping to share her body heat and warm her uncharacteristically weak husband. They both lay like that for several minutes before Tryggvi passed out from exhaustion. Not wanting to wake him, Anna carefully removed the cloth from around his head to inspect the wound. It was far worse than she had hoped, but at least it looked like the bleeding had stopped.

Slowly crawling out of bed, she grabbed some warm water and a fresh bandage. She cleaned the wound, applied the dressing, and made sure that he was comfortable. Not wanting to leave her husband alone, she slipped back under the covers and put her arms around him. She stayed awake as long as she could to keep an eye on his condition, but, eventually, she too drifted to sleep.

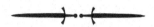

She awoke several hours later, deep into the night. The sun had long since ceased shining through their windows, and the only light in the room came from the glow of the smoldering embers in the fireplace. She carefully slipped out from under the covers and crept over to the pot of stew over the hearth. Dipping her spoon into the surface, she gave it a few good swirls and tasted a tiny bit. It was still warm and felt good in her stomach. Lying with her frozen husband for so long had sapped the heat from her body, and the chill was hard to shake off. She reveled in the warmth as it flowed through her.

Anna wanted to wake him to get some food into his system, but he looked comfortable in his sleep. She would warm the soup up again in the morning. Carefully lifting the lid from the rack above the fireplace, she covered the pot and slipped back under the heavy blankets.

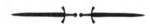

In the morning, they sat up in bed together to eat the reheated stew. Skùli Tryggvison, who had been out on a camping trip with his friends in the forest nearby, came in from the cold. Seeing his injured father in bed, he was elated to see him home again.

"Dad? Dad! You're back!" exclaimed the young lad. He ran across the room and launched himself up onto the bed. Coming down hard, as he had grown into a strong, tall lad for his age, he landed like a rock upon his father's legs.

"Ooh!" yelped Tryggvi, louder than he would care to admit.

"Ah! Sorry, Dad!" exclaimed the young boy. "What happened? Are you okay?"

After recovering from his son's affectionate attack, and moving his sore body out of the way to make room for everyone on the bed, Tryggvi explained what had happened during his trip over their breakfast together. He was more embarrassed than anything in his telling of the accident, but his wounds and throbbing pain could not be readily ignored.

Once breakfast was finished, the village doctor came while Skùli left to play outside with his friends. The prognosis was not good. Tryggvi's head wound would not stop bleeding, and it was beginning to develop an infection. The pain was mounting and worsened with each passing hour. Additionally, several toes and fingers had frostbite on them that did not appear to be healing on their own, and would most likely need to be amputated. The doctor gave him some roots to chew on for the pain, but given their medical technology of the time, there was little that he could do for the man besides waiting and watching to see how his body mended itself.

Tryggvi took the news better than most. He was a brave man who had enjoyed a full and hearty life. He had experienced more than most, explored many new lands and lived to tell the story. If the end was near, he was ready for it.

Anna, on the contrary, was distraught at the thought of losing her husband. She had already lost one husband and was unprepared to lose another. She feared that young Skùli would grow up without a father in his life.

The family spent the rest of the day together, lying in bed resting, reading, and trying to relax. Anna kept the fire going and made sure her boys were warm and fed. Tryggvi's pain increased substantially throughout the day, but he did his best to hide it, at least from Skùli. Anna could not be tricked as easily. She grew nervous watching her love suffer. As the day turned to night and the sun set behind the mountains, the village grew dark and the temperature dropped lower than they were used to. The family huddled together in Tryggvi and Anna's bed and soon drifted off to sleep.

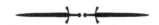

Late into the evening, Tryggvi awoke to find his head hurt more than before. He wasn't sure what was happening, but he feared that his time left on Earth was short. If he were to pass on to Valhalla that evening, he had one last thing to do.

Carefully slipping out of bed so as not to disturb his slumbering family members beside him, he walked over to the kitchen table and lit a candle. Glancing back over his shoulder to see if the candlelight had alerted his wife or son to his activities, he was relieved to see that it had not roused his loved ones. Opening the cabinet door, he pulled out two pieces of parchment.

Taking his ink and quill, along with the blank parchment, he went back to the table and sat down in his favorite chair. Rubbing his hands along the well-worn arms of the chair, he reflected on the many happy memories formed in this house. Meals with his father, drinks with family and friends, and ten long years as a family of three, much of his life had passed by sitting here. He would miss those moments the most. With a heavy sigh, he proceeded to write. When he was done, he left two folded letters, one addressed to his wife and the other to his son, and got back to his feet.

Limping back across the room to his bed, he bumped into the shelf on the wall. The gusset supporting the shelf creaked under the impact, but held. He chuckled to himself, remembering when Anna had offered to fix the shelf all those years ago. It looked like it might finally fall, but that wasn't a concern to him anymore. He gently pulled back the covers, crawled underneath, and fell back asleep with his family.

As the hours passed and the first rays of the morning sunlight crept over the village, the heat from the morning sun reached the outside walls of their home. As the heat warmed the wood and caused it to expand, a slight groan ached through the structure of the home as timbers were stretched and nails and pegs adjusted in their holes. As the wood shifted ever so slightly from the expansion, the creaky old shelf on the wall finally collapsed, sending its contents to the floor. While most of the objects fell to the dusty floorboards and bounced in different directions, a lone object, the old stone from Tryggvi's childhood trip, hit the top of the headboard of the bed, bounced, and landed next to the sleeping man. Slightly disturbed by the impact, Tryggvi rolled over and put his arm around the stone. Pulling it in close, he fell back asleep.

A short time later, after finally succumbing to the damage done to his body, Tryggvi's heart gave up and he quietly slipped away.

Later that morning, while still half-asleep, Anna awoke and lovingly looked over her sleeping family next to her. Confused by the mess beside the bed, she glanced upward and noticed that the shelf was hanging on by just one nail. Pulling herself upward to lean on her right elbow, she noticed the old, smooth stone by Tryggvi's side. Sadly... she also realized that he was no longer breathing.

With a tear rolling down her cheek, she carefully slipped out from under the blanket and walked around to the other side of their bed. She didn't want to wake Skùli before knowing the truth. She leaned in close to her husband's face, but felt no breath from his mouth or nose. Gently placing her fingers upon his neck, she searched longingly for a pulse, but could feel nothing. Leaning down over the bed, she embraced her husband and wept.

After several long minutes, the sound of her crying woke their young son. Pulling herself together, she broke the terrible news to the young boy and comforted him. The loss of a parent at such a young age is an unimaginable experience, and it hit Skùli hard. They huddled together in their sadness and wept for a long, long time.

After a spell, Anna left the bed to begin making preparations. She needed to be strong for her son and could not let him see how badly this affected her. Walking to the kitchen to get a drink of water from the pitcher on the table, she noticed the two sealed letters sitting there. She couldn't recall those being there last night, and realized that Tryggvi must have written them during the night while they had slept. Her heart instantly warmed knowing that through all of his pain and agony, he still had the strength and love for them both to leave them a final message.

Calling Skùli over to the table, she handed the boy the letter addressed to him. Unsure of what to make of it, he took the letter and stared at it for a moment. Glancing back over his shoulder to his father still lying in their bed, he made the connection and realized what it was. Turning to his mother, he looked up into her eyes, imploring her to tell him what to do.

"Let's read them together, shall we?" she asked. "I think that's what your father wanted us to do." Sitting down at the table side by side, she put her arm around her son and pulled him in closely. Opening hers first, Anna read the message, first to herself, and then again aloud for Skùli to hear:

> *To my wife, Anna,*
>
> *Anna, my love. I am deeply sorry that I am leaving you in this manner. I have never known anyone quite like you and dreamed of a long lifetime together. To cut it short like this brings great sadness to my heart.*
>
> *What brings me relief, however, is knowing that our love produced the greatest child in the world. Skùli is a blessing to our lives and a boon to the village. I know that he will grow up to be big, strong, and a capable leader. Our love and guidance will make him a compassionate man who will lead our people fairly and justly. While I regret not being there for both of you, I know that you'll be strong enough to endure it and you'll love and care for Skùli enough for both of us in my absence.*
>
> *I look forward to joining you again in the next world, but do not rush to get there. Live a long,*

prosperous life and I will see you when the time is right. I love you.

Tryggvi

When she had finished, they both sat still and just hugged each other. Both mother and son quietly contemplated the words they had read with moistened eyes.

After a few more heartbeats had passed, Anna looked down at her son and said, "Now your turn, my dear. Let's see what Dad wanted you to hear." With shaking hands, the lad took the letter from the table, unfolded the parchment, and began to read:

To my son, Skùli,

Son, you are the best thing to have ever happened to me. I have been to the most amazing places in the World on my many adventures. I have fought beside the bravest of all the Viking men and women. I have encountered the most interesting and unusual creatures in my travels. But, none of this compares to the first time I laid my eyes upon you.

Since the day you were born, you have brought a new light into our lives. I thought that I had everything I wanted in life. But you truly made my life complete. I cannot imagine not spending every day with you, and if I die today, losing you will be the saddest part of it all.

Do not mourn me. Do not dwell on my absence. Go live your life to the fullest. Take good care of yourself, your mother, and all those around you. Go find someone whom you love, start your own family someday, and make the world a better place than you find it. We will meet again on the battlefields of Valhalla and celebrate our lives in

the mead halls in the next life. Until then, just know
that I love you.
Dad

Glassy-eyed, the young boy stared absently at the letter. He was still in disbelief, but thrilled to once again hear how his father had felt about him. He would dearly miss his father's help and guidance, but his love would burn on in Skùli's heart.

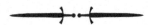

The following day, the villagers gathered in the town square to pay their respects to their departed leader. Some brought flowers and parting gifts for Tryggvi, while others brought food and tools to help Anna and Skùli in their loss. Tryggvi's body was placed upon a simple wagon, prayed over, and loaded with his gifts.

Later that evening, after everyone had said their final goodbyes to their beloved leader, Anna and Skùli each took a handle of the wagon and gently pulled it along the path out of town. There was a cave a mile outside of the village proper, where Tryggvi had often taken his son on hikes and expeditions. It was a fitting place to inter the man, and it held a special place in Skùli's heart.

Upon reaching the cave, both mother and son prepared the space for the body. As daylight was waning, the two quickly cleared a spot along the back wall. Laying the body down on the cold granite, they carefully piled the rocks on top of his body. They stopped once the pile was about two feet tall and fully obscured any sight of the man inside.

Stepping back, they both hugged each other and looked over the shrine to the man whom they loved. Remembering something, Skùli turned and went outside for a moment.

"Where are you going, my dear?" asked Anna.

"Just one minute, Mom. I have a surprise," replied the boy.

A moment later, Skùli returned with something in his arms. Anna squinted in the dim light to see what he was carrying with him. Bending down to the rock pile, the boy placed the smooth, blue stone his father had been holding when he had passed. Neither of them fully understood the significance of the stone or why Tryggvi had kept it all of these years, but he had liked it and would have wanted it buried here with him.

Standing beside each other, mother and son remained still for a while. Skùli thought of the father whom he loved, but would never go adventuring with ever again. Anna thought of the husband and longtime friend whom she would miss dearly. When the sun had passed beyond the horizon and left them standing in the pitch-black cave, the two walked back outside, grabbed the cart, and returned home.

As the years went by, very little changed in the village. A brave young warrior had taken up the mantle of leader. Anna and Skùli went out to the cave from time to time and to visit Tryggvi's burial site, speak over him, and pray as needed. Some of the villagers went out occasionally to pay their respects to their former leader, but they were few and far between.

Years later, Skùli fell in love, married a fellow lass from the village, and started his own family. When he had his children, instead of carrying on the surname tradition of his people by giving them the surname "Skùlison" or "Skùlisdottir," he decided to break new ground and stuck with Tryggvison. He wanted to keep the memory of his father alive, even if only through a small symbolic gesture such as a name.

And so, time passed on in the mortal realm. Seasons turned from one to the next, and the years ticked by one after another. Generations came and went, and ultimately, Tryggvi and his burial cave were long forgotten. His descendants stopped visiting as frequently, and soon, all together. His stories were told less often in the mead halls of the village and other nearby towns until they were eventually replaced with new tales of adventure and intrigue.

As the centuries progressed, the Tryggvison family migrated further south in search of warmer climates and better hunting and growing. They would come to settle in the region known today as New England.

PART THREE
EMERGENCE

CHAPTER EIGHT
CRACKS

From the outside, little had changed over the past three centuries. The unusual stone still sat atop the pile of burial stones that covered the body of Tryggvi Brynjarson. As the years passed, the village elder went from being a lost loved one to a distant memory. With the lack of visitors, the cave was eventually overtaken by nature. Persistent plant growth soon crowded the trail to the mouth of the cave and all but erased the path that wound its way through the forest. Tree saplings were allowed to take root in the trail, having no consistent passersby with trampling feet to slow their attempt at life. The trees grew, leaves fell, and eventually, all evidence of the path to cave was erased from time. The cave opening was obscured from view and disappeared into legend.

During a particularly harsh winter, after an extremely rainy fall season, the water-soaked ground quickly froze and shifted the rocks and dirt on the hillside above the cave. The expanding ice cracked rocks, broke tree roots, and dislodged a sufficient amount of earth to cause a landslide further up the hillside. As rocks and debris cascaded down the slope, the mouth to the cave was all but covered. Only a tiny opening remained at the top of the entryway, leaving just enough wiggle room for a small animal to pass through cleanly.

Through all of the years and all of the natural transformations happening outside of the cave, very few changes occurred inside the protective stone walls of the burial chamber. While dust collected and spiders built their intricate webs, Tryggvi's old stone sat in uninterrupted silence. No human eyes were there to witness it, but the stone grew a deeper shade of red as time passed. If the young boy from long ago thought that the stone was peculiar back then, he would have been even more interested in it now.

And so, the stone continued to sit. And wait. And wait it did, until one fateful day during an exceptionally hot summer. As the surface of the Earth was being scorched by continual weeks of hot sunshine and elevated air temperatures, the air inside the cave began to heat up beyond its average cooler temperature. While the sun bombarded the cave with heat from above, another change was taking place, deep within the planet. An earthquake, while relatively minor in nature, released a reservoir of molten magma from below the continental plates to a chamber closer to the surface of the Earth's crust.

While the magma never breached the surface, the sudden increase in proximity to the large store of heat energy, coupled with the intense summer sunlight, caused a dramatic localized increase in the ground temperature. As the ground continued to absorb the newly unleashed thermal energy, the air inside of the cave became a natural oven, baking everything inside of the cavern in the increasingly uncomfortable temperatures. All living creatures, spiders, flies, mice, snakes, and anything else with the ability to move, walked, crawled, or slithered their way out of the cave to more comfortable environments. While it continued to offer protection from larger predators and the normally cool weather, the heat was more than they could take.

Yet, the stone remained. As the internal heat increased and countless Joules of energy were conductively and convectively transferred to every square inch of the smooth, hard surface, the reddish hue of the rock changed to a rich crimson. The red slowly gave way to gray, and then again, to a deep, dark black.

As the summer months transpired and the heat remained, the stone's surface began to form tiny, nearly imperceptible hairline cracks. It started with just one, lonely little crack, no larger than a blade of grass or a bit of spider thread. But it soon began to grow and propagate in random directions around the outside of the curved surface. Oddly enough, the stone also began to bulge.

Darkness. Warmth. Moist. Cramped. These four sensations dominated the infant mind of the imprisoned creature. Not able to fully comprehend what was happening, the young creature struggled to understand his current situation. He was stuck, but yet, felt oddly safe and secure. Part of his brain told him that he could move, stretch out, and even leave this place, yet, how would he know? As far as he knew, he just became conscious for the first time.

Unable to move, unable to see around himself or where ever he was, he felt that he should be able to at least see something with his eyes. But the darkness enveloping him obscured all of his senses. Also, how did he know that he was a 'he', and what did 'he' even mean? These strange questions, and a slew of others, swirled around his brain.

As time carried onward, he began to grow hotter, more uncomfortable, and no longer able to cope with all of these strange sensations. For the first time, he became aware of his physical form. He could feel arms, legs, and other appendages. Much of this was still very confusing and he didn't know how to act or respond to any of this newly acquired stimuli. The only thing that made sense in this dark pool of confusion was to move.

Walk.

Run.

Escape! Somehow, to somewhere, he had to escape. He did not know where 'here' was, but he didn't want to be here anymore and needed to find somewhere else that made more sense to him. Squirming and flexing his newborn muscles, he began to stretch and move in any way that this prison would allow.

At first, he felt nothing give. A slight twinge of panic crept into his mind as he feared that he would be trapped in this darkness forever. However, after several attempts, the area above his head started to feel like it would give a little. Stretching his legs more, he heard a cracking sound, and a sliver of dim light trickled in through the surface of whatever it was that was holding him hostage. Ecstatic, he pushed again until the material gave way. As he threw himself upwards in one final surge of aggression towards his unknown foe, a large chunk broke away and fell to the ground.

The creature stretched his head out of the cage and looked around. He was surrounded on all sides by a low mound of similar looking objects. These were "stones," he somehow remembered. He must have been trapped in a stone of sorts, as well. As his curiosity continued to grow, his mind quickly grasped onto two concepts: he had a lot of weird memories of this place within seemingly no understanding of why he would know, and two... it was hot in this place. He knew that it was hot, and that it should bother him, but he felt strangely comfortable in this temperature.

Determined to finish his escape, he strained against the walls of his enclosure, mustering every ounce of strength until he felt them flex and snap. With a final push, several large chunks fell to the ground around his feet.

Looking down at the broken pieces, he extended his limbs, stretched his cramped muscles, exercised the motion of his joints, and took in several deep breaths of hot, dry air. Another word was stuck in his mind: egg. He wasn't sure yet what an egg was, but he knew somehow that he had just come out of one. And there was something oddly familiar about the color of the pieces. The texture of the material. The size and shape of what the egg must have looked like before he had broken out of it. He didn't know how, or why, or when, he would have ever encountered this object before, but it seemed familiar.

Regardless of what this stone-egg thing was, the creature had more basic biological needs to address. He felt a growing pang in his stomach and his base desires told him that he needed to do one thing and one thing only: consume. Nothing in the cave looked edible. He didn't know exactly what he wanted, as he had never eaten anything before, but he wanted to find something that moved.

Shaking off the last parts of the broken egg, he quickly whipped his body around to shed himself fully from his former prison. Stretching out, he felt another appendage flopping around behind him. Turning to see what it was, it instinctively curled towards him. "A 'tail,' I think?" thought the creature. He had never seen a tail before, but that was the word that came to mind.

Shaking slightly on untested legs, he took a few nervous steps forward into the rest of the cave. Finding himself oddly steady, he confidently moved around the stone pile that he was still standing on and sniffed the air. The cave was stagnant, hot, and seemingly devoid of any other life. Nothing grew in the hot, dark cave, and he didn't see anything else moving around him. Looking up and to his right, he noticed a small shaft of light burning through the darkness.

Slowly making his way over, the creature found a sloping pile of rocks and dirt leading up to the source of the light. Having never seen light like this before, but knowing that there wasn't much for him in this cave, the small creature began to carefully pick his way up and around some of the more stable rocks in the pile towards the top. While the climb itself was no more than nine or ten vertical feet, it was a challenge to the small, inexperienced legs of the young creature. Upon reaching the top of the mound, his new eyes squinted in the bright light.

Taking a moment to acclimate to the brightness, the creature mustered his courage and slowly stuck his head into the opening. He was able to put his head and neck through at least half of the length of the opening. He tried climbing the rest of the way through, but found that his body was getting stuck on something. He tried again, and again, but kept having sharp pains along his shoulder.

Pulling his head and neck back through the hole, the creature looked backwards to see what was hitting. Given the extremely low light within the cave, he could not see anything in particular that would be getting in the way. But... there was something there. From what he could see in the dark, he saw that there were things on each of his shoulders that kept him from crawling through. Growing anxious, the creature roared and lurched at opening. Using his front feet, he dug into the dirt and rubble with his claws and furiously scraped away everything in his path. Rocks and dirt were flung between his legs. Dirt was thrown in every direction as he cleared a path to the outside world.

As the top, harder layer of detritus was cleared away, the work became increasingly easier. Soon, the relentless clawing and scraping of the creature's powerful front limbs had cleared out most of the tiny tunnel. The small opening which had originally cast a narrow beam of sunlight into the cave was now a two foot diameter passageway leading upwards towards the light.

While obviously successful, the progress was coming at a price. With each additional scrape, lunge, push, and pull of his body, the young creature was quickly draining itself of energy. Having just hatched and now fighting for escape without food, water, or rest, he was quickly working himself into exhaustion. Seeing the end in sight and almost being able to stick his head out of the end of the hole, the creature dug with more intensity. After another few minutes, the last bit of earth burst outward as the creature pushed with all of its might, flinging itself out into the world for the very first time.

Blinded by the bright afternoon sun and covered in dust and dirt, he slid down a small, rocky hill and landed with a thud on the grassy surface below. Through squinted eyes, the creature saw tall trees and rocky outcroppings and heard water moving nearby. With hunger and thirst on its mind, the creature collapsed in a heap and passed out.

Several hours later, after the sun had set and the air temperature dropped dramatically, the young creature slowly awoke from its involuntary nap. Looking around, he noticed that the world was upside-down and that something pinched on his back. Giving his head a shake, he realized that he had fallen onto his back and that his arm was asleep and giving him a pins-and-needles feeling. "But, how could my arm be asleep? My arms and legs are here under me," thought the creature. Giving his "arm" a shake, he let out a surprised roar when he realized what was actually on his back.

Protruding from his lower shoulders, a powerful set of scaly wings were folded against his back. In their current position, they went from his shoulders all the way down to the tip of his tail. Again, he wasn't familiar with wings, what they did, or why he had them, but for some reason, he found this to be an exciting discovering. Twitching his muscles in unison along his shoulders and back, he discovered just which sensation he needed to trigger to control these newly discovered limbs. Focusing on his wings, he stretched them out sideways and marveled at their impressive extended span. Holding them out flat, the spread ranged almost ten feet from tip to tip. He was still unsure of how to use them, but he would find out soon enough.

After a few minutes of stretching his muscles and testing his body out, the newborn creature eagerly started to explore his surroundings. While the area around him was new, it oddly felt familiar. Tall, solid trees extended hundreds of feet into the air, and mountains dotted the horizon as far as the eye could see. The warm air was chilled by a cool breeze blowing in from the north. Gazing around the landscape in front of him, the creature spotted a lazy, meandering line of blue moving across the field to his right. Instinctively knowing that this was something that he wanted, he quickly set off in that direction to satisfy his thirst.

The young one soon found himself at the edge of a small stream. Water moved rapidly from his right to his left, heading downhill to the lowlands in the distance. Following the direction of the stream he saw that the stream eventually joined with several other smaller streams to form a river, which then emptied into the vast blue water in the great distance. Lacking the geographical understanding of exactly what it was that he was looking at, but knowing what extreme thirst was, the creature lowered himself to the bank and lapped up the cool water.

Oddly, the creature noticed thin tendrils of steam rising from its mouth. When he had finally quenched his thirst, he noticed movement in the depths below. Curious as to what he was looking at, he stuck his head under the water and gazed at the moving colors in their territory. He saw a school of fish swimming in formation from one rock to another. They darted behind logs and hid amongst the plants. The skittish fish moved in jerky motions, only stopping only to nibble at bugs, smaller fish, or anything else that looked appetizing.

He didn't know what to make of them, but was entertained by their exciting nature. He watched for a few seconds more before realizing something felt wrong. He needed to breath. Whipping his head up out of the water, he quickly exhaled the breath that he was holding and filled his lungs with fresh, cool air.

Panting for a few moments at the minor scare that he just experienced, he rapidly resumed his normal breathing. Contemplating whether the fish were something that he could eat, he leaned back over the water's edge and scrutinized the area before him. In this section of the stream, a natural dam had formed behind a pile of rocks. This feature had caused the flow of water to divert around the outcropping and run more rapidly on the other side of the stream. On his side, though, the water was moving very slowly, and its surface had a reflective sheen.

Looking down at the pool, he saw trees, leaves, the sky, and other things that were above the water. Confused, he glanced back and forth several times between the real things and their reflections. Still unsure of just what he was actually seeing, it took him a few repeated glances to conclude that he was looking at a different view of the same objects. This mirror property seemed familiar to him, as with many other new things today, but yet he could not explain how he knew. Taking another step closer, the creature looked straight down into the water's surface. He gasped in surprise when he saw another face looking back at him. He had gasped so strongly that the force of the powerful gust of air leaving his mouth rippled the water and made the reflection scramble and seemingly disappear.

Continuing to stare down into the water, his eyes darted back and forth as he wondered where the other face had gone to. The face soon came into focus as the water calmed and returned to its previous, flat state. Not surprised to see it there in front of him this time, he moved closer and inspected the visage from various angles. He noticed that with each movement of his head, the other creature mimicked his every motion and did likewise, but backwards. He even experimented by moving his head back and forth, up and down, jerking from side to side, and winking with his eyes, and the face did the same each time. Ever curious, he reached down with one of his claws and poked the other creature on the nose. As soon as his claw came into contact with the image, the water rippled again and it disappeared.

As the water settled and the reflection reemerged, it finally hit him. The creature froze, as did the other face down in the water. A multitude of thoughts quickly formed within his head. In the end, they all narrowed down to one, all-encompassing train of thought. "That is me," thought the creature. He didn't know how or why, but that image in the water was of himself. But, his vague memory of his own appearance was drastically different than the image that he was looking at down below. It was at this moment, that he realized there was only one thing to say that made any sense at all. "Huh," thought Tryggvi.

Tryggvi spent the rest of that day walking around his new home in a daze. When he had first hatched from the egg and awoken into his new life, he was confused about the world around him, as any newborn creature would be. However, it was not as simple as that. It was compounded by the duality of mind that he kept experiencing. Not only was he confused about his body and environment, he was also confused because some things were brand new to him, but there were other things he could clearly remember.

One thing he knew for certain was that he was hungry. Memory of a past life or not, he instinctively knew what he wanted to eat. Meat. A lot of meat. He ran back to the stream to where the fish had been before. Crouching back on the river bank, he drove his head into the cool water and gnashed his teeth at anything that moved. Given his lack of experience with hunting in his current form, he was not as successful as he once was. Due to his unfamiliar physical geometry and unusual reaction speed of his muscles, he continued to go hungry for the first few minutes. Time and again, he reared his head back up out of the water only to have caught weeds, grasses, and the occasional stick caught in his teeth.

After an hour or so of determined, but unsuccessful, hunting attempts, Tryggvi decided to lay on the bank and watch the fish more carefully. He noticed a flock of long-legged birds standing in the water about a hundred feet upstream from his position. Seemingly unaffected by his splashing and raucous attempts at trying to catch the slippery little swimmers, they remained very still and stared into the water. Every few minutes, one of them would spear its head into the water and come back with a fish caught between its beaks. Mesmerized by both their patience and success, he carefully studied their technique and resolved to mimic their behavior. He had vague memories of fishing, but they involved large bodies of water and using tools of some sort. He wasn't sure what these tools were, how to get them, or if his new body could even utilize them, so he pushed those thoughts to the back of his mind. It didn't help him now to dwell on this dark, elusive past. The key was adapting to the present and going from there.

From what he could gather, the key to fishing was to get into the water with your whole body, stand there, and wait. Anxious to try this out and get some food, he braced himself for the cold water and jumped into the stream with the entirety of his mass. As he plunged into the stream full on, he splashed a large volume of water up and onto the bank. His tail sloshed the water behind him as he aligned himself with the stream and quickly sank into the water with all of his body. Between the impact of his body hitting the water and his massive might blocking the continued flow of water coming down the stream, even more water was splashed up onto riverbank. While this wasn't the most graceful of maneuvers, Tryggvi was pleasantly surprised to see a small, stranded fish flopping on its side next to him in the mud. Not wanting to waste a chance at a meal, he waddled over and grabbed the fish with his front teeth.

Swallowing the fish down his long neck felt better than he could believe. Apparently, he was very hungry. All of that energy spent digging and hunting must have added up and worn down his nutritional reserves. While his hunger was not yet satiated to say the least, it was a good start and felt great to have something down in his stomach. With this small meal swallowed, his hope was renewed and his spirits buoyed. He watched the birds continue to hunt for a few minutes longer and decided to revise his strategy.

Lifting himself up and out of the water, Tryggvi rose on his four legs while maintaining a slight crouch. He kept his underbelly just barely above the surface of the stream and got ready to strike. Looking down into the water he realized, unfortunately, that he couldn't see a single thing down there. His previous actions had stirred the river bed up so much that the stream was now full of silt and debris. All that he could see was a brown cloud drifting with the current below and around his legs. After waiting a few minutes for the silt to clear, he could once again see fish darting back and forth under the water. Slowly lowering his face towards the glassy surface, he took a deep breath and submerged his head into the stream.

As he looked around, his mood improved immediately. Just before him, where there used to be a cloud of silt obscuring his vision, was a group of five fish. The fish, seemingly unaware of his presence, were facing upstream as they swam into the current to maximum the oxygen entering their gills. Careful not to displace too much water, he slowly crept up behind two of the fish which were swimming closely together. From his estimate, they would both just barely fit within the width of his jaws. Watching their movements with more patience and attention than he could remember doing anything else in his short life, he rose above the two fish to better angle his attack. Should he miss them on the first strike, he wanted to be in a good position to catch them afterwards. Following their every motion and matching the timing of his actions to theirs, he prepared himself for the right moment. Sensing a small pause, he launched himself at the two fish and gulped them both in one fell swoop.

This second meal felt even better. Eager to hone his new hunting skills, Tryggvi continued to prowl the stream for more fish. Looking to avoid the silt issue that he caused before, he moved upstream a few steps before trying to hunt again. By keeping fresh areas ahead of him each time, he never had to worry about the disturbed debris stirred up by his previous attacks. After an hour or so of near misses and happy catches, he found himself with a full stomach and a strong desire to rest.

Climbing out of the stream, he walked up onto the dry land and shook vigorously to rid himself of any water still clinging to his hard scales. Looking up into the sky, he squinted against the bright sunlight. It felt uncomfortably warm standing out here in the open. He considered returning to the cave before remembering how hot it had been inside. While he could try to climb back in there, he would rather wait until the sun had set and the air had cooled.

Feeling sluggish and lazy, he ultimately decided to lay down in the shade of a nearby cluster of trees. Wrapping his wings over his face to block out more of the sunlight and curling his tail around his body for a better sense of protection, Tryggvi quickly fell asleep. It had been a long day full of new and unusual experiences.

Waking several hours later, Tryggvi looked around the tree cluster that he was hiding under and determined that no other animals or predators were nearby. Feeling safe to emerge from the relatively small amount of protective camouflaging that he had to work with, he returned to the stream for a long drink of water. Taking a few minutes to hunt again, he filled his gut with three additional fish.

Lifting his head out of the water, he scanned the area around him and remembered that he was still interested in checking out the cave again. While the sun was slowly disappearing over the horizon, enough light was shining into the mouth of the cave that he could investigate a little. Sensing that it would be dark soon, he jumped into action and ran to the mouth of the cave that he had violently exploded from earlier this day.

Approaching the place where he had hatched, his eyes adjusted to the lower light level inside the chamber. While he waited, he sniffed the rocks and ground around him. With a keener sense of his abilities and a better understanding of the world, he spent some time investigating the cave's floor, walls, and ceiling to look for food, natural protection, and just to understand the place better. Not finding food or anything else of significant interest, he made his way back to the stone pile and began to inspect the fragments of the egg from which he had escaped.

Seeing the fragments in a better light now and not fraught with the anxiety of escape, Tryggvi approached the small pile of random pieces and shards and sniffed them closely. Smelling of organic matter, he curiously took a larger piece and licked it. Confused about the taste, he was not sure if this was something that he could, or should, eat. He took a small bite of larger part sticking up into the air and chewed it a few times. Unhappy with this experiment, he spit the now-smaller fragments out and lashed his tongue about trying to get rid of the taste.

The larger, bottom section of the shell still pointed upward and was mostly intact. He was amazed to think that he had actually been inside there. How long had he lived inside the egg before he hatched? He could not imagine that it would have been very comfortable to have stayed in there for any period of time.

By now, the sun had set. He decided that this cave was warm, offered protection, and would be a good place to sleep for the night before it got too warm during the following day. Finding a smooth, flat section of rock on the floor near the stone pile, Tryggvi walked around in a circle a few times, determined how he'd like to lay, and gently dropped low to the ground. Curling his wings and tail around himself, he rested his head onto one of his arms and drifted off to sleep.

Morning came quickly for the young creature. The long night of rest was exactly what he had needed, and he felt renewed and rejuvenated. Feeling hungry once again, he made his way back outside for a drink of cool water and a few choice fish who made the mistake of swimming too closely by his perch on the bank of the stream.

As he pulled his head back out of the water, he looked down into the water again and gazed at his reflection. It was occasionally broken by small ripples in the water from water droplets falling from his jaw. As the droplets stopped falling and the reflection became more clear, he continued looking at his own image in fascination. He stared into his own eyes and pondered why they looked so familiar, yet different. As far as his memory was concerned, this was the only face which he had ever seen. He could only remember back to yesterday morning, and he only knew himself to have ever been this creature looking down into the calm water.

However, he felt that he had looked at himself before and seen a different face. A different body. A different... life. This unusual feeling disturbed him. Why would he have feelings like this? What other life could he have had, and why would these feelings be so overwhelming to him? The more that he thought on this, sitting on the bank of the stream in the early morning light, the more he wanted an answer. Not knowing anywhere else to look, he decided to go back to the cavern and check for clues. Turning around quickly, he ran back to the mouth of the cave and scurried inside.

Approaching the stone pile, he once again inspected the shell fragments. Again, nothing seemed significant about the pieces. However, the colors and shape of the egg still held some unknown significance to him. It seemed old and familiar to him, like something that he should know but just could not seem to remember. Gingerly, he gripped the shell fragments with his teeth and carefully set them, one by one, off to the side of the stone pile. After a few minutes of delicate work, he finally had the egg shells pieces collected in a small pile off to the right and could freely investigate the stone pile. He sniffed each stone, licked several, and stuck his head into a few crevices to try to get a better look in some of the cracks. Unable to discern anything new from this cursory investigation, he started taking the pile apart, rock by rock, using his teeth and front claws.

The pile, standing approximately seven feet long, three feet wide, and two feet tall, did not take very long to disassemble. Emulating the same care and attention to detail which he had used in moving the egg shell pieces, Tryggvi placed all of the rocks in an empty spot next to the original pile. As he neared the bottom of the pile, he began to see odd details and objects appearing under some of the stones. Long, white objects, some slender and long, others stubby and short, appeared in an increasing frequency. He felt like he had seen them before, but was not sure where or when. Or why. Again, these memories haunted him and clouded his understanding of the world around him and his place within it.

It wasn't until he got to the far end of the pile when things got weird. As he removed more rocks, a new word came to his mind: bones. He didn't really understand what bones were, but he knew that these were bones. Bones of another being who must have died long ago. On top of some of the bones in the middle, a long, sharp object rested amongst the rubble, with some of the bones wrapped around one end. These bones resembled the shape of Tryggvi's clawed hands. A rectangular piece of stone, different in color and texture than the stones around it, sat on top of the being's chest. Odd markings had been carved into its upper surface. Tryggvi looked at the markings from several angles. He felt like they had some form of importance, but could not figure them out.

At the far end of this collection of bones, another oddity appeared. It was at the very end, and it seemed to be the last of them. But it was different than the others. While it gave him the impression that it was composed of the same material, it was vastly different. It wasn't long or slender. It was roundish, with holes in multiple places. In one of the holes was a collection of... what were they? ... Teeth? Not sharp, pointy teeth like he had in his mouth, but flat and smaller. Remembering back to his reflection, Tryggvi concluded that this 'bone' must have been a similar head of another creature. It was like his own head, but much smaller, and from a different type of creature.

Not sure what to make of all of this, he spent a few long moments staring at the pile and pondering what it could all mean. Also, why had he been sitting on top of this pile inside of his egg? After a while, he grew tired of this onset confusion and needed to clear his mind. Heading back towards the light shining through the opening in the cave, he quickly made his way out into the fresh air and bright sunlight to escape the gloominess of the cave behind him.

The rest of the day was spent practicing how to hunt and learning more tricks and techniques. Growing bored of fish, he branched out into the wooded areas and tried searching out some smaller, non-aquatic game. He managed to catch a rabbit, some bugs under a fallen tree, and unfortunately, tried to hunt down a porcupine. Fearing the sharp-looking quills as he tried to bite at the pointy critter, he found that the quills broke and bounced off of his tough scales on the outside of his skin. However, the softer, inner tissue of his mouth and nose were not so impervious to the animal's defensive attacks. Letting out a short yelp as one quill poked his tongue, he decided that this meal was not worth the trouble. Thankfully, he found that his clawed fingers could easily grasp the quill and pulled it out of his body.

As he grew tired of hunting and the sun began to slip below the nearby mountain range, he headed back to the cave to hide for the night. Making his way to the same spot where he had slept last night, Tryggvi repeated his circle-walk, settled in on the smooth floor, and fell asleep shortly after closing his eyes.

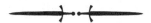

Almost immediately, he found himself to be awake again, in the cave still, but it was slightly different. For starters, it was substantially brighter and cooler than it was just a moment ago before he fell asleep. The entrance wasn't caved in like the opening was just a few moments ago, and air was able to move in and out more freely. The air smelled fresh and clean, full of organic smells from the outside meadow. He noticed that the pile of stones was at his feet in its original assembly, but there was no trace of the egg from which he had hatched. The stones also looked cleaner and less dusty than he remembered.

"Am I dreaming, or is this some sort of vision?" Tryggvi thought to himself. Unsure of exactly what it was that he was currently experiencing, he continued to gaze around the cave to absorb all of the details that he could. From behind him, he heard a light scraping on the floor of the entryway. He turned and watched in awe as a woman and a young boy entered the cave. The boy carried a large oval stone that appeared to be very similar, if not identical, to the egg from which he had hatched. It also seemed familiar from another manner, as if he knew that stone, the egg, from another part of his mind. An unknown distant trace of a memory eluded his thoughts and prevented him from pinpointing how or where he knew this stone from. But it was there at the back of his mind, bugging him and gnawing at his consciousness.

The two people were also familiar to him, and he had a sense that they were very important to him, as well. Their manners, their faces, their voices, all and felt like... home. Again, the word "home" didn't mean anything particular to him, but he knew that it was important to him, something that he missed and wanted in his life. He watched as the two stood at the base of the rock pile and stared down at the stones. Both looked deeply saddened and openly wept as the woman comforted the young child and held him close.

What he hadn't noticed before, and only became clear to him when he walked around the scene playing out in his mind's eye, was that the pile of stones was only complete from the end where he was originally located. As he made his way around the pile, he noticed that some of the stones were missing at this end. Coming closer to the incomplete end of the pile, he immediately froze in his tracks. Looking down, he saw the full image of what was missing from his non-dream view of this cave.

Down at his feet, amongst the stones, was a man lying on his back. He was dressed in full war gear, with a sword and a stone tablet on top of his chest. The man lying there, in the place of where he previously saw a collection of bones, was Tryggvi himself. Everything now made sense. Forgotten memories flooded back into his consciousness and it all became clear to him. He was not the dragon he had seen looking down into the pool of water. He was Tryggvi Brynjarson, leader of the Viking people and great traveler of the North Atlantic. The sword there was his sword, the very sword given to him by his father. Looking closely, he could now read the words written on tablet: "Tryggvi Brynjarson. Leader. Husband. Father."

Confusion turned to panic, which in turn, became a complete and utter meltdown of his psyche. None of this made any sense whatsoever. The last that he had known, he was a living man. He had a wife, a son, friends, and a village to look after. He wasn't some dragon living in a cave struggling to eat fish. And a dragon?! Dragons did not exist. They were merely mythological creatures that he and his people told their children about in fairy tales of long lost days in history. Weren't they?

As his confusion continued to take over his body, mind, and emotions, he saw the dream sequence continue in front of him. His wife and son had left the cave, and he was alone again. The pile of stones was now completely covered as he had first found it, but they were cleaner and more akin to their state at the end of the funeral scene which he had previously experienced. The sun must have gone down and turned to night, as it was very dark now in the cave. However, a faint light emanated from the stones and cast a warm, white glow on the area before him. He watched in awe as a small, dimly lit orb, no bigger than one of the tiny fish that he had been catching, appeared from the center of the pile of stones and rose up in front of him. It hung in the air for the briefest of moments before floating towards the egg that sat atop the pile. Reaching the surface of the egg, the light passed through the outer shell and disappeared deep inside.

Fascinated, yet equally horrified, Tryggvi could not look away from the scene unfolding in front of him. The light began to return, but this time as a pulse coming from deep inside the egg's shell. It started very slowly and with a dim magnitude of light. But as the pulses continued, the frequency and intensity began to increase. The light came faster and stronger, and before long, it was almost painful to watch. He put up one of his hands to block the light, but even that was not enough. The light continued to pulse, brighter and brighter, until he finally wrapped both of his wings before him to shield his eyes from the light and energy projecting from the core of the egg. The energy became so intense that it finally overloaded his senses and he passed out on the spot. His body, no longer under his control, slumped to the rocky floor in a heap of limbs and wings.

Light. The light was blinding Tryggvi, and he defensively put his hands back up in front of his face, still under the belief that the pulsating light was overwhelming his brain. He was still unsure if what he had experienced was imaginary or not. It felt real, but how could it have been? He had seen himself dead, and his wife and son were there in this very cave, with his body, but he was still very much alive. Incomplete strings of thought flooded his mind, clouding his sense of the world and diluting his understanding of what was real or fake, imaginary, a dream, a vision, or a nightmare. His heart raced, and the blood boiled inside his veins.

Finding himself short of breath, he immediately sought fresh air. He longed for the warmth of the morning sunlight on his scales. "Scales?" he thought. Why wouldn't he think "skin," like he felt he should have? He burst from the cave and ran straight to the stream nearby. Jumping directly into the water and splashing the shoreline and plants around him, he tried to cool himself off in the refreshing waves. He drunk deeply from the cool water surrounding his body. While it sated his thirst, it did little to cool the heat that burned within his heart.

He raced back to the cave to see the body again for himself and used his clawed hands to remove more stones from the skeleton beneath. Looking again, it was clear that this was a human body and similar in size and shape to his old body that he had seen during the dream. Looking down at the tablet and sword again, he mind began to race. It clearly said his name. He could not have read it before, but the words were clear as day now. His pulse increased, his blood pressure rose, and he did the only thing that made sense to him in that moment. He roared.

Having never roared before, the sound surprised him at first. But as he continued and the anger propagated from his jaws, he washed the inside of the cave with violent sound waves as his unrestricted emotions were unleashed. Fear. Anger. Disbelief. Curiosity. Anxiousness. Excitement. Despair. Worry. Sadness. Longing for his family. All these feelings culminated in one very unusual and entirely new feeling within him.

From the back of his jaw near the top of his neck, his mouth began to feel extremely hot. As his mind filled with anger and fear, his promethium glands activated for the very first time. Instinctively, unaware of what he was doing, he unleashed a blazing salvo of dragonfire. The fire poured out of his toothy maw and scoured the stone walls of all life: animal, plant, bacterial, and fungal.

As the seconds continued to tick by, Tryggvi felt drunk with the raw power that raged within his young body. He dug into the stone floor with his clawed hands and feet, braced his mass lower and more powerfully to the ground, and arched his neck around the room. The fire only increased as his anger grew and the sound became deafening to his relatively young ears. Lost in the moment, he felt only one, all-encompassing desire: to destroy.

Without letting up, he turned his head sideways and blasted the stone pile, egg shards, and remains of his former body with white-hot dragonfire. The fire washed down the walls, like some living, breathing entity of its own. As he looked down upon his grave site and saw that his remains were now reduced to nothing more than a pile of scattered ashes, his anger and regret rose to unbearable heights.

He blindly swung his head towards the mouth of the cave, unable and unwilling to cease this mass destruction of everything around him. The hot gases pushing through the entryway of the cavern as they escaped the column of death flowing from his body ruptured the top of the opening and obliterated all support material around it. The tunnel he had worked so hard to dig finally crumbled and collapsed right in front of him.

Blocking off the only source of oxygen to the fire-breathing monstrosity which Tryggvi had become, the fire spread and licked every surface of the cave and everything within it. As the daylight was shut out from the cave and only his fire lit the room around him, so was his source of breathable air and fuel source for his anger. While his body went unscathed from his fiery onslaught, his lungs still required an oxygenated atmosphere to survive. As he continued to unleash his uncontrollable fury upon the interior of the cavern, he rapidly used up all of the fire's fuel in the air. He couldn't breathe... but the fire kept pouring from his mouth. Unable to think clearly, Tryggvi belched flame until there was nothing left to burn. As his lungs exhausted themselves and denied his brain oxygen to keep functioning, his body gave in, and all turned to black.

Chapter Nine
Vibrations

When Tryggvi realized that he had not only died, but that his soul had been transferred to a dragon's egg, his confusion and anger nearly led him to suffocate himself. Any other creature would have perished with no breathable air or water to drink. Tryggvi, however, was a hardened, robust dragon and was capable of long periods of deep hibernation.

After closing off the mouth of the cave and passing out, the dragon slumbered, hidden from the world, for many, many years. Undisturbed by nature or humankind, the young creature slept and slept. Thankfully, some rubble eventually fell from the sealed opening, allowing a miniscule amount of air to seep in. His body, in its dormant state, only required small breaths from his tired lungs. Additionally, his body sustained another function: he continued to grow.

It had been two centuries since Tryggvi the Dragon unleashed his anger upon the cave. In that time, his body had fully rested and healed itself of its injuries sustained during his violent outburst. It had also grown much larger than before.

When he woke up, confusion set in. Having not used his body in many years, Tryggvi painfully opened his eyes to the light shining through a crack between the large boulders blocking the cave opening. It took a moment for him to remember who he was and why he was there. There was another feeling: discomfort.

Years ago, the cave had been a good size for his newborn dragon body. However, with his increased size, he was now feeling cramped and needed to stretch his limbs. His legs felt tight, and his wings ached behind his back. He tried to squeeze through the opening, but his body would not fit. He backed up, got a better look at the shape and size of the opening, and tried to walk through again. After three attempts, he realized that his body was just too big. Through his years of rest, his body had grown impressively.

Lying down on the smooth stone floor, he stretched his arms through the opening and tried to wiggle his body through. The best that he could accomplish was to get his head and one of his arms through most of the cave opening. Looking back, he could see that he was stuck at his shoulders and the rest of his body would not budge. Creeping backwards, he got himself back into the confines of the cave.

Looking closer, he noticed that some of the rocks were cracked and looked weaker than the rest. While he wasn't a wrecking ball, he did have the size and mass to potentially cause some damage to the rock if he hit it hard enough. Tucking in his wings, he backed up as far as he could to the far wall of the cave, dug in his claws, and charged the opening with all of the force he could muster.

The impact on his shoulders and upper back was unexpectedly intense. After years of hibernation, his muscles had grown strong, and he could now run incredibly fast. The contact with the rock opening sent pain shooting up and down his spine. He looked up at the top of the cave opening and saw that nothing had moved, but that the cracks had propagated ever so slightly. The result of this experiment wasn't anything to celebrate over, but it gave him hope.

Backing up again, he repeated this process several more times. Each time, he ran harder and faster, hurling himself against the rock opening with more might than before. The pain continued to wrack his body and his shoulder was beginning to feel like a pile of mush. But he needed to escape this stony prison. He needed to get free. So he crashed himself into the wall. Over, and over again. Each time feeling closer to freedom. On the final attempt, he rushed the opening with more force and anger than he could imagine possible in his exhausted state, and slammed into the rock with all the energy that he had left in his body.

When he hit the rock this last time, the earth shook, and the hillside rumbled. The impact reverberated through the dirt and stone as far as ten miles away. Trees shook and leaves fell. Soil drifted down the hillside in dusty streams. The powerful adolescent dragon forced his way out of the ground at last and burst into the sunlight of the bright, warm day. Shielding his eyes from the shattered bits of rock and rubble, Tryggvi flew to the ground and rolled several times head over heels through the grass. He landed in a heap and didn't move for a solid minute. The ground continued to rumble, and the air was littered with fine dust.

As the ground settled and he could see once more, he looked over with great satisfaction to see the enlarged opening of the cave and the wreckage that he had left in his wake. His entire body ached, but he was breathing fresh air again and he could finally stretch out. Of course, it hurt to do so, but staying compressed in that cave any longer would have surely killed him.

Limping over to the nearby stream, which was now slightly wider than he remembered it and had developed an oxbow lake along one of the turns, he drank deeply from the cool, refreshing water. He left his head there for a minute more, enjoying the feel of the cool liquid flowing around his mouth and nose. Lifting his head back up, he scanned the area. It was still the same place that he recognized from before, but it felt different. Some trees were gone where he recalled them being formerly, while others had grown up in places that he remembered to have been bare.

"How long was I asleep for?" he wondered.

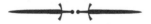

And so, Tryggvi returned to his daily routine and started adapting to the new, slightly different environment. He drank, hunted, ate, slept, and explored. His old cave was too small for him now, so he had to find a new lair to dwell within. Thankfully, the mountains' rocky terrain provided many outcroppings and water worn areas along the rivers, with nooks and crannies for creatures of all shapes and sizes.

Eventually, he found a cave larger than his first and made himself at home. He had to chase the family of bears out first, but that didn't take too long as they were easily frightened away by the sight of their first dragon. Oddly, he found himself to be inherently frightened of the bears when he first saw them, but he couldn't remember why he would be. He had a fuzzy memory of something about bears from his previous life, but he couldn't recall what it was about.

And so, like the hermit crab, Tryggvi spent the following centuries moving from one lair to another. Each time, he slept and hibernated while the days and nights crept by in the outside world. After a spell, he would awake, find himself trapped inside a rocky prison, and once again fight his way out. With each escape, the animals and people of nearby villages and towns would feel a slight tremor vibrate through the ground. Some of his escapes were pretty minor, while some actually caused low-magnitude earthquakes in the surrounding regions. As the years progressed, Tryggvi became more adept at selecting larger and larger caves with smoother openings, knowing that he would someday awaken and need to escape once again.

CHAPTER TEN
THE CAVE

On one occasion, Tryggvi awoke and found that not only was he not uncomfortable with his body size in the cave, but that he could easily walk through the opening. As he had spent most of his life constantly growing and needing to fight his way out of his lair at some point, finding out that he had stopped physically growing was an unusual surprise to the young adult dragon. Tryggvi, in his draconic persona, was now close to seven hundred years old, a young adult in dragon years. As each year came and went, he remembered less about his former human self than before. With each passing day, the glorious leader of the Viking village was not only forgotten by his ancestors and historians, but by himself as well.

Happy to remain in his current dwelling, Tryggvi relished in the opportunity to simply search for food and water in the nearby land. It was fall in New England, and he lived in what is now the state of Maine. He took to the skies and hunted through open fields and clearings, skimming low over wide rivers. On these flights, he opportunistically caught fish from the rivers, birds that made the mistake of venturing too closely to his flight path, and even snatched up a moose on an open expanse of grassland. The region was rich in animal life, and the dragon enjoyed the tasty menu laid out before him.

What was surprising, however, was the number of humans that he spotted. These two-legged creatures could be found chopping down trees in the forests, hunting animals in the thickets, and working the fields. Tryggvi once approached a group of humans to see what they were and what they smelled like. When they saw him, however, they reacted very harshly and attacked him with their tools and weapons.

Over the years, they shot at him with arrows, rocks, pointed sticks, and even metallic balls that travelled faster than he could fly. He rarely suffered any serious injuries, but their advances were unfriendly and quite annoying. Eventually, he grew tired of these creatures not wanting to be his friend and began to fight back. He never attacked first, but he refused to let them assault him anymore. He would often retreat, take to the skies, and try hunting somewhere else. But, sometimes, their attacks hurt.

It was due to such attacks that his approach eventually differed. He found that they were more consistently employing these metallic lobbing weapons that made a very loud boom at the start of the attack. Unlike their other weapons, which were laughable, these could sometimes penetrate his scales and cause him sharp pain. While he had yet to actually be seriously injured by these, it would still hurt for several days, and he believed that he still had a few of these metal chunks stuck in his skin somewhere. Tired of being shot at, he decided to satisfy another of his curiosities: to see what they tasted like. He would fly in quickly, dodge their attacks if possible, and pluck them from the ground.

These creatures were much different than the other animals that he caught in the forest. Unlike the other animals, with their soft fur, warm meat, and tiny bones that he'd have to pluck out with his claws, these animals wore unusual outer coverings. Sometimes, they were easy to eat and were covered in very soft material, and most often than not, they were covered in the skin of other animals. This provided him with an unusual mixture of flavors and textures to his meal.

As time went on, though, they were increasingly more difficult to eat. They began to be covered with hard outer scales that stopped his claws and teeth from penetrating on the first attempt. He found that he had to chomp more furiously and swipe with more power than he had in the past. Unable to eat this protective covering, he would need to rip it off of their bodies before proceeding with his meal. Besides this "armor" (as he had heard some of the humans call it, which he still was not sure how or why he could discern their language), they often carried sharp objects that made eating them painful. He grew more careful over time and would pick out these knives and tools with his claws. Once finished, he could fill his belly with warm meat.

These attacks also changed his eating habits over time. In the past, when he simply hunted fish from the rivers and lakes, deer on the open ground, and animals hiding in trees, he would catch them where they lived, eat them there on the spot, and then be on his way. He would continue his hunt until he had had his fill and then return to his lair to rest. However, these attacking humans were dangerous. Unless he killed everyone there at once, it would be hazardous to remain in one area for too long.

As he fought with the smaller creatures to defend himself, and secure his next meal, he would often grab two or three of them at once. He could take one in each hand and then one more in his mouth. Rapidly pumping his strong wings, he would thrust up from the ground and be airborne again within seconds. With this maneuver, he'd be on his way before they could muster their numbers and mount a counterattack. Flying back to his lair, he could then eat in peace without having to be constantly on his guard.

Returning to his lair, he would kill his recent catch, if they weren't dead already, settle into the security of his deep cave, and consume his meal. As time progressed, he developed a system to keep his cave clean and tidy. He still wasn't entirely sure why he did this, but some deep-seated part of his brain compelled him to maintain order in his life and domicile. He would pick the humans' armor and weapons and fling them to one side of the cave. He found these consistently interesting as each person had similar, yet different suits of armor, weapons, and trinkets on their bodies. Even more interestingly, he found that some of them carried round and shiny golden coins. He was magnetically attracted to these and kept them in a nook behind where he slept. He felt the need to collect and guard these objects, despite not knowing what purpose they served.

After eating, he would throw the bones outside his cave near the entrance. He had no use for them and disliked the odor. However, he found that other animals, which might be looking to enter his cave and steal his possessions, or worse, attack him in his sleep, were afraid of the smell of the rotting leftovers and stayed out of the cave. The cave was deep enough, fortunately, that he couldn't smell it from the back where he slept. A small price to pay for the added protection it provided, so he compromised on this bone collection.

One day, however, his relative friendliness towards the humans changed. Every so often, when food was hard to come by or he just needed a change of scenery, Tryggvi would stretch his wings and travel further from home. He had a natural curiosity with the land around him, and felt compelled to explore, find new things, and see what was beyond the horizon.

While out on one of these extended hunting trips, he found himself flying around several large bodies of water. Today, we know them as the Great Lakes. He heard yelling and various loud "booms" coming from the humans down below. Many of the noises were from the sticks that some of them carried, but others came from longer cylinders lower to the ground. Not sure what they were, he swooped in low for a closer look.

As he approached, he heard several of the tiny creatures scream in surprise at his sudden appearance. He had heard this many times in the past, and it often brought him great amusement to hear them squeal. As in previous run-ins, they took shots at him with their metal lobbing sticks, but either missed or connected with grazing shots that didn't really faze him.

Coming up on one of the large, hollow cylinders, he quickly dodged out of the way as he realized that they were shooting at him... with larger, more dangerous metal balls. With a loud blast, the cylinder fired a round past his body so fast that he barely got a look at it. He wasn't sure just what this thing was, but he wasn't taking any chances.

Swooping back around in a long, lazy arc, he lined himself up with the humans and entered a quick dive. Tucking in his limbs and wings to decrease his drag, he quickly picked up speed. On his first pass, he had noticed that the cylinder, while appearing to be made of metal like other human artifacts, had a different base material. This lower part, which the humans were using to aim the weapon, appeared to be made from the wood of a tree. As he had learned in the past, wood burned. It burned especially hot under a blast of dragonfire.

Taking careful aim, he unleashed a salvo of fire upon the weapon. As the blaze erupted from his mouth and raced towards the ground, the two humans operating the weapon dove out of the way in opposite directions to avoid the incoming fire. The weapon, or a cannon, as we know it to be, was directly hit by the sustained blast of Tryggvi's wrath. The body of the cannon itself withstood the blast, but the base, however, quickly caught fire and burned to ash within seconds. The cannon barrel limply held on for another few moments before rolling off to the side and lodging itself into the soft ground below. Without proper support to aim and relocate, the weapon was rendered useless, at least for this battle.

Content in the weapon's destruction and assuming the threat had been neutralized, Tryggvi let up his guard and circled the area in search of a new target to befriend or destroy. It was at this moment that everything changed.

Low to the ground and off to his right side, just out of his field of vision, another cannon was being loaded by a crew intent on evening the odds with this flying monstrosity. As they loaded the barrel with gunpowder, they readied a different form of projectile, one that Tryggvi had never seen before: grapeshot. Unlike the large, single-piece cannonballs, which the dragon could easily dodge given enough distance and advance warning, grapeshot consisted of many small pieces of lead, iron, rock, or anything else that was handy on the battlefield. While each projectile alone would cause little harm to him individually, grapeshot has a higher probability of at least hitting the intended target with something, if not multiple objects. This is why grapeshot, much like buckshot in a shotgun, is good for hunting fast, flying targets... like dragons.

Tryggvi, unfamiliar with this weaponry and ammunition, was completely unprepared for what came next. Still flying low to the ground looking for food and new curiosities, he heard a loud explosion to his right. Glancing over his right wing to see what was going on, he felt his right leg, parts of his tail, and the underside of his wing being peppered with tiny, red-hot objects. They stung and burned like nothing that he had ever felt before. The humans had shot at him in the past with their guns, but this was different. He could not even count how many small places hurt on his body as they all seemed to blend into one large, throbbing sense of pain.

Fighting through the agonizing torment ravaging his body, he banked hard to the right to swoop back around towards the source of the attack to get a better look at whatever tricks the tiny humans were up to this time. Lining up on the cannon that fired at him, he was about to unleash another fusillade of burning death upon the weapon and the crew surrounding it, when a loud bang went off from just underneath him. He was moving so quickly that he had failed to notice the third crew hiding just below his field of view.

The shot struck his underside, hitting his chest and stomach as well as the inner surfaces of his arms and legs. He could feel the hot projectiles burning through his scales and scalding his inner skin. Unused to feeling pain on his typically protected, softer inner tissue, the new pain surprised him almost as much as it physically hurt. Unlike before, however, this attack had the added advantage of close proximity and succession to a previous attack. Already wounded from the first blast at a longer distance, this close attack packed more of a punch, and he momentarily lost flight control.

Flinching from the impact and instinctively pulling his limbs in towards himself to ward off further attacks, he lost altitude, caught his tail on a tall tree, and crashed into the dirt below.

He hit head first into the ground and lost consciousness. When he opened his eyes again, he found himself flipped over and lying on his back. Still disoriented and wincing from the agony in his scales and shaking off the confusion in his head, he failed to notice the armored men running toward him on all sides. He aimed to roll himself over and plant his feet in the dirt to push off and take back to the air, but before he could even land back on all four limbs, he felt a great, heavy, rope net fly over his body and pull him down to the ground. Four men, evenly spaced around him, each held a corner of the large net that was currently restraining him sufficiently to prevent him from flying away. He could still move on his legs, but even that provided to be difficult for the injured dragon. Tryggvi pushed and tugged against the restraints, and almost found amusement in the fact that several of the men were whipping through the air as they held onto the wildly moving ropes. He jerked his head from side to side to try to free himself, but stuck beneath the small square lines of the net.

Realizing that the only way out of this trap was to burn his way through, he warmed up the promethium glands in his throat. He was about to unleash his anger upon the group when a sharp pain shot up through his chest. He cranked his head to the left and saw that a human had just jabbed a long spear between a gap in his hardened scales. This last bit of pain was the final fuel that he needed to grant his deep-seeded anger the retribution upon the world that he desired. Letting out a pain-driven roar, he poured burning hell upon the spearman, as well as the surrounding land and vegetation. He had never found joy in killing other sentient beings, but this time it was different. This time, it was about self-preservation... and revenge.

The man died almost immediately. Not only did the fire incinerate the man's flesh upon contact, but all of the oxygen around him was consumed to fuel the continued salvo. Tryggvi twisted his body, grabbed the man's corpse with his front claws, and pushed the body to the dirt. Pressing closer and firing a second time, he reveled in hysterical rage as he watched the flesh and bone melt away into a pile of ash. The fast flow of air and fire blew the ash away as it was produced, leaving nothing but a burnt circle on the ground below.

Turning his attention to the others, Tryggvi first set the net ablaze. The rope strands instantly caught ablaze and turned into a checkerboard of ash hanging frozen in the air. He continued the blaze as he swung his head to the right, and set two of the men alight with a long, deadly arc of dragonfire. After roasting the last of his captors, he whipped his tail out from behind and swept the legs of the other two men standing behind him. Before they could rise to their feet, he raised his tail high into the air and brought it down with tremendous force upon the man on his left. He crushed his skull with the solitary impact and permanently removed him from the fight.

The last one still alive frantically tried to gain traction on the soft earth below him. Unable to scramble up and away in time, he was easy pickings for the blood-thirsty dragon. Tryggvi violently grabbed the puny human around the legs with his toothy maw and bit down until he heard bones crunch. Reaching for his upper body with his arms, he wrapped his claws around the man's chest and pulled. He kept pulling until he could feel the muscles and joints within the still living man pop and stretch to their breaking points. The man's body snapped in half just above the waist and came apart in two wet chunks.

Tryggvi threw the lower half to the side, swallowed the torso, and lifted his head to the sky. In that moment, overcome with anger, pain, and victorious glee, he roared to the heavens. The remaining humans hiding in ambush fled the battlefield for fear of being slaughtered next when the dragon came to its senses.

He bellowed his anger into the air for a minute longer before realizing just how weak and exhausted he really was from his near fatal encounter with the humans. What he once thought of as curious creatures worthy of getting to know better, were now dangerous beings to be killed on contact. Never again would he let his guard down and suffer like he had today.

They would suffer. They would suffer until there were no more left to threaten him and his way of life ever again.

After Tryggvi had calmed down and caught his breath, he mustered his remaining strength and took to the air. As he was a long distance from home, he flew as far as he could until he found a cave big enough to fit his body within and hide from sight. He crawled inside, curled into a circle with his head hiding behind his tail, and passed out.

Nestled within the relative protection of the new cave, he rested for several days. By the time he awoke, it was already growing dark on the eve of the third day. Carefully sticking his head outside of the opening to the cave, he looked around to make sure that there were no human or animal attackers waiting for him. Sensing that he was safe, he fully emerged from the shelter and stretched his wings out as far as they'd go. Shaking off dirt and debris, he laid out on the nearby grass and took note of where his body still hurt. He maneuvered his neck around to get a better view of the different wounds and tried to see what was wrong. As the sun was already setting, he'd need to either wait until the following morning or create some light for himself. Not wanting to wait, he came up with an idea.

Using his teeth, he collected some dry trees in the area and piled them up in the clearing outside the cave. Stepping back, he gave the pile a small wash of dragonfire and lit the wood into a rapidly roaring fire. Content with his newly created light source, he continued with his bodily inspection. He found several chunks of grapeshot still stuck in his flesh or wedged under loose scales. Using his claws and teeth, he managed to slowly, but surely, remove each piece. He noticed that his skin was exposed where several of the scales had been broken off. He'd need to be mindful of those in the future and keep those spots better protected from harm.

Instinctively, he felt compelled to clean the wounds of anything that might cause further pain or injury. In some places, he was able to twist his body into different positions to use his tongue to lick the wounds clean. However, some places were too hard to reach, and he grew increasingly frustrated trying to reach them. Recalling that he had flown over a river on his way to the cave, he quickly ran through the forest until he came upon the water from his memory. Jumping into the river, he splashed about as he painfully, but joyfully, cleaned off his skin, scales, and flushed the wounds with the cool, refreshing water.

After satisfactorily removing all foreign contaminants from the battle, he felt relieved and was able to relax for a while. Reflecting back on the past few days, he realized that he was now living in a whole new world. These strange human weapons had nearly killed him, but he still had explored many miles of new lands. If he healed properly, this trip would not have been a total waste of time and effort. Feeling tired and a little light-headed from the running around and painstaking extraction of the grapeshot, Tryggvi went back to the cave for another night of rest and recuperation.

After his slumber, Tryggvi headed home. Waking up with the morning light, he exited the cave and spent some time hunting for his morning meal. He spotted a few deer and managed to catch one with his hungry, drooling jaws. After eating the delightfully tender meat from the fit animal, he took to the skies again, headed east, and made his way back to his lair.

Opportunistically eating along the way, he spent his time flying, looking for food, and trying to avoid any further human contact. While not necessarily afraid of the humans and their unnatural weaponry, he was wary of entering another fight in his current state. After a long day of flying, he finally made it back to his lair as the sun's last rays were kissing the Earth with their warmth and light.

Alighting on the soft grass just outside of the opening to the cavern, he noted that the air felt unusually cold. It was late fall at this point, so it wasn't entirely surprising, but he had hoped for it to stay warm a little while longer this season. Ambling through the mouth of the cave, he smelled something strange coming from within. Moving past the bone pile at the front of the cave, he found a family of foxes sleeping in the dirt depression that he used for a bed. Breathing in a lungful of air, he let out a low, deep growl and released a quick gout of fire across the ground. He didn't want to hurt any of them per se, but he was not above scaring them a bit to get his bed back.

The foxes jumped up from the ground in a panic and screeched before scrambling out of the cave. Grinning to himself, Tryggvi walked over to the depression, circled a few times, and slumped down into a comfortable ball of scales and spikes. He quickly fell asleep with little regard for what was happening outside.

During the night, the air turned crisp, and the temperature dropped into lows that Maine had not experienced in years. The upper atmosphere had been collecting water vapor into dark, angry-looking clouds over the past several days, and they now hung ominously over the landscape. Late into the evening, when the last Joules of heat energy from the sun had long since been exhausted, the winds hammered the mountainside as the clouds released their moisture into the freezing air, producing a thick flurry of snow. For the rest of the night and into the early hours of the next morning, the region was blanketed in dense layer of snow and ice. The humans stayed bundled in their cabins, their roaring fireplaces and woodstoves burning brightly to stave off the encroaching cold. Animals hid in their burrows and caves, curled up in their furry protective layers.

All the while, deep in his dark cave within the mountain, Tryggvi slept. He had no reason to worry about the cold. Buried so deeply into the mountain, his lair was kept warm by the Earth itself, protected from the cold winds by a series of twists and turns in the layout of the cave. Hiding in the back, it was difficult for any passerby to know of his existence, and prevented the cold weather from reaching him.

As the snow continued to accumulate, a precarious snow drift formed near the top of the mountain, directly over the opening to Tryggvi's lair. With each passing minute, more and more snow built up overhanging a cluster of loose boulders, which were barely held in check by a small grove of trees. As the weight of the snow increased, the trees, rocks, and the hillside itself experienced higher levels of stress and strain from the unusually large amount of force being constantly applied to them. As the stress increased on the trees, they began to creak and lean out over the side of the hill. Their roots gradually pulled out from their earthen foundations, and the rocks shifted behind them.

Early in the morning, the perilous balance was finally defeated by the power of gravity. All that it took was one piece of the puzzle coming undone: a single tree. With a sharp snap, the final root holding one of the trees in place let go and the tree leaned out further over the side of the hill. As it lurched forward, the rocks behind it gave way and took out more of the trees. The energy and momentum of each object joined together to create a monumental landslide.

Tumbling and sliding down the mountainside, the boulders, dirt, trees, snow, ice, and everything else which happened to get in their way came flying down the mountain. A tremendous roar built up as the objects crashed down and continued taking out more and more objects along the way. A mighty boom echoed around the valley as the mass slammed into the ground at the bottom and spread out in every direction. All living things for miles around were woken from their slumber.

All, that is, except for the dragon sleeping deep inside the mountain. Tryggvi, exhausted from his long flight and the battle with the humans, slept soundly as all of this transpired. Even the roar of the landslide failed to rouse him. As the entrance was directly under the origin site of the landslide, the majority of the material naturally fell straight down below. The mouth of his cave, while large, was soon blocked by the random assortment of broken tree trunks, shattered rocks, and dirty snow as the landslide finally came to rest.

For many long minutes, the air was eerily still. Dust, wispy snow, and particles of ice hung in the air. The snow continued to fall, covering the mountain in an even deeper blanket of snow. After a few hours more, for all anyone could have been concerned, it was as if nothing had ever happened.

Deep inside his lair, Tryggvi continued to sleep, more deeply than ever before. Sleep was the best thing for healing his skin, scales, and pride. As the hours passed, his large lungs soon consumed the oxygen in the air. The landslide, however, had sealed off the deep tunnel and chambers from the outside world. The cave's breathable air continued to diminish, leaving the sleeping dragon in a thick cloud of carbon dioxide. His body, though, was well adapted for long-term survival in extreme environments. His breathing slowed as his heart rate plummeted, and he slipped again into a deep hibernation. There he stayed, hidden away in the cave, for many years.

PART FOUR
HELLFIRE

CHAPTER ELEVEN
THE ENCOUNTER

It had been over three hundred years since the night of the landslide. Tryggvi the dragon, stuck in a deep hibernation and unbothered by any outside stimulus, had been all but forgotten by the outside world. The four seasons came and went with each passing year, and the land around the cave slowly changed. The snow around the mountain eventually melted, but massive boulders still blocked the mouth of the cave.

However, the cave mouth wasn't entirely blocked off from passage. As the snow and ice melted in the warmer months and water ran through the cracks, the debris covering the entrance eventually relocated and settled. Gaps formed, replenishing the cave with enough cool, clean, breathable oxygen to keep Tryggvi alive.

While he slept, his body remained in a near vegetative state. His breathing was slow, his heart rate almost negligible, and his body consumed his stored calories and fat reserves at an extraordinarily slow rate. Unconscious, his mind drifted in a very long dream where time knew no bounds. As he had already grown to full size centuries ago, there was no risk of him getting stuck in this cave as he had been in previous hibernations.

In all those years, nobody had ever made their way into this cave to disturb his slumber. As the mountain was in what is today the remote Territory of South Oxford, there were very few people living nearby who would accidentally wander into his lair. Small rodents, reptiles, and insects found their way in, but none dared approach the sleeping monster.

The truck bounced from one bump in the road to another. Gripping the steering wheel tightly, Liam struggled to keep his old 1995 pickup truck straight and true in his lane. He was beginning to regret going this way, but he had never driven this route and wanted to see something new. After leaving his great-uncle's cabin in North Conway, New Hampshire, he cut over on Route 302 and was now heading north on Route 113.

Trying to maximize his summer vacation, Liam had just spent the weekend in the White Mountains hiking and riding his mountain bike every chance that he could. He was now en route to Kingfield, Maine, to spend a few days with his grandfather, Pop. Pop was his paternal grandfather, and an avid, lifelong hunter. From an early age, he had taught Liam about hunting, firearm safety, shooting, and tracking wildlife in their natural domain. The plan for this trip was to scout out the region for new hunting areas. With luck, they might chat up a few farmers to get permission to hunt their lands in the fall.

As for this little out of the way trip addition, he wanted to check out this route on the journey up as it was closed for the winter each year. That meant that it was much less travelled than other roads in the area. Less travelled to him meant that it featured cleaner side trails and more pristine rivers and pools to explore. He loved going out in the woods but hated seeing trash left by lazy visitors and the erosion caused by too many visitors coming through trails and scenic vistas each season. There were many beautiful spots to see in Maine if you were willing to go out of your way, leave your comfort zone, and do some adventuring.

Shortly after passing through Stow, he entered the White Mountain National Forest once again. This region was one of his favorite places to visit, and he tried to make his way up here as often as possible. Growing up in Manchester, New Hampshire, just a little to the south, he had spent most of his life in heavily settled areas with more buildings and houses than trees. Up in the mountains, he was able to really stretch his legs, breathe deeply, and relax.

Driving along, he felt his phone vibrate in his pocket. Pulling it out, he saw an incoming call from a 603 number that he didn't recognize. Realizing that he only had one bar for reception, he decided to answer before he lost the caller.

"Liam Tryggvison," he answered.

"Hey bud, how's the drive going?" asked Jim Tryggvison. Jim, Liam's dad, was a robotics engineer who worked for an R&D lab down in Manchester. Normally, he'd be right there with Liam on this adventure. But today he needed to stay behind for work and catch up on a project.

"Oh! Hey, Dad. I didn't recognize your number," replied Liam. "It's going fairly well so far. I hiked Washington yesterday, and now I'm heading up to meet Pop at Art's camp in Kingfield."

"Awesome, I'm glad to hear it. I don't want to keep you long. I just wanted to call and see how you were doing," said Jim. "I have a lot of great memories of the Whites from when I was a kid. It makes me so happy to see you enjoying it as well. Keep your eyes on the road, I need to get back to work, anyways."

"Ugh, Dad, you know that I'm a safe driver. I'll be fine!" the teenager retorted.

"I know, I know. I just worry about you, bud" replied his father. "Give your mom and me a call later tonight when you get to camp. And say 'Hi' to your Pop for me."

"I will, Dad."

"I love you, Liam."

"I love you, too, Dad."

Liam smiled as he ended the call and put his phone into the cup holder in the center console of the truck. It rattled back and forth as he swerved around potholes, evidence of frost heaves from previous winters. This road was pretty rough, and the aging automatic transmission occasionally slipped as it tried to keep the inline-six happily connected to the tires.

Reaching into the other cup holder, he plucked out his heavily-sweating iced coffee cup and let it drip for a moment over the floor mat. He had learned a long time ago that accidently letting condensation drip onto his khaki shorts gave the other kids the wrong impression, and often led to laughter at his expense. Sipping happily at the cold, energy-providing liquid, he continued down the lonely road in search of fun.

About a half hour later, he found what he was looking for. At the base of a large, looming mountain on the eastern side of the road, there was a sign for a trail leading up into the woods. He pulled out the *Trails and Waterfalls* guide he had picked up from the visitor center. Locating the name of the trail, he confirmed that it led to the pool he wanted to see.

Reaching into his backpack on the bench seat beside him, he made sure that he had a few essentials for the trip: a towel, his digital SLR camera, a flashlight, his water bottle, and some snacks. He checked to see that his knife was clipped into his left front pocket and threw his wallet, cell phone, and keys into the outer pocket of the bag. He slipped off the seat and dropped onto the grassy parking area near the trailhead. Swapping his sandals for hiking boots, he tightened the laces, gave his leg muscles a stretch, and made his way for the trail.

After an hour of hiking, he found himself in a cool, shaded area of the trail and he stopped to listen. Deep in the distance, he could hear the flowing water from the stream that he was searching for. From what the guide said, the pool should be just a little further up from where the trail intersected the stream. Smiling, he picked up his pace and broke into a light jog. Five minutes later, he struck gold. The stream was crystal clear and flowed gently from the northwest. He looked down into the water to see if anything interesting was living in there, and was delighted to see a tiny school of minnows swimming around.

Kneeling down on the edge of the bank, he gently reached his arms into the cool water and began picking up rocks to see if any crayfish were hiding underneath. It took a few tries, but he finally found a big one sitting in the shelter of a flat rock covered in moss. Approaching the dark brown crustacean from behind its eye stalks, he gently gripped the little guy behind the arms and lifted it out of the water for inspection. The crawfish, obviously unhappy about the disturbance, defensively waved his claws towards the boy and snapped them open and shut. Impressed by the show of valor, Liam let out a little chuckle. He put the crawfish back down and delicately replaced the stone.

"This place is awesome," he said to himself. There were no signs of human impact here. No trash. No other footprints. No trees chopped down needlessly, and no names carved in the bark. This place was a good find, and well worth the extra added time that it tacked onto his drive up north. Rising to his feet, he adjusted the weight of the pack back onto his body, cinched up the straps, and continued his way up the stream. In only a few minutes, he reached the small pool of water that he was hoping to find.

The pool was about twenty feet in diameter and four feet deep, and sat in a clearing at the base of a low waterfall. Looking into the glass-like surface of the water, he could see dozens of larger fish swimming around, and several turtles were sunning themselves on a submerged log that had fallen from the shoreline.

Seeing the strange human approach, the turtles darted into the water with a loud splash and retreated to safety. Watching where they went, Liam grinned as they predictably poked their heads back up above the water, just high enough to expose their noses and eyes, to study him from safety.

He bent down and stuck his hand into the water. It was comparatively warm from sitting in the bright sunlight before flowing downstream, and was a welcome feeling for the anxious boy. Quickly unlacing his hiking boots, he pulled them off, ripped off his socks, and stuck them into the boots. After removing his shirt and hanging it from a tree branch, he waded into the water.

Having planned this activity ahead of time, he was already wearing his bathing suit to save time and the need to change. Slowly dunking his head under water, he looked around and watched the aquatic ballet unfold before him. The fish swam back and forth, either hunting smaller fish or bugs; others were fleeing from hunters themselves. Several frogs swam near the water's surface. He noticed that a large turtle, clinging to a black rock at the bottom, carefully watched the newcomer to its domain.

Happy with his finds, Liam planted his feet on the bottom of the pool, pushed upwards, and brought his head back up to the air above. Filling his lungs with fresh air, he waded over to the side of the pool and sat on a large, warm rock in the sunlight. Leaving his feet in the water, he gingerly lifted some of the rocks below, looking for more crawfish. He was intrigued by how they created little lairs under the water, hiding and waiting for tiny fish, bugs, and other scraps of other creatures' meals to pass by. They were very opportunistic like that, and he marveled at their patience. Always on his feet and going from one place to another, he was far too curious and anxious to operate in such a manner.

Liam got down into the water and scooted his butt around in the gravel to make a little seat, then leaned back against a large, smooth stone protruding from the edge of the pool. He rested his head against it, closed his eyes, and soaked in the rays of the sun shining down upon his white skin. Hours of playing outside kept his hair a light blond color, unlike his dad's, which had reverted to a light brown over the years of being stuck at a desk. Liam hoped that his hair would stay like that, as girls told him he looked cute. Others had said they liked his bright blue eyes. Hearing such compliments made him blush, but he was starting to get used to it.

Finding this position to be extremely comfortable, he sat there in the pool like that for almost an hour before feeling a tiny tickle on his toes. Opening his eyes, he glanced down at his feet and saw a blur moving below the water. Curious as to what was venturing around his foot, he slowly lowered his head towards the water and let his face slide below the surface. Looking underneath the light ripples in the water, he saw that one of the larger fish, about ten inches long from nose to tail, was taking tiny little bites at his feet. He had experienced smaller fish doing this to his hands and feet before, gobbling up the flakes of dead skin, but this was a new experience. The fish proceeded to nip at his pinky toe, and Liam was surprised to find that it actually stung a little. The fish had very tiny serrated teeth that probably wouldn't do any significant damage, but it still hurt a little and he found it annoying, anyways. Giving his foot a shake, he laughed as the terrified fish darted away to the opposite side of the pool to hide behind a submerged log.

Lifting his wrist up a little to glance at his watch, Liam noted that he had been in the woods now for almost two hours and should probably be on his way. He wanted to reach Kingfield before dark, and if he left soon, he would pull into the campground just before sunset. Standing up, he shook the sand off his bathing suit and stepped back onto the grassy shore. Picking up his backpack, he retrieved his towel from the bottom of the bag. Quickly drying off his skin, and patting the bathing suit dry as much as he could, he put his clothes back on and prepared himself for the return to the truck.

While tying his boots, he looked up at the mountain and noted a large, haphazard pile of trees at the base of the hillside, together with boulders of various sizes. More interesting, though, and the source of his real curiosity, were the tiny birds flying in and out of the pile. Most birds slowed down dramatically before landing on a twig or nest. These birds, however, still moved at a decent clip as they flew back and forth. The only conclusion that he could reach was that there must be open space behind the pile.

"I bet there's a cave back there!" he excitedly proclaimed. Looking down at his watch, he wondered whether he really needed to leave so soon. He could probably check it out, jog back along the length of the trail, and still make it to Pop's cabin before dark.

Feeling a tingle moving through his veins at the prospect of exploring a new cavern, he set off toward the mountain.

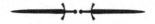

Given his excitement, and the fact that he was in good shape, Liam covered the distance in just under ten minutes. Slowing to a halt, he let out a low whistle as he inspected the gargantuan pile of rocks, tree limbs, trunks, and roots, many rotted from the years of rain, snow, and exposure to the sun. It was as large as the house he'd grew up in, and some of the boulders were bigger than his mom's car.

As he got closer, he noticed that the wood itself looked to be ancient. Jumping up on top of one of the larger trunks, he noted that with the number of rings within the diameter of the trunks, these must have been hundreds of years old already when they had fallen. And given how decayed some of them were, he wouldn't be surprised if they had then sat like this for a few centuries more. Giving the pile a quick scan, he plotted out a route in his head and started jumping from one trunk to another, from rock to rock and branch to branch. In a matter of minutes, he reached the top.

Crouching low, he saw several birds flying in and out of a gap between the top of the rubble and the underside of a large radius curve in the rock. Feeling confident in his guess of there being a cave behind there, he picked his way carefully over the rubble until he got to the gap. Getting down on his hands and knees, he stuck his head into the opening and looked down. However, he could only see a few feet into the murky darkness. Remembering that he came prepared for situations like this, he sat back up and pulled out the trusty flashlight that he had had since Scouts as a kid. Thumbing the power button, he shone a beam of light into the cave and peered around.

From his current vantage point, all that he could see was more rubble and continued inky blackness in the cave beyond. Given his height and the path that the cave appeared to follow, he could only see a little further, about twenty more feet into the opening. But, this knowledge told him two things: one, there was more to see, and two, the cave was big enough for him to easily walk into while still standing upright. Nervously looking back at his watch, he realized that this would ruin his plan to reach camp before sunset. However, this was way too cool to pass up. "That's what headlights are for, right?" he thought. "Let's go!"

Gripping the flashlight tightly in one hand, he carefully climbed down the backside of the rubble. Thanks to gravity, and his excitement to go exploring, it only took another minute or so to reach the smooth stone floor of the cavern. Aiming the flashlight down the length of the main chamber, he realized that the cave was even deeper than he had expected. Shining the flashlight around the floor, walls, and ceiling, he couldn't see anything of note, so he started walking while continuing to casually scan the area.

As he walked, he noticed that the floor of the cave pitched slightly downward, almost imperceptibly. Testing his theory, he gave a small stone a kick and noticed that it kept rolling out of the range of his flashlight, way past the point where it should have stopped on level terrain. This cave was going deeper into the earth. After another minute or so of continued walking, he found himself to be slowly arcing towards the right around a bend in the path. As he rounded the bend, he came upon a disturbing sight. Bones.

Not just bones, but a lot of bones. Walking more closely to the collection of white death in front of him, he played the light across the pile to get a better sense of what he was really seeing. The mound was about eight feet in diameter and came up to his shoulders. While no expert, he was knowledgeable enough to recognize the remains of wolves, bear, deer, large birds, and moose. He even saw some cattle bones in there, based on what he'd observed at the butcher shop in town over the years. But in addition to these, he saw many bones that were very apparent in origin to him... human bones. He saw rib cages, skulls, spine segments, and various limbs strewn about. One thing was certain: the creatures here had obviously met a violent end.

Feeling his stomach churn, Liam was glad he had only eaten a small lunch early this afternoon. Anything more down there, and he would probably be throwing it all up right now. Looking around, he realized that he couldn't see any tracks or physical evidence that anyone, or anything, had been here in recent history. Whatever had done this must be long gone. Confident that he was alone and not about to be ambushed in here, he decided to press onward. Pulling out his camera, he snapped a few photographs of the bone pile for evidence. He didn't think that anyone would believe him, so he wanted some good pictures to share later.

Coming around another bend to the left, he found a small rounded out nook large enough to park a car. However, what he found inside was no vehicle. Instead, there was, essentially, a museum exhibit on historical warfare in North America. Similar to the previous accumulation which he found, this was a haphazard collection of swords, knives, antique firearms, shields, armor, and uniforms. While placed in a fairly sloppy manner, it was apparent that whoever had placed these here knew what they were, how they were used, and was trying to organize them in some fashion.

Growing up in the Tryggvison family, Liam was familiar with modern weaponry. Both his father and grandfather owned a variety of pistols and long rifles. And he had spent much of his childhood playing video games and card games with his dad that featured weapons such as these. But this was amazing. The only thing he could compare it to was the Tower of London in England, which he had visited on a family vacation.

As before, he pulled his camera out and started taking pictures, wanting to capture everything as best he could the first time around. He already imagined himself of writing a book, or at least making a cool website when he got home. After taking dozens of photos of the armor and weaponry, the camera's flash was starting to give him a headache. He decided to conserve his camera's battery power and move on. Who knew what else he would find?

What he saw next, he could not explain at first. Reaching the end of the cavern, he found himself in a large, roundish room. In the middle of the room was a giant mound of green material with an odd looking texture. From his current distance away, it looked like a large stone sitting in the middle of the expanse. As he shone his light around the room, he noticed a golden glint reflecting from the other side of the mound. Walking around the perimeter of the room, he felt a strange sense of nostalgia, almost, as if, he knew what this was, even though he had never seen it before. It just seemed... somehow familiar.

Playing his flashlight's beam across the surface of the mound, he noticed that it was covered in what appeared to be an overlapping diamond pattern. Almost like scales on the bearded dragon he had kept as a pet a few years back. Compelled by an intense sense of curiosity, he reached out to touch it, but stopped just before making contact. Could he sense warmth coming from its surface? Moving his hand the last quarter of an inch, he gently touched the palm of his right hand to the surface of the mysterious object. Oddly enough, his suspicions were correct: it did feel warm. The heat issued by the Earth's core must have kept this cave warm even in the dead of winter. Pulling his hand back, he swung the light to the right to inspect the collection of shining objects.

Walking around to the far end of the room, he approached the shiny conglomeration and let out a gasp. The golden twinkle had come from an enormous conglomeration of coins and other random expensive looking trinkets. Some were carelessly thrown in place. Others were stacked neatly in tall, spindly towers. Picking up a handful of coins, he shined the flashlight on them and inspected their faces with delight. The coins were all dated from the late 1600s yet were still in remarkably good shape. It seemed as if they had gone untouched since their minting over three hundred years earlier. Looking closely, he noted that they originated from the eastern colonies of America, France, England,

and several other European countries. How they wound up here was a mystery in itself, but it just added to the suspense and amazement that this cave had already offered to his pondering mind.

Wanting to take some pictures of the small mountain of gold, he placed the flashlight in the crook of his armpit, tossed the gold coins back into the mix, and picked up the camera still hanging from his neck. As he started to adjust the focusing ring on the lens, one of the tall, narrow stacks tipped over, impacting the others and creating a small landslide of gold. As each coin fell with a ping, the sound of crashing gold echoed within the chamber, reaching a loud crescendo before fading into silence.

Standing perfectly still, Tryggvi didn't know if he should be laughing or feeling utterly embarrassed. He had just knocked over, by his estimate, several million dollars' worth of gold coins, let alone whatever their numismatic values might be. A slight grin started to develop on his face as a thought occurred to him.

I'm rich.

Of course, he would need to haul all of this gold out of here, and he'd probably need to properly report it to the police and some local university for study and analysis. He'd probably also have to pay taxes on the value to the IRS, but either way, this gold was his. He was rich! Thoughts began to swirl around in his mind of all of the things that he could buy: a new truck, better clothes, college tuition, parts for his combat robot that he was building, a 3D printer, or even a house! The world was his oyster if he could even net a fraction of what this gold was worth.

While Liam stared in awe at his newfound riches, the large green mound behind him moved. It moved so imperceptibly that unless you were staring at it, you probably wouldn't have even noticed it. But in the middle of the mound, a foot or so off of the ground, a quick flash of green unveiled a white circle. An eye. An eye that was now slowly taking in the objects within the room and eagerly focusing in on the young man standing beside it.

It started as a small sound, metallic in nature, in the back of his mind. Tryggvi didn't know what he was hearing at first, but it startled him and stirred his ancient, slumbering body to awareness. Startled, Tryggvi shot open his left eye and took in what he saw. A young human man, or a tall boy, was standing just a few feet away from him. In front of the boy, his precious collection of gold had been spilt all over the stone floor of the cavern. He had spent years curating his collection, and it angered him to see this stranger desecrate his hoard.

Not wanting to give away his presence, Tryggvi inhaled very slowly, deeply filling his lungs with new oxygen and relishing the revitalizing sensation. It had been a long time since he had tasted fresh air, and it felt fantastic. He smelled sweat, dirt, vegetation, stone, and blood. These things were all familiar to him. But, he also picked up strange new smells, several of which he could not discern their nature. Whoever this boy was, he represented a people with whom he was not entirely acquainted. Additionally, this boy, somehow, in some way, was recognizable to the dragon. Playing into his curiosity, he decided to make his presence known.

"But wait!" a part of his brain cried out. "This boy, though young, is still a human. He is one of those who tried to kill you with their deadly cannon."

"Yes, yes, he was," mused the dragon. "This boy was one of them, and he must pay!"

Tryggvi slowly stretched his wings, then his arms, and then his back legs. As his claws scraped the stone floor, the startled young man turned and shone his handheld torch onto the face of the dragon.

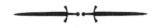

Liam felt a slight breeze behind him and swore that he had heard some light scraping on the stone floor. Expecting to find a mouse, some small critter, or at the absolute worst case scenario, a black bear, he turned and saw what appeared to be an extremely large lizard... with wings... and a large gaping maw full of knife-like teeth. He paused, momentarily lost for words.

"AAAAAHHHHH!" was all that managed to escape Liam's mouth as his brain finally communicated with the vocal cords in his neck. While he normally considered himself to be a fairly brave young man, at this very moment, here in this ancient cavern in the middle of nowhere Maine, face to face with what appeared to be, but he must be crazy for even thinking it... a dragon, he could think of nothing better to say.

Clutching his flashlight with a white-knuckle grip, he frantically looked about for the best means of escape. Seeing an opening, he leaped over the long tail of the beast and bolted straight ahead, following the curve of the stone walls out of the room.

"How curious," pondered the dragon. "In the past, these nasty humans attacked me outright, even knowing what I am and what I could do to them. This little human is running away. It's been so long since I've had such an easy target." Raising his head up to the full height of the ceiling, Tryggvi built up the rage in the back of his mouth, opened wide, and unleashed his fury into the air.

"Oh crap! Dragon! Crap! Crap! Crap!" was Liam's personal mantra for the next several seconds. While he had read about dragons in his dad's library and played with them in his collectible card games, he had never dreamt that dragons were real. But this was more like a nightmare than a dream. He looked back over his shoulder as he ran, and saw that the creature was rising up to his full height allowed by the ceiling of the cavern. If he had thought that the beast was large when curled up into a ball, its current size was even more impressive. The dragon was huge, and it was following him.

Turning back, Liam put all his power into his legs and tried to put more distance between him and those teeth. While running, he tried to keep the flashlight beam ahead of him on the floor where his feet would hit next. This did technically help the dragon follow him, he couldn't afford to not know where he was going. The cave was pitch-black otherwise, and he would be as good as dead without his sight. While he ran, he noticed that the cave walls around him were growing brighter and brighter. Glancing back over his shoulder in between strides, he saw the last thing that he had expected to see: fire. And not just any fire. A ball of fire blasting from the mouth of the dragon in his direction.

Thinking quickly, he looked next to him and saw a large boulder on his right. Throwing himself behind it, he huddled as far behind it as he could just as the inferno struck the rock. The fire slammed into the opposite side with such force that the stone shifted forward several inches. He was no geologist, but he estimated that the boulder easily weighed several tons. As a salvo of liquid fire sprayed overhead, he was grateful for the protective eclipse created by the stone.

Squinting and turning his face away from the onslaught, Liam saw the edge of the stone next to him was beginning to turn colors. It turned a shade of red first, then yellow, and then white. As the heat quickly spread through his stony shield, his back was getting very hot. Crouching forward, he leaned off of the stone to prevent himself from being scorched by the very thing keeping him alive right now.

Feeling physically drained from the first sustained burst of fire generated since he awoke, Tryggvi cut off his fiery attack and took a deep breath of comparatively cool air. As his eyes were still adjusting to the lower light levels, as staring through his fire breathing for several long moments had screwed with his pupils, he could not see as clearly as normal. Dragons can see quite well in the dark, but even a mighty beast like Tryggvi had his limits. Waiting for his eyes to adjust to the blackness now that the fire was no longer illuminating the surrounding area, he tried to spot the human in the twisting cavern ahead.

"Surely," mused the ancient one, "I must have turned him to ash. Nothing could have survived that blast." Although, he had to admit, he had rested for a very long time and it was his first fire in who knows how long. He might not be as good as he once was and would need practice hunting again. What he could see, however, was a small shadow sprint out from behind the large boulder in front of him and disappear out of sight down the length of the cave. Fearing that his quarry would escape, he stretched his limbs, shook off centuries of dust and debris, and took off down the tunnel in a crouched sprint.

Liam had never been so afraid of anything in his life. "Where did I go wrong on this trip?" he wondered. "One minute, I was relaxing in a mountainside pool. Now, I'm being chased by some mythical creature intent on obliterating me!" Not letting up for one second, he sprinted through the shaft of rock as quickly as possible. Bouncing up and down, the camera dangling around his neck was smacking into his chest and hurting more and more with each consecutive impact. His chest was probably bruised by now, but he wasn't willing to stop and fix the situation just yet. Grabbing the camera with his free hand while still gripping the flashlight, he tried to keep it all together while putting as much distance between himself and his pursuer.

Looking ahead, a dreadful thought crept into his brain: He wasn't going to make it. He could sense the dragon getting closer and closer behind him, and knew that the debris wall was still far up the length of the corridor. He would most likely not make it in time before the dragon caught up, and even then, he would still need to climb the wall of debris to the other side to safety. On top of that, he was pretty sure that this wall wouldn't stop the mighty fire blast of the dragon, so even 'if' he managed to escape, the dragon would still be behind him out in the open. Without any kind of weapon, he stood very little chance of defeating the hunter behind him in the wide-open expanse of the woods.

"Wait a second," he realized, as an idea came to him in between breaths. "What about the weapons stash further up ahead? There are swords, axes, and shields there, just waiting for me to use them." While he didn't have any false hopes that he could get there in time, suit up in some dead warrior's old armor, and still have a chance of even fighting this thing in the close confines of the cavern, he did think that he could probably find a strong shield to hide behind. With enough luck, the dragon might not see him and assume that he had already escaped.

And so he ran. Tryggvi kept his head low, wings folded down the length of his back. This little varmint was fast, but he was making pretty good time considering. Each step, if he wasn't careful, would cause his back and shoulders to grind into the sharp rocks of the ceiling above. Hoping to scare his prey and force him into making a fatal mistake, he occasionally let out little gouts of fire from his deadly maw. They were unlikely to hit him from this far back amongst the twists and turns of the cave, but it would be enough to keep fear in his heart.

Pounding along the rock floor, the dragon could feel the angle of inclination steadily increase towards the surface of the ground above. Fighting the fatigue building in his muscles, Tryggvi gripped the rock with his claws and propelled his massive body through the cavern. He could hear the tiny footfalls of the trespasser, which only increased his desire to find out what he tasted like.

Recalling from memory, he should be just about to the weapons dump by now, followed by the bone pile on the way out of the cave. If Tryggvi could not catch him before the opening, he could easily take to the skies outside and burn his prey from above.

Tearing through the cavern, Liam rounded the last bend in the path before the weapons stash which he had previously encountered. High-tailing it through the opening in the wall, he dashed into the mounds of weaponry and armor. He was looking for one specific item: a large shield. Especially, a fire-resistant shield.

Careful to avoid the business ends of the swords, spears, and glaives amassed before him, he found several shields of various sizes and build qualities. He quickly picked them up one by one, rapidly assessing their combat effectiveness. After all, the dragon was just a short distance behind him.

Grasping several of the shields, he easily threw aside some obvious options to eliminate. A few were constructed of lashed sticks and animal hides. Others were just a few boards fastened together and cut into a circle with leather straps. His eyes lit up when he found a tower shield made of solid bronze. Grabbing it by the handles, he tried to hoist it up in front of him. Caught off-guard by the sheer weight of the massive piece, he lost his footing and fell backwards. The shield toppled down with him and landed on top of his body.

More embarrassed than hurt, Liam almost laughed out loud but stopped himself short. Peeking above the top lip of the shield, he saw a gout of flame shoot out into the corridor, followed by the massive head of the dragon. Ducking his face behind the ancient shield, Liam held his breath and waited.

Exhaling more fire as he ran, Tryggvi rounded the last corner just before the weapons stash. He dug his claws into the ground and skidded to a halt. Catching his breath with a few quick, deep lungfuls of increasingly fresher air, he swung his head from side to side while sucking in every scent possible with his powerful nose. He could smell the human nearby, but couldn't make out just where he was. Lowering his nose closer to the cavern floor, he sniffed along the path of the corridor, the walls, and even the ceiling, trying to figure out where he went. The trail was weak, but the boy might be somewhere near the weapons nook. Advancing a few more steps, he peered inside, but saw nothing aside from his trophies.

Annoyed at losing is quarry, he roared down the length of the cave and grinned at the echoing sound of his anger. He hoped the young creature was shivering in fear from his deafening bellows. Pausing to listen for any sounds or signs of the creature's reaction, the dragon became annoyed at the apparent lack of fear. Angry at possibly losing him, he reared his head back, charged his glands, and unleashed upon the space in front of him. He coated the walls and floor of the corridor and the weapons nook, and the weapons themselves, with red-hot, liquefied fire. He reveled at the sight of everything burning or melting before him, even if he destroyed some of his spoils of war.

Satisfied with this small act of vengeance, he barreled forward through the last section of the cavern. Picking up speed as the cave's diameter enlarged closer to the entrance, he was finally able to use the full stride of his legs and spread his wings a little more. Coming upon the mound of debris, he opened his mouth again and blanketed the trees, boulders, and dirt with flame. Watching the wood and dirt turn to ash before his angry eyes, he continued blasting as rocks popped and shattered from the heat.

Not waiting for anything to cool, he pushed on and crashed through the burning mess. Stretching his wings to their full width as he ran the last few yards to freedom, he burst out in the open air for the first time in three hundred years. Roaring in delight and flapping his leathery wings, he lifted his bulk from the earth and took to the air. Circling the entrance to the cave, he scanned the mountainside and forest for the little creature.

"He must be here somewhere," mused the beast. "I hunger for meat, and that trespasser will be my first meal before I take to the skies again."

And so he circled. Flying around the mountain, he grew disappointed at how easily he had let his prey get away from him. He had been asleep for a very long time, and must have grown rusty in his hibernation. Flying back to the mountain, Tryggvi perched himself atop its peak and rested his tired wings.

"Whoa," the usually articulate Liam muttered to himself. He was typically more adept at coming up with witty commentary on things, but what he just witnessed had left him speechless. Peeking out from over the shield, he realized that the piece of armament, which was formerly protecting him, was now simply burning his left palm and right forearm as he continued to hold onto the hot bronze. Slipping his arm out of the melting leather strap, he kicked the shield off and sent it clattering to the floor.

Looking around, he realized that everything nearby was also hot or in some stage of melting. That dragonfire was potent stuff and would have surely killed him but for the shield. He held his breath for a moment and listened for the hulking beast. Confident that it was gone, he picked his way through the burning mess of formerly beautiful antique weapons and armor. Seeing that the coast was clear, he made his way back into the main tunnel.

Looking off to the right, Liam saw that the impressive landslide, which had once closed the cave off from the outside world, was now burnt and smashed to pieces. The dragon must have obliterated the blockade as it escaped from the cavern. At least his way out would be a little easier.

Realizing that he hadn't taken a relaxed, deep breath to slow his heart from hammering itself to death in his chest, he leaned forward and rested his hands on his knees. Feeling the weight of the objects in his backpack shift forward, he slipped the pack off, and gently dropped his belongings to the ground. Taking inventory of what he still had with him, disappointment quickly took over his previously relieved mood. Looking down at the camera dangling around his neck, he frowned at his camera, now a mostly melted hunk of plastic and aluminum sitting in his blistered hand. The lens was drooping down, the glass on the outside was warped, and the body of the SLR had lost all of its color, shape, and defining features. Several of the buttons were gone, as well. He almost smashed it to the ground in frustration, but stopped himself short. While the camera itself was ruined, the memory card inside might still have some data left on it to retrieve. It was a long shot, but he was willing to give it a chance.

His canvas bag, while durable, had melted in places, and the zippers were still hot to the touch. Without the bag on, his back might have taken some of those burns. His flashlight had been lost somewhere along the way. He certainly wasn't going back into the cave to look for it, at least not yet. Some of his clothes inside were a little charred, but overall, his things were in good shape.

Collecting his things, he cinched the bag back onto his shoulders and shifted the weight into a comfortable position. He knelt down to tighten up his boot laces, while mentally preparing himself for what may be waiting for him outside. Taking a deep breath, he clenched his fists, gritted his teeth, and slowly made his way to the mouth of the cavern.

CHAPTER TWELVE
THE ATTACK

Perched atop the mountain peak, the dragon sat and watched. He had not spent centuries living amongst these humans without learning a little patience. He was however, a little annoyed. He had been so close to catching that young man, and he couldn't believe that he had let him get away. Of course, he was hunched in the cave and it had been a long time since he had actually hunted something, so he should be a little easier on himself. But still, he was angry about the intrusion, and, most importantly, he was hungry.

Tryggvi scanned the forest for signs of movement. He saw birds, deer, and some rabbit moving around, but nothing large enough to be the human. "How had he gotten away so quickly?" Tryggvi pondered. "I was right behind him, and I can't believe that he would have climbed that wall of detritus any faster than I could burn it down and run through it." And so, he continued to wait. Three hours were spent staring, waiting, and watching every movement within the full circle of the landscape before him. As dragons have very good vision for hunting, and he had an unobstructed view of everything around the mountaintop, this time he would not fail.

"Come on!" Liam muttered. He was still down in the mouth of the cave, peeking just barely enough past the edge of the cavern entrance's sidewall to allow one eye to see beyond the stone walls. For what must have been the hundredth time in the past couple of hours, the teenager discretely spied on the dragon waiting a thousand feet above.

While Liam considered himself to be a fairly patient person, even he was growing tired. He was pretty sure that the dragon did not even know that he was still in the tunnel. Otherwise, he would probably be dead right now. Based on the way that the dragon continued to pan back and forth and swiveled his head around, the creature must suspect he was down here somewhere, but not know specifically where. For now, the only safe plan was to wait.

Peering off into the distance, Tryggvi spotted a bird. An unusually large bird, which made a strange droning sound he had never heard before. Feeling his stomach growl, and remembering that he didn't even know how long it had actually been since his last meal, the dragon took a few final glances around the mountain. Coming to terms with the fact that the human must have escaped, he decided to let that one go and pursue this new target.

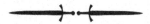

Taking another risky look, Liam peered over the edge of the stone again to see if anything had changed in the dragon's position or stature. Sure enough, he was still sitting there, tirelessly scanning the ground, woods, and anywhere else which Liam might choose to escape into.

Ducking back into the protection of the cave, Liam sat down on the rocky floor and leaned up against the wall of the opening. If he would have to wait it out, he might as well save his energy and rest up a little. Pulling his legs and feet up closer to himself, he tried to minimize his profile in case the dragon was able to look downward and see him sitting there. Leaning his head back until it lightly touched the stone, he closed his eyes and took in a long, quiet, deep breath to calm his nerves.

With his eyes still closed, his ears perked up at the sound of an unnatural whine coming from far off into the distance. He opened his eyes and strained to listen to the new sound. It was a single-engine airplane, probably a few miles out by the sound of it. Normally, this would be a commonplace occurrence and he would think nothing of it. But this situation was anything but commonplace. Looking up at the top of the mountain, a dark thought crossed his mind. Could the dragon fly?

Extending his wings out to their full reach, Tryggvi looked like a gigantic gargoyle sitting on top of his perch at the apex of the mountain. Giving his wings a few easy flaps, he stretched out his muscles to prepare them for their first use in hundreds of years. Increasing the force behind his flapping, he rose several feet into the air, pitched forward into the wind, and dove off of the side of the mountain, head-first into the forest below. Catching a strong thermal updraft, he flapped hard with the wind and launched himself after this noisy bird in the distance. His breakfast awaits.

"Eastern Slopes Ground, Cessna Tango Kilo Four Two One, twenty miles northwest. I have an unidentified aircraft on an intercept course. He is not responding to radio calls." the pilot nervously radioed to ground control.

"Cessna Tango Kilo Four Two One, I have both of you on radar. Descend to five thousand feet and continue on your original heading," replied the comms officer.

"Wilco," the pilot returned, wiping a bead of sweat from his forehead. He had never had another craft completely ignore him like this before, let alone fly straight at him. And worse still, he had no idea what it was, or why the wings appeared to move.

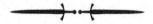

Liam didn't know whether to cheer or scream. A few hours ago, he had thought that dragons were a myth from the past, tales told by his ancestors on his family's Nordic side to scare little children. Now, he was watching a dragon soar through the air. It was the coolest thing that he had ever seen.

But, it was also the scariest. Liam had to warn that pilot, if at all possible, and he had to do it now. Feeling safe that the dragon had lost interest in him and not coming back around, he bolted from the cave and ran through the woods, following the trail back to his truck near the main road.

Tryggvi climbed rapidly as he approached the strange bird. He wanted to surprise his new prey and attack from above. Still several miles away, he was now about one thousand feet above his target and closing rapidly. The bird had either not seen him or was unafraid of the approaching dragon, because it was still heading his way.

Liam hustled down the trail, intent on getting to his truck as soon as humanly possible. Leaving the serene pool in the distance, he covered the same trail length in less than half of his original time while walking.

Emerging from the edge of the woods, Liam ran towards the truck and started pulling off his backpack as he approached. After fumbling through the backpack for his keys, he started it up and peeled out of the parking area, leaving behind twin rooster tails of dirt. A cloud of dust was all that remained of his truck as it disappeared into the distance.

Far exceeding the posted speed limit, Liam grabbed his cell phone out of the center console of the truck and punched 911 into the keypad on the touchscreen. Keeping his eyes on the road ahead, he glanced down in confusion as to why he didn't hear a dial tone. He had no signal. This far into the woods, he should not have been surprised. The cellular coverage this far out was pretty bad, but he usually had at least one bar for signal strength.

Given his options, he decided to continue on to Kingfield to meet up with his Pop. He would check his phone every minute or so to see if he had any bars and call the police as soon as he could. He needed to let them know about the dragon and get a warning relayed to the airport and that pilot. For all that he knew, it was already too late.

High in the sky, just below a layer of white, puffy clouds, Tryggvi soared along with the wind and watched his target far below. He noticed that as he had been climbing, the strange bird had been descending closer to the Earth's surface. While he had closed in on his target from a horizontal distance, their altitude difference negated some of that previous gain.

Tryggvi flew closer but could not figure out what it was. He was unsure if it was living or not, but it moved of its own accord. Given his persistent hunger, the dragon would still investigate, regardless.

It wasn't until a short while later that Liam was finally able to get a signal strong enough to place a phone call. Triumphantly hearing a dial tone, he waited for the other line to pick up.

"Bethel Police Department. This line is being recorded. Please state the nature of your emergency," stated the officer.

"My name is Liam Tryggvison and I'm currently heading on Route 2 east towards Bethel," began the teen. "There is a small aircraft heading southbound from this position that is about to come under attack. You need to contact the Fryeburg Airport immediately and get that plane on the ground."

"Sir, what do you mean, 'under attack'?" the officer replied. "Under attack from whom?"

Unsure how to answer, Liam paused and found himself momentarily speechless.

"Sir?" the officer pressed.

"Um, this will sound really weird," started Liam, "but, it's... um... a dragon."

"Sir, this is an emergency line, and we need to keep it clear for actual emergencies" snapped the officer. "This line is not for prank calls from high schoolers."

The line went dead as the officer hung up on him. While slightly irked, Liam couldn't really blame him. What he had just said was ridiculous. And prior to this afternoon, he wouldn't have believed it either.

Pulling over onto the shoulder of the road, he quickly brought the truck to a halt and held the phone out in front of him. Punching "Fryeburg Airport" into the search bar of his phone's browser, as he knew that to be the closest airport around where he last saw the dragon and the plane together, he quickly found the phone number for the airport, listed as Eastern Slopes, and pressed "dial" when the menu popped up.

Waiting for the airport to pick up, he tried to think of a more vague way to describe the situation that sounded less crazy. He couldn't think of one. When the receptionist picked up on the other end, he had almost the exact same conversation as he had just had with the police station. He explained the situation, pleaded with the responder, and was promptly hung up on. Unsure of what else he could do besides jumping into a plane himself and attacking the dragon, he continued onward and made his way north to Kingfield. He tried calling his Pop while he drove, but he had already lost his signal again. Gritting his teeth, he mashed the gas pedal and focused on the road ahead.

"Get a load of this, Bob," started the receptionist at Eastern Slopes Airport. "Some kid just called me and said that a dragon was chasing an airplane heading our way from the North. I don't know what kind of television shows these kids are watching these days, but their imaginations are getting a little too creative for my liking."

Bob, over in the control building, chuckled over the phone. He was about to respond with another joke when he noticed that the radar scan showed that there were, in fact, two small craft approaching their position. One was a small Cessna, identified as TK-421, flying at 5,000 feet. The other was unidentified and flying around 6,000 feet. Staring at the screen, he absentmindedly hung up the phone.

"Hey Mike," Bob said nervously. "Weren't you just trying to reach an unidentified aircraft in the area?"

"Yep!" Mike exclaimed. "That bastard up there is really starting to piss me off. First, he's scaring this other plane who keeps trying to get him on the radio, then he's tailing it, and now he's ignoring my calls. I was thinking about calling the Air Force tower on him."

Just then another call came in on the radio.

"Eastern Slopes Ground, Cessna Tango Kilo Four Two One again. This guy is making me nervous, and I want to put down immediately," the pilot said.

"Cessna Tango Kilo Four Two One, we can't blame you. You are clear to land on Runway One" replied the comms officer.

"Roger, wilco. Coming in now," the pilot answered.

On the radar screen, the tower controllers saw the Cessna descend towards the designated runway. Looking through the windows, they watched the plane as it approached and readied for landing. Curiously, they noticed that the second object was also coming in, and travelling faster than before.

"Mike," Bob said, "hand me those binoculars over there, will ya?" Taking a better look at the sky before them, Bob finally got a good visual inspection of the second thing. It was a large, flying lizard, all right. And it was coming this way.

Tryggvi, carefully watching the every movement of his prey below, noticed that it was picking up speed and descending towards a big, long line off in the distance. Wanting to catch it in the air before it could land, the dragon tucked his wings in close to his body and rapidly dove towards the unsuspecting bird below.

Looking through their binoculars, the two men in the control building watched helplessly as the thing closed in behind the Cessna. As they both drew near to the airport, the men's fears were confirmed: it was definitely a dragon.

Bob called the local police station and asked for responding officers, a fire truck, and an ambulance. He purposely left the dragon portion out of his description, knowing that they wouldn't believe him. Mike, in the background, reconnected with the Cessna and helped talk the pilot in to land on the tarmac.

Coming up on the bird, Tryggvi didn't know what to make of it. It had a metallic nature and didn't flap to fly. It just flew straight where it wanted to, perhaps with the help of the unusual spinning wheel on its nose. He closed to within five feet of the airplane's tail. Sniffing the air, he smelled burning oils and minerals.

Banking to the right, he flew alongside of the bird to get a better look. What he saw next, he could scarcely believe. Inside the bird, through some clear material covering the outer surface, was a very frightened human staring back at him. The bird-human suddenly dove sharply, putting distance between them. Tryggvi, still hungry and much angered by this deception, tucked his wings in and sped after the descending prey. Catching back up with the flying object, he began warming up his promethium glands and prepared to attack. Opening his mouth, he lined up behind the tail and unleashed a burst of fire.

The gout struck the rear of the aircraft and burned away a chunk of the tail rudder, but it remained airborne. Tryggvi lined up again and shot another burst of flame at the right wing.

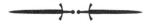

Watching in horror from the control building, Mike and Bob stood frozen in fear. All they could do was try to talk the pilot in, but he went hysterical the moment that the dragon started shooting fire at the plane. And who could blame him? They watched as the plane rapidly dropped to just about one hundred feet over the runway, thankfully, still on an acceptable approach vector. The dragon followed closely behind, shooting small gouts of flame at the plane as they both came in close to the ground. It almost seemed as if the dragon was merely toying with the pilot.

The plane choppily approached the runway and touched down lightly with one wheel, and then two, leaving behind a small cloud of smoke as the rubber tires heated up on the asphalt. Swaying dangerously side to side from the lack of control panels left to the pilot, the two men couldn't believe that he had actually pulled this landing off.

As the plane came to a halt, they watched the pilot frantically undo his harness. Just as he was about to open the door, the dragon alighted beside the plane and ignited the side of the aircraft with a dousing of dragonfire. Covered in light oil spatters from the barely operational engine, the sheet metal of the craft lit up brightly as the flames consumed the material.

The pilot jumped away from the torched side and tried to open the other door, hoping that the dragon would not see the change of tactic. Realizing that his prey was trying to escape, Tryggvi jumped onto the left wing of the aircraft and tipped it sideways until the wingtip crumpled into the ground. The craft kicked up at a 45-degree angle, rolling the pilot across the cabin until he fell against the hot metal interior of the cabin. Tryggvi crunched his way along the wing, digging his clawed feet into the light sheet metal skin of the mechanical bird. As his weight moved along the length of the wing, the plane slammed back down onto its wheels and leveled out again. The pilot was rocked back against the other wall as it fell to the pavement.

Just as the dragon was rearing its head up to unleash another torrent of liquid fire against the injured craft, a string of vehicles with lights and sirens blazing came flying around the corner of the road and quickly drove onto the tarmac. Police cars, of both local and state troopers, converged around the burning airplane and surrounded the dragon in a semicircle.

Tryggvi, surprised by the intruders, paused mid-breath and let the fire extinguish in his mouth. Despite his rage, flashbacks of cannon fire filled his mind with dread. Looking around, he noticed that each man and woman pointed similar weapons in his direction, yelling commands back and forth to each other that he could not comprehend. While he had learned many human words over the centuries, these words were coming out too quickly from too many sources, and many were words that he had never heard before. Panning his head back and forth across the gathering of humans, he noticed that several were looking a little jumpy. While they all had their weapons drawn and pointing at him, two were shaking their hands slightly and looking ready to attack.

Tryggvi would not let them have the advantage. If he was going to act, he needed to do it now. Feeling an imminent threat coming, Tryggvi roared at his challengers, gnashing his teeth in the air, hoping to provoke a reaction. The frightened officers clenched down on the triggers of their rifles, firing two concurrent three-round bursts at him. Several rounds pinged harmlessly against the hull of the aircraft, but two of them grazed the scales on Tryggvi's back and deflected off into the air. While these failed to penetrate his natural armor, they did hurt quite a bit. The dragon realized that these weapons were far more advanced than the weaker weapons which he had encountered in the past.

After the first two humans shot at Tryggvi, the rest joined in. They fired countless rounds at the dragon, who ducked behind the plane for protection. He roared at his attackers, hoping to scare them off.

Lying still on the floor of the plane behind the front seats, the pilot felt the plane slam back onto the pavement as the sounds of police and fire rescue sirens filled the air. Holding on to anything that he could, he fought to arrest his movement with each violent jolt of the small craft. Afraid to expose himself to the dragon, which was still sitting on top and next to the plane, he kept his head low below the line of the windows.

Trying to slow his breathing and calm down his racing heart, he didn't want the dragon to hear him. With everything going on outside, the dragon might just forget that he was still inside and leave him alone. He had almost convinced himself to remain in the plane and just hope that the dragon would go away, but then the shooting started.

Hearing the bursts from the officers outside, he decided that it was time to go. Hoping that the dragon would be sufficiently distracted by the gunfire, he carefully pushed the door open. Looking outside, he froze in terror.

Keeping his head below the top of the mechanical bird, Tryggvi shielded himself from the human's gunfire. While some of the impacts were barely perceptible, he knew that a direct hit to one of his weak spots would cause immense pain. He did not wish to relive those experiences, if he could avoid it. As he tucked his head below the wing, a tiny door popped open right next to his face. Inside the new opening, there was a human staring directly at him. This was the same human who had taunted him up in the air with his abominable false-flight, trying to take to the air in contrast to how nature had designed his puny little body. Startled by his sudden appearance and suspecting that the man had summoned the other warriors to attack him, Tryggvi decided to strike first before this creature could cause him any further harm.

Grabbing the door with his front claws, he braced himself against the frame of the craft, opened his mouth, and roared a fiery discharge of physically-manifested anger into the cabin. The pilot, and everything else inside, were incinerated, melted, and blasted into their base elements as the dragon unleashed his rage. The windows burst outward as jets of flame propelled shards of glass and debris out into the atmosphere.

The humans attacking Tryggvi ceased firing as they braced themselves behind their vehicles for cover. Blocking their faces with their arms or jumping inside the doorways, they tried to shield themselves from the heat washing off of the burning plane wreckage. Fearful that a continued conflict may spell doom for him now that his protective cover was diminished, Tryggvi decided to create a distraction and flee the scene.

Whipping his body around, he slammed what was left of the plane with his massive tail and launched the metallic scrap at the closest police car in the surrounding cluster. As the wreckage soared across the tarmac and crashed into the cruiser, Tryggvi belched a long stream of fire from left to right in a gigantic flaming arc of destruction.

Watching the humans jump for cover and flee their burning vehicles, Tryggvi pumped his wings, pushed off with his mighty feet, and took to the air. As he flew away from the landing strip, he heard tiny shots being fired in his direction, thankfully, all in vain. He was too far away by now for them to pose much danger, despite their valiant efforts. It was time to return to his cave and plan his next move.

Triple checking his control board, the fighter pilot noted that he was still at 30,000 feet and travelling close to Mach 1. The call had come in to Hanscom ten minutes ago, and his current mission necessitated speed and efficiency. He wouldn't leave anything to chance.

Checking his radar again and confirming the target zone on his paper map on his sleeve-insert, Rob "Nighthawk" Grady saw that he was about halfway to the epicenter of his predetermined search area. He wasn't travelling to Eastern Slopes Regional Airport, where the alleged attack occurred. Rather, he was headed to a point several miles north based on the reported direction and speed of the fleeing target.

Grady still wasn't entirely sure of what to expect, but that was why they had sent him for this mission. He had seen some strange stuff in his career and wasn't about to be jostled by an unusual creature. His CO had publicly stated that Grady's mission was to pursue an unidentified flying object. That usually spread gossip about alien spacecraft swooping in to beam up unsuspecting people in the night. However, after the others in the briefing room had left, his captain leaned in and whispered in his ear that it was a dragon.

"A dragon? Doubtful," Grady thought as he sped through the atmosphere in pursuit of his target. Whatever it was, the thing had reportedly killed several people, and it was his job to take it down. From what he had read, at least one victim had been burnt beyond recognition. A creature that could do such a thing did not deserve share his airspace. Noting the time on his chronometer and referencing his original flight plan, he should be coming up on Fryeburg soon.

"Eastern Slopes," he began, "this is Lieutenant Commander Grady on approach to your position. Do you copy?"

"Roger, we have you on our radar," replied Bob in the ground control building. They had just finished extinguishing the flames that had been licking the side of the building since the dragon took off. Thankfully, very little inside had been damaged, and all his controls and instruments still functioned.

"I need a status update on the location of the target," Grady said. "Do you still have it on radar, and what is its vector?"

"The target appears to have stopped eighteen miles from your position, on a bearing ten degrees due east," Bob answered. "That's all that we can really give you, sir. Watch out up there.... he's big. Good luck and happy hunting."

"Roger. Over," the Lt. Commander tersely replied. It was time to enter battle, and he needed to focus. Several minutes later, as he neared the last reported position, he eased back on the throttle and gradually dropped to five thousand feet.

He circled the area, searching for any sign of the "dragon." Finding nothing significant on his first few passes, he dropped even lower to the ground, just around eight hundred feet, and circled the area in five-mile diameter circles. Bringing the F-16C down to as slow as he could go without stalling, he rolled onto his side to get a better view through the glass of the cockpit window. Targeting cameras were good for some functions, but it was often better to just see it for yourself.

After several long, lazy circles over endless miles of Maine forest, he spotted something green on top of a mountain that shouldn't have been there. Sure enough, the crazy reports coming in from the witnesses on the ground were true. Sitting atop that peak, jutting up into the skyline, was a large lizard with four limbs, two large wings, and an angry set of teeth in a head that was now looking in his direction as he approached.

"Eastern Slopes, this is Nighthawk. I have eyes on the target," he transmitted. There was a long pause and a few audible clicks as the radio connection was transferred between several relay stations. A second later, the response that he was hoping for came through.

"Nighthawk, this is Hanscom Control," replied an unidentified speaker on the other end. "Green Light. You are free to engage with extreme prejudice."

"Acknowledged."

Having just set down on the mountaintop above his lair, Tryggvi was still catching his breath from the long flight when he heard a roar in the distance. Looking to the south where it sounded like the roar was coming from, he saw a shiny speck moving overhead at an extremely fast speed. Crouching low to the rock and side-stepping slowly, he positioned himself behind a copse of trees to make his profile less obvious. Turning his head to track the path of the new craft, he watched the deadly-looking thing fly in wide circles over the forest below. Clearly remembering what had just happened when he tried to attack the last one, Tryggvi was less than eager to engage this new mechanical bird.

Watching intently, he grew nervous as he saw the plane roll sideways and arc around his mountaintop. Looking up, he could see the pilot as he flew only a few hundred feet before disappearing around the side of an adjacent mountain. Fearing what this one may do to him, Tryggvi decided to flee for the safety of his cave, several hundred feet below him. Leaping off the side of the cliff, he pumped his wings and slowly arced around to the opening of the cavern.

As he approached the cool darkness of his home, he heard the jet swoop around the mountain, followed by a rapid series of thuds. With barely a pause in between, he felt three tiny, burning impacts slam into different parts of his body. Looking over to his right wing as he continued to soar, he saw a tiny hole in the thin membrane. A similar pain radiated from his side and the base of his tail. He could see blood oozing from the hole in his wing and imagined that a similar fate had fallen to the other impact sites. Hoping to avoid further damage, he tucked his wings more closely to his body and executed a tight dive towards the mouth of the cave. He twisted his body at the last minute and unfurled his mighty wings to arrest his descent. Slamming his legs into the ground with much more force than he had anticipated, he heard a sharp crack from his ankle and knee joints, which had absorbed the brunt of the impact. Adding to the intense pain that was already pulsating throughout his body, he mentally pushed it aside and carried on.

Looking up, he saw the jet loop back around for another attack. Limping closer to the edge of the rock, he hid most of his body behind the protection of the mountain itself. Just as the plane came within range, he pointed his head upwards and launched a long plume of fire into the sky, just in front of where the fighter jet would predictably pass through. The dragonfire struck the underside of the craft, setting several parts of the mechanical abomination ablaze. He launched several follow-up gouts after the jet, but the pilot easily dodged them, now knowing what to expect.

Finishing his last maneuver, Grady let out a sigh of relief as he dodged several additional blasts of dragonfire. Now that he had a better idea of the dragon's attack patterns, he felt more confident in anticipating his moves. Glancing down at his control panel, however, his mood instantly changed. A fuel temperature warning flashed red on his panel, indicating that his external fuel pod was reaching above nominal temperatures. Thinking back quickly to where it felt like the fire had impacted on his craft, he realized that parts of his craft were still on fire. On the jet's underside of his aircraft, there was a centrally mounted external fuel pod, and three weapons pylons were on each wing. The fighter had been loaded with two 500-pound bombs and four Sidewinder missiles, symmetrically positioned to balance the weight. He wasn't sure of exactly what he would run into out here, and figured that he would best be prepared with this arsenal.

Toggling the controls on his display screen, he switched to his external underside camera to see what was happening down below. What he saw drained the life from his face. The fuel pod and both bombs were on fire. If the fire penetrated the housings or caused the temperature inside to reach critical levels, they would explode... and take him with them.

Ordinarily speaking, the next move would be unheard of in a populated area. However, given the remoteness of the location, and his own desire for self-preservation, Lt. Commander Grady only had one option left: Dump everything that he didn't need.

Flicking open the safety cover on one of the switches that he never wanted to touch, he jettisoned the external fuel pod. With his other hand, he simultaneously armed and dropped his two dumb bombs. Hoping to escape the impending explosions, he banked hard to the right and sped away from the direction of travel which all three objects should be taking after the drop. Looking back over his shoulder, he watched with relief as the fuel pod exploded harmlessly in the air above the tree canopy. The bombs, however, struck the earth and leveled an acre's worth of beautiful forest. He winced with regret, but he had no other choice.

Returning to his external camera, he was relieved to see that the majority of the flames had gone away with the dropping of the ordinance and the extra fuel, but, there were some portions of the sheet metal that were still on fire. Wisps of smoke shot off in straight lines behind the jet as it screamed through the sky. He appeared to be safe for now, but he had no idea how much more fire was back there and when it would put itself out. Travelling at his current speed was both a blessing and curse. While the wind put out some of the flames, it was also force-feeding fresh oxygen to the fire, which would just allow it to burn more intensely. He needed to figure out how to put out the flames, or he would be forced to ditch the jet before it blew up. Thankfully, it looked like the remaining ordinance, his four Sidewinder missiles loaded further out on the wings, were currently safe. But for how long?

Rolling to the side and pulling back on the stick, he brought himself around in a tight loop to set up for another attack run. After completing his turn, he was surprised to see the creature waiting for him at the base of the mountain. This presented an easy target, but he was curious if the dragon had some sort of trick planned for him. Thumbing the safety cover on his rocket controls, Rob armed all four missiles and prepared to attack.

Still recovering from the pressure wave that slammed into his body from the three explosions that went off a few hundred feet away, Tryggvi anxiously tracked the jet through the sky as the pilot looped back around again. Remembering how badly those bullets had hurt from the first attack, he moved more cautiously now.

Recalling that the attack happened when it was pointed at him, it was clear that the pilot needed a straight line of sight to fire his weapons. Moving side to side while keeping the larger boulders between him and the approaching plane, Tryggvi made himself a moving target. He couldn't run or fly away; the plane was obviously too fast. And he didn't want to hide in the cave, because then he'd be trapped and at the pilot's mercy. So, he instead waited patiently and looked for his time to strike.

He didn't have to wait long. Watching the craft come closer, he saw two small tubes with fins emerge and separate from just underneath the body of the mechanical beast. They seemed to be alive and move on their own accord. They also seemed to be moving very quickly and were coming straight for him. Not knowing what these were, he angrily blew fire straight at them with the most powerful stream he could muster before crouching behind the lip of the cave. He wanted to see what would happen next.

As the dragonfire connected with the two objects, each exploded on contact, spreading large plumes of flame in the sky above. Whatever devilish form of weaponry this was, it would explode if it connected with him. He had never been hit by one of these, but, Tryggvi knew enough to keep his distance from it. Continuously moving, he remained hidden from the plane as it overshot the mountain and circled back around, then let off a stream of fire at the belly of the beast as it flew overhead. Tryggvi was delighted to score another direct hit.

Swooping back around the mountain, the pilot lined up for another attack. He didn't know how many of these weapons the pilot was equipped with, and he wasn't looking forward to finding out. He was unsure of just how long he could play this game before he grew tired and made a mistake. As expected, the pilot lined up on him and Tryggvi heard another quick succession of thuds and watched as bullets struck the boulders around his hiding place. Each bullet either obliterated the rock or left deep impact craters where they struck the stone. Small, sharp shards of rock flew through the air all around him and pelted his scales.

The plane overshot him, arced through the air once again, and lined back up on the dragon's position for another missile attack. Watching with a small wedge of his head exposed, Tryggvi saw the tell-tale sign of one of those self-guided weapons coming at him again. The pilot didn't shoot two together this time, but instead shot one, waited a second, and then shot the second. Knocking these out in the air would be more difficult this time. Sticking his head above the rock, Tryggvi lined up with the first shot and launched a massive fireball. The fire streaked through the air and impacted the rocket as before, detonating it in midair with a shockwave rippling through the immediate atmosphere. As treetops caught on fire, he shielded his face with his wings to block his eyes from the burning light.

Almost forgetting about the second missile until it was too late, Tryggvi launched his massive bulk away from the mouth of the cave in a last-ditch effort to save himself from the anticipated explosion. Glancing backwards as he hit the dirt, he watched in delight as the second missile followed the smoke trail of the first missile without arcing down towards him. The missile punched through the dissipating cloud of fire and continued onward, having lost its previously locked-on target.

The wayward missile carried on, entered the mouth of the cave, and detonated just inside the entrance to the cavern. Though some distance away, the massive concussion knocked Tryggvi several feet backwards. He wasn't seriously injured by the man-made fire, but the concussive shockwave blew him into a large boulder, and he felt something crack in his back from the impact.

He found it hard to breath and he felt dizzy. Rising oh shaky legs, he looked over at the cave in dismay. The entire mouth of his cave was destroyed. The explosion had ripped apart the ceiling and walls and collapsed the entryway to his home. Looking at the size of some of the rocks blocking the way, he wasn't sure if he could even move them after healing from his current injuries.

Remembering the human still buzzing around trying to kill him, Tryggvi scanned the skies and spotted it a few miles out. He watched in relief as the plane finally succumbed to his flaming onslaught and exploded in midair. The battle had cost him his home and almost his life, but he had finally eliminated his foe. Curiously, he noticed a small, black speck hovering near where the plane had just exploded. As the wreckage rained down upon the forest, he saw a white cloth unfurl from the speck as it slowly drifted down into the woods below. Flinching as the largest chunk of the jet landed with a boom, Tryggvi decided to leave before things got any more exciting.

Still unsure of what had attacked him and how it had even tracked him down, he didn't want to wait around for any other of these metal birds to attack. Looking back over towards his cave, he sadly realized that he was homeless. His centuries of collected gold, human weapons and armor, and the best lair that he had ever resided in, was now gone. He needed to find new shelter, and soon. Despite the pain in his wings, he was still able to fly. Pumping mightily and pushing off from the ground, he took to the blue sky above and headed westward.

CHAPTER THIRTEEN
PANIC

"Woah! Wait, don't change the channel, Pop!" Liam urged. "Turn that up, I want to hear this." Running from the kitchen to the Spartan living room of the hunting cabin, Liam jumped over the back of the old couch and landed down hard on the cushion next to his grandfather. The decrepit furniture creaked under the impact, and Pop gave him a look of clear annoyance. Too distracted by what the reporters on the television were saying, Liam brushed it off and turned the volume up.

"We're here live at the Eastern Slopes Regional Airport in Fryeburg with a breaking news story," the reporter began. "Earlier today, a single-engine airplane was attacked by a mysterious creature in midair and then brutally destroyed on the ground. My sources tell me that the pilot was killed in the encounter. Several law enforcement officers, both from county and state agencies, were injured as well. Their individual conditions are unknown, but anonymous sources from the hospital have told his reporter that at least two emergency personnel also died in the attack."

"Susie, from what I understand, you have an actual witness on the ground with you," the anchor said.

"That's correct, Toby," she replied. "The ground controller, Mike Long, was the one in charge of the small, single landing strip airport before and during the attack, and watched the whole event transpire. Mike, what can you tell us about the attack on the airplane, its pilot, and the officers around us?"

"It... it, it, was big... really... really big," Mike managed to stammer. "It burned that pilot alive. I watched him die with my own eyes."

Liam sat in silence as he watched the man stop talking and just stare back into the camera. He appeared to still be in shock from the encounter.

"What else can you tell us, Mike?" the reporter asked. "What was the creature, and where do you think that it came from?"

The ground controller merely continued to stare into the background and didn't even acknowledge the further questions. The reporter awkwardly waited for another few seconds before nodding to someone off screen. "This was obviously a traumatic event for all involved. We will be standing by to update you on any further developments in this tragic story. Toby, back to you in the studio."

Pop grabbed the remote and changed the channel back to the local hunting station. "Turn off that silliness, Liam," chastised his grandfather. "I know what you're already thinking. It's not that creature that you saw, and there are no such things as dragons. You must have seen some large bear or something. And that guy on TV was probably attacked by some crazy person with a flamethrower."

Feeling defeated, Liam rose from the couch and went over to his bed on the bunk. Checking his cell phone again, he noted that he still had no signal and couldn't call his mom and dad. There was a pay phone back in town, so he could at least take a ride in the morning and give them a call.

Taking a notepad out of his duffel bag, he started sketching out the dragon and the cave from memory. He wasn't sure if he would be able to salvage anything from his melted camera, so he wanted to record his memories while they were still fresh. He sketched, wrote down notes, and even drew a rough map of the area around the cave. Pop came over at one point, looked at what he was doing, chuckled while shaking his head, and climbed into the bunk below him. Liam continued to work for a few more hours before realizing how late it was. He and Pop had an early morning planned, and he should probably get to sleep soon or else he'd be a zombie the next day. Closing the notebook, he slipped into his sleeping bag and turned off the light. He stared into the darkness before falling into an uneasy asleep.

After several long, sleepless hours interrupted by occasional stints of slumber filled with nightmares involving dragons and fire, Liam decided to call it quits and just stay awake. Feeling his stomach growl, he looked over at the wall clock and saw it was just past four in the morning. Swinging his legs around, he climbed down off of the top tier of the bunk bed and gently dropped to the floor. He didn't want to wake up Pop just yet, but he was too hungry to wait for breakfast time.

Skilled in the culinary arts, Liam had cooked with his parents from an early age and was adept at preparing just about anything that you'd want to eat. Grabbing ingredients from the cupboard and refrigerator, he went about making Eggs Irish, hash, and bacon. Smelling the waves of deliciousness now circulating around the cabin, Pop eventually rose and wandered over to the stove.

"Dude, that smells great," Pop muttered while rubbing his eyes. "I can't even remember when I last had homemade Hollandaise sauce. Give me a few minutes, and I'll be out to help you finish up."

"No worries! I'm almost done anyways," Liam replied. "Get yourself freshened up, and we'll fill up before heading out."

The two spent the next hour eating and preparing their gear for the day. They were looking for new woods to hunt in, so they primarily needed their hiking gear, maps, and cameras for recording tracks, tree rubbings, and tufts of hair caught in branches, or better yet, deer themselves. Liam wasn't a fan of actually hunting, but he loved to eat venison, spend time with his grandfather, and hike. So these trips were well worth the effort.

After they had loaded up his grandfather's truck and headed into town for coffee and gasoline, Liam dialed in his father's cell phone number in the pay phone. After a few rings, his dad picked up, and Liam filled him in on what they were up to today and when he was planning on coming home. Once the easy topics were covered... he told him about the dragon.

Amazingly, his dad listened patiently and let his son recount the day's events in minute detail. After five minutes of story-telling, and convincing his dad that he was alright, Jim filled him in on what he had heard on his end via the local news and stories on the Internet.

The Governor of Maine had just come on and declared a state of emergency for the entirety of Oxford County, and the Governor of New Hampshire had done likewise for both the neighboring Coos and Jackson counties. While the attacks had all taken place in and around Fryeburg, the latest reports coming in from witnesses showed that the creature was headed west and may now be in New Hampshire. Given its proclivity for mountains, the White Mountain National Forest was an obviously attractive target for the creature's next destination.

Jim said that a pilot had been rescued after ejecting out in the woods, but the Air Force had quickly scooped him up and were not releasing any information. Whatever had happened at that airport was being rapidly scoured and hidden from the public. However, there were spotty accounts circulating around social media and various local newspapers' websites of farmers having cattle and other livestock attacked by a flying creature, with wildly differing physical descriptions, and either eaten on the spot or carried away. Each of these eyewitness accounts, while varying, all corresponded in one shape or form to the dragon that had nearly taken Liam's life. And it seemed that the dragon was on the move.

Thanking his dad for the information, and assuring him that he was alright, Liam said his goodbyes and hung up the phone. Walking back to the truck, he jumped into the passenger side and buckled in as his grandfather started the engine. Rumbling out of the parking lot, the two men headed out into the woods for a day of exploration and reconnaissance.

Four days later, Liam sat down with his father at his desk back in Manchester. As Liam pulled his camera out of his backpack, Jim let out a gasp at the sight of the expensive, formerly-functional digital SLR camera. The lens and body, mostly plastic, had melted heavily under the tremendous heat from the dragonfire. Jim was amazed that his son was still alive based on the dismal appearance of the camera. Taking the camera gingerly from his son, Jim held it over a metal bowl. Putting on his safety glasses, he popped the battery compartment door open with a flat-head screwdriver. Sure enough, as he expected, some battery acid dripped down through the compartment. The casing had been ruptured from the heat and blew up inside of the camera. Pulling the melted battery out with a pair of needle-nose pliers, he dried out the cavity with a rag and immediately threw it away.

The door to the memory card slot had fused to the housing of the camera during the blast. Jim took a sharp hobby knife and carefully cut around the area of the door. Popping it open with the screwdriver, they finally got to see the condition of the memory card. It wasn't promising. The unit had a shiny look to it from where the plastic had melted and smoothed out upon cooling.

Liam let out a sigh and slumped down in his chair. Not so easily defeated, Jim continued working at it and managed to extract the card from the slot with the help of another knife and a pair of locking-jaw pliers. Pulling it clear of the camera wreckage, he slid the card into the reader slot on his laptop and waited.

It took a minute or so, but the laptop managed to connect to the memory card, albeit slowly, and opened a new window on the screen. There were a few hundred image files on there, but many produced an error when he tried to open them. The heat had evidently corrupted much of the data on the storage device, and it was doubtful that many, or any, of these files would even open for their viewing. After another thirty minutes or so of patiently clicking on each file and hoping that it would open, the two managed to collect several usable files and transferred them to the laptop's hard drive for further investigation. Disconnecting the camera's damaged memory card from the laptop's reader, they put the camera and card aside and dug into the photographs more carefully.

What they could recover, sadly, was a mishmash of blurry photographs and corrupted files. There were some good pictures of the mountains, the pool, the waterfall where Liam had swam, and of some animals in the woods where he had hiked on previous trips. However, there were very few images pertinent to the investigation. Several photographs featured a hazy green and red object, a pile of gold coins, some of the armor and swords that Liam had found, and many randomly snapped images of the cavern itself. But only a couple were of the dragon, and these were either fuzzy, out of focus, or had been partially corrupted by the heat. This was very disappointing, as Liam had no physical evidence aside from these pictures that the event had even occurred.

His father, to his credit, helped his son review the pictures for the remainder of the afternoon. Having spent much of his life reading science-fiction and fantasy novels, the idea of real-life dragons was not that far-fetched for Jim. In his heart, Jim wanted to believe that such mythological creatures existed. And in his years of playing collectible card and role-playing games, dragons had always been his favorite fantastical creature to portray, fight, and imagine playing out in the world around him. Naturally, he also believed in his son and would help him in any way possible.

Jim uploaded the image files to his son's online storage drive and transferred them to a different folder on his desktop for his own viewing. This wasn't the end of Jim's investigation into this matter.

Thanking his dad for his help, Liam made his way upstairs to his bedroom and plopped down on his bed. He lay there on his back for a while and stared at the ceiling, replaying events from the past week through his head. Some were extraordinary, some horrific, some still unbelievable even after experiencing them for himself. Rolling to his side, he grabbed his tablet from the nightstand and pulled up the photographs. He pored over every detail of each one for an hour or two, and completely lost track of time.

It wasn't until much later when his mother called him down for dinner that he realized how much time had passed. Turning the tablet off, he hopped off of the bed onto the floor and made his way downstairs to the kitchen. This mystery wouldn't be solved anytime soon, so he might as well think about it on a full stomach.

Over the next several months, the panic over the dragon situation peaked, plateaued, and eventually fell from popularity at the lack of firm evidence and facts. Initially, the three-county state of emergency put air travel and tourism on lockdown. State troopers and local police departments canvassed the area and interviewed possible witnesses. The National Guard was activated to patrol the streets and woods. Local airports and weather stations worked with the Air Force to watch for any unusual activity in the skies.

Liam, feeling personally responsible for all of this, as he had originally awoken the creature from its slumber deep within that mountain, had almost immediately contacted the Manchester Police Department to tell them everything that he knew and to offer his services in the matter. He volunteered to help out with anything and everything that he could. While thanking him for the call, the authorities, already swamped with tips and volunteers, declined his offer to help in the search effort.

Liam begged his parents to let him return to the mountain to investigate, but they firmly said 'no'. It was far too dangerous, and he was too young to go gallivanting all alone into the wilderness on a wild goose chase. While not the answer for which he was hoping to receive, he couldn't disagree with them and relented to staying at home.

A search effort can only be maintained for so long without some sign of success. After a solid month of combing the mountains and caves around the areas where the dragon was last spotted, little concrete evidence was found. Aside from the farmers who reported their livestock to be eaten or maimed, there had been very few others coming forward with stories. One set of footprints had been found at a local farm, but most reported that the creature had snatched up their livestock without even landing on the ground. Whatever this creature was, it was smart, fast, and knew how to be invisible when and where it wanted to be. As quickly as the dragon had come into everyone's lives, it had disappeared, and the public eventually lost interest.

While disappointed in the outcome, Liam could find no one to blame. He decided then to take matters into his own hands and began his own research into what had happened, what this creature was, and where it had gone to next. Given that it was still during his summer vacation between his junior and senior years of high school, he more or less had available time on his hands. Without telling his parents, he quit his part-time internship at a local machine shop and dedicated every waking moment to his investigation. He couldn't wait for the authorities to uncover the truth, and who knew whether something worse might happen.

He turned his bedroom into an impromptu crime lab. He bought several large cork boards and hung them from his walls. Where once hung posters of superheroes, characters from action and adventure movies, or his favorite bands, he now had various forms evidence thumbtacked all around his room. He had collected a massive depository of newspaper clippings and Internet printouts. He scoured every website that he could find related to the dragon situation and poured over every detail. He even found some social media pages dedicated to dragon sightings around the region and contacted the people posting there. He emailed and messaged back and forth with members of the community, swapping pictures and information.

Next, he purchased large-scale maps of Maine and New Hampshire and hung them on the last available bit of wall space, sticking tacks and pins wherever there were documented sightings or clues. He wrote down bullet points concerning each sighting. He then connected the pins to the bullet-points with pieces of string and red yarn to help him find information more quickly. What had once been a clean, tidy bedroom of a seventeen year-old boy, was now an information-packed war room of an amateur private investigator. In a matter of a few weeks, the room of an innocent young man now showed signs of someone growing up too quickly. Intensely focused on a solitary objective, he was unable to slow down.

This was the scene that his father took in one night when he walked upstairs to get Liam for supper. After several calls of increasing volume up the open stairwell to summon the typically hungry lad, his father was confused as to why Liam wasn't coming downstairs, let alone answering him. Walking up to the boy's room, Jim noticed that the door was slightly ajar and peered through the open crack. Seeing his son lying down on the bed, fast asleep, he opened the door quietly to go in and wake him up.

Upon entering the room, Jim stopped dead in his tracks and merely gazed around. He hadn't been in his son's room in a few weeks and couldn't believe his own eyes. Encompassing the room, there was the evidence of hundreds of hours of ceaseless research to the dragon and all things dragon related. He knew that his son was looking into the matter after his run in with the creature up in Maine, but he had no clue that it was this intensive. While Jim was a little shocked, he was also extraordinarily proud to see this level of passion and dedication. He may not fully understand the boy's obsession with the dragon, but he at least respected it.

Looking back down at the bed, Jim decided to let his son sleep. He would put some food in the refrigerator for him and heat it up later when he woke up. Quietly walking backwards out of the room, he carefully closed the door behind him and went back down to the kitchen to eat with his wife.

After another long, intense week of work, Liam had finally built up the courage to ask for permission to personally search for the dragon. He had thought about it extensively for the past few days and had the perfect sales pitch formulated in his head. He had even practiced in the mirror to make sure that he looked and sounded convincing. He had been denied once before, so if he was going to try this again, he wanted to do it right.

After dinner one night, as the family enjoyed some ice cream for dessert, Liam made his pitch. After several long, arduous rounds of begging and pleading to his parents that he had researched the matter more thoroughly, that he knew what he was up against and where he'd begin his trek, and that he'd be safe and stay in near-constant cell phone contact while he was gone, he found himself silently looking back and forth between two non-verbal parents. He was so sure of himself that he had either fully convinced them or had put the last nail into the coffin of his plan. When they neither congratulated nor yelled at him, Liam froze in confusion and just stared at them open-mouthed.

After what felt like an eternity, Jim finally spoke. Glancing over to his wife with a slight nod, he explained how he had been impressed by Liam's diligent work and was extremely proud of him.

"However... we can't let you just drive up to Maine by yourself to hunt around the countryside for a dangerous creature," his dad simply stated.

Staring back in defeat, Liam couldn't talk. His brain wanted to say a thousand different things: ranging from anger, denial, disappointment, defeat, and acceptance. But, at this moment, his brain just shut down. "I understand, Dad," he muttered with a sigh.

"But," his father continued with a smile. "I do have some vacation time that needs to be used up before it expires, and I haven't been up to the woods of Maine in quite some time. Would you like to take a trip with me for a week or two?"

Liam froze. Surely this was a trap. Or was it? He knew for a fact that his dad's company issued vacation days bi-weekly, and that they needed to use them up before he hit a maximum running number. He might really have a large chunk of time saved up. And he used to love hiking and camping, but hadn't gone in years given how busy things have been around the house and with a new project that he was working on.

"Liam, are you in there?" his Dad queried.

"YES!" Liam proclaimed, somewhat louder than necessary. Leaping from his chair and nearly upending his dinner plate, he launched himself at his still-seated father, wrapped his arms around him. The duo fell backwards in his father's chair, laughing all the way to the floor.

A week later, the plan was finally ready. Jim and Liam would return to the cave where it all began, visit the airfield in Fryeburg, and then head west into the White Mountains to follow the trail of sightings. After packing the pickup with their hiking and camping gear, several days' worth of food, and most of the boy's documentation and evidence, the two men said goodbye to Mrs. Tryggvison, who gently pleaded for them to stay safe, pulled onto Route 93, and headed north.

While Jim drove, Liam continued to pour over all of the information that he had, in addition to new information that he pulled up on his phone as they rode along. That is, until they hit the last of the cellular coverage in southern Maine. As they made their way towards Fryeburg, Liam switched his focus to the hard copy documents and photographs that he had brought with them from his document collection back at the house. He wanted to be as familiar with each and every detail as possible to streamline their efforts on this trip.

Stopping for gas only once along the way thanks to the large, dual gas tank setup on the truck, Liam and his dad made remarkable time. They had already called ahead and were en route to the Eastern Slopes Regional Airport to speak with some witnesses who were there that day and had seen the dragon with their own eyes. Given the amount of speculation that was being tossed around online, it would be good to start with some first-hand accounts of what it looked like, its characteristics, traits, and any other tiny details that the authorities might have overlooked in their investigation. About two and a half hours after leaving Manchester, the father and son duo pulled into the parking area at the seemingly deserted air strip.

Jumping out of the passenger side of the truck, Liam stretched his leg muscles and did a few quick squats to shake out the tightness in his body. It wasn't a long drive, but it was long enough to cramp up his back and legs. His father did likewise, but with a slightly pained expression on his face. Liam almost made a quip about him being an old man, but remembering that he was currently on this expedition only through the good graces of his father and his desire to help his son out, he respectively held back.

As the two walked towards the control building, Mike Long opened the door to wave them over. Before walking inside, they looked around at the airstrip and took in the barely repaired damage caused by the attack. The dragon really did a number on this place.

The meeting went more or less as they had expected it to. Mike claimed that he was under strict orders by the police and military officers, of whom he wasn't even allowed to say their names but only rank, to not speak with anyone. His job at the airport was threatened if he mentioned anything of the sensitive nature to the media or anyone else snooping around. He wouldn't even allow them to go out and look at the strip today as he was paranoid that the government was watching their meeting from satellites above.

After only a few minutes, Mike proceeded to quickly rush them back out the door and made an elaborate display of kicking them off the property to anyone who might be watching from the concealment of the nearby trees. What wasn't expected, however, was what he did as they were walking out the door. Although he made it blatantly clear, both physically and verbally, that he wouldn't tell them anything, he placed something into Liam's hand and closed the young man's fingers around it. While he said 'goodbye' and shook his hand, Mike leaned close and whispered, "Stay nearby for a few hours."

Liam was unsure of what just happened. But, eager for more information, he played along. Jim shot him a weird look trying to figure out what was happening, but Liam just gave him a quick nod and they got into the truck.

Driving down the road, and waiting until they left the line-of-sight of the air strip's buildings, Liam finally opened his hand to find a small prepaid phone in his palm. He instantly knew what Mike had meant and a smile crept onto his face.

"What are you so happy about over there?" inquired his father, trying to keep the old truck straight on the bumpy road. "And what did that crazy guy give you? I can't believe that he would have us drive all this way up here just to turn us back and kick us off of the property when we arrive."

"Oh, he might be crazy," replied Liam. "But he's apparently not done talking with us. He gave me a burner phone and said to stick around. I think that he wants to call us later to talk when he's not so worried about being watched or listened to. Let's find something to do in the meantime and see what happens."

A few hours later, Liam and his father sat in a nearby coffee shop reading the regional newspapers and listening in on the local gossip. The only mention of the dragon attack came from an op-ed in stuck in the back section of one of the fringe papers. The mainstream news had all but dropped the story. Liam was reading an article about a new solar farm when the phone started to vibrate on the table in front of him. Looking around for eavesdroppers, Liam picked up the phone and listened to the speaker on the other end. After a pause, he looked at his father and said, "It's time to go."

Getting up from the table, Liam dropped enough money to cover the food plus tip next to their empty plates and glasses. As the two men walked outside to the truck, Liam broke the simple flip-phone into two pieces at the hinge, wiped each half off with his t-shirt, and dropped them into a nearby trashcan. Jim put the truck into reverse, straightened out, and pulled back onto the main road. Looking over at his son, he simply smirked and shook his head.

"What?" asked Liam. "The guy told me to do it. He's wicked paranoid and thinks they'll come for him just for speaking to us. He was probably wearing an aluminum foil hat when he called. Regardless, he said that he has information and wants to get his story out."

"Fine," retorted his father, "but if we get killed, it's all your fault. Where does he want to meet?"

"He said that there's a little cemetery over on 302, just a mile or so away. He asked to meet him over in the back row and pretend to visit a grave." With that, they sped off towards the next phase of the adventure.

By the time that the two approached the cemetery, the sun had already begun to set and darkness crept over the area. Jim turned off the headlights and drove through the quiet lanes between grave sites using the daytime running lights. He figured that he'd probably spook the guy if he drew too much attention to their approach. Seeing only one other car there, Jim parked several spaces away from a beat-up sedan.

Remembering to play their parts, the two solemnly walked to a stone several plots away from where a lone man stood. Glancing over, Liam confirmed that it was in fact Mike from earlier at the airport, except he was now wearing a comically large hat and a full-length trench coat, which must have been swelteringly hot inside given the weather for that day. Thankfully, he was sans aluminum hat.

They greeted each other in low tones. Convinced that they were alone and it was safe to do so, Mike pulled a thick manila envelope out of his coat and laid it down on the ground before the gravestone. He nodded to them, walked back to his car, and quickly drove away.

Waiting until he had disappeared into the distance, Liam casually walked over to the adjacent stone and knelt down as if to pray. Picking up the envelope, he slid the package beneath his shirt and pressed against his stomach with one hand to keep the contents from falling out. After waiting a respectable amount of time to convince any onlookers that he was legitimately praying over the grave of this anonymous witness to their clandestine meeting, he stood back up and the duo made their way to the truck.

Clutching the envelope to his chest as they drove to the motel that they were staying at for the night, Liam smiled. Their adventure was just beginning. He couldn't wait to see what was inside and where it would lead them!

Back at the motel, Liam and Jim relaxed on the couch in the room watching the late night local news on the television. While his father and mother talked on the phone, Liam had the envelope opened and spread the contents out on the rickety old wooden coffee table before him. He divided the material into several piles: web printouts, newspaper clippings, a series of 8"x10" photographs, and photocopies of some official-looking government documents. The envelope had been over an inch thick, so there was a lot of material to digest.

He spent the next few hours carefully reviewing each piece of evidence, careful not to miss any details. Keeping his notebook next to him as he read, he jotted down important details and flagged interesting bits with a sticky note. He had learned that what seemed important at first often turned out to be bogus, while trivial things sometimes turned out to be monumentally important.

Some of the photographs showed the dragon clearly for the very first time. From what Liam could tell, they had all been shot with a camera phone, but from a remarkably short distance. Most were blurry, mainly due to the fast motion of the creature and the intense light coming off of the fire emanating from the beast's mouth, but a few were very good. They clearly showed a European-style dragon with four limbs and a broad pair of wings coming off of the back. The dragon was obviously fast on its feet, and appeared angered by the presence of the people around it. From what he could tell by pictures of the creature lifting off to fly, the dragon had extremely strong wings and was able to rapidly propel itself into the air.

Sadly, the photographs also revealed the harsh reality of the attack: death. Liam counted seven individuals who had died at the hands of the beast. This was surprising, as the news only reported on the deaths of five individuals. For whatever reason, the media was covering up two of the deaths. Liam made a note to follow up on this matter later.

From what he could see, each person who died suffered agonizing fates from the encounter. Most were severely burned by varying degrees depending solely on where they were at the time of the attack and how long the dragon had focused on them. Some were burnt from the waist up if they were standing behind one of the many vehicles at the scene, while some were burnt on their entire bodies if they were not lucky enough to be standing behind shelter at the time. Some probably died from breathing in the hot gases, while others had been incinerated to the point where much of the contact area was simply gone. Two of the victims had been reduced to blackened ash, and nothing more.

Leaning back into the couch, Liam needed a moment to pause and clear his mind of what he had just seen. Closing his eyes, he tried to think of literally anything else that he could, if only to would give him a momentary respite from the images that now swirled around in his head. The fact that this dragon was capable of so much death, destruction, wholesale violence, and was still on the loose did not sit easily with the teenager. How this had fallen so quickly from the public eye amazed him. Then again, every time he turned on the news he saw stories about normal humans committing similar crimes upon other humans. What makes an unexplained mythical source such as a dragon any different? Rubbing his eyes, he took a deep breath and tried to focus. Losing track of the conversation besides him, he wasn't even aware that the phone call had ended between his mom and dad, and that his dad was now speaking to him. Feeling his dad's hand on his shoulder, he opened his eyes and looked next to him.

"Are you in there, bud?" his father asked.

"Yeah, these pictures are just getting to me," started Liam. "There's a murderer still on the loose. We need to find this thing, and we need to find it now. It's my fault that it's out there and killing these people, and I won't be able to rest until I finish what I have started."

Staring back in amazement, Jim had never felt so helpless. He was simultaneously worried about Liam's growing guilt, scared for what may come, and proud of his son's accomplishments so far. While the idea of fighting a dragon, a creature he'd only recently accepted was real, frightened him deeply, Jim admired the teen for his dedication and sense of responsibility. Liam had grown up a lot since this all began.

"Well, why don't we shift gears a little and give your eyes a break?" Jim said. "Looking at these pictures all night won't get you anywhere. We should look through the witness sightings and radar information, and try to determine where the dragon might have gone. Also, we need to discuss another imminent attack that may happen at any moment if you don't take the proper action."

Alarmed, Liam exclaimed, "What's happening now?!"

"Your mother, Liam," his father said, smiling, "is still on the phone waiting to talk to you. If you don't pick up that phone and tell her 'good night,' the dragon will be the least of your worries."

The next morning, after a long night of study, Jim and Liam loaded the pickup and headed out for breakfast. Over several cups of iced coffee and a hearty meal, the two worked out a list of places to go for the day. The plan was to head west and visit several people who claimed to have seen the dragon. Liam marked each location on the map and saw that they more or less formed a straight line heading west. Always to the west. The dragon was going somewhere specific. Just where was what they needed to find out.

The duo spent the rest of the day meeting with the first two people on their list. The first witness, a middle-aged man, had seen the dragon fly away due west from Eastern Slopes after the attack. He had little else to contribute, though, and they thanked him before moving on. The next person lived near Redstone and owned a small restaurant in town. The woman had been outside tending tables when she had looked up and noticed something funny flying just below the clouds. She thought little of it until she had seen the news reports on TV.

And so, the next week was spent in a similar fashion. The truck continued west into New Hampshire as Liam pointed the way and fed his father one address after another. They spoke with each witness on the list, and even a few extras along the way, as they cut through a large swath of the White Mountain National Forest. They visited a barkeep in North Conway, a gas station owner in Bartlett, some employees at a rest stop in Crawford Notch State Park, a farmer in Livermore, and a hut worker near Zealand Notch.

Their last visit, however, was the most exciting. While at the Zealand Falls Hut, situated along the Appalachian Trail, they spoke with a man who claimed that his friend had seen a large lizard flying through the air, and then settle into a forested patch near the base of Mount Lafayette. After getting the hiker's contact information, they immediately reached out to him and set up a meeting to discuss the details. The hiker sounded excited and was very eager to share. They met later that day at a small restaurant along the Daniel Webster Highway, just north of Lincoln. The place was fairly deserted, as it was halfway between lunch and supper, but they spotted a young man in his early twenties who matched the description that the hiker had given them over the phone. He had long hair pulled back into a ponytail, a thick beard that reached his chest, was dressed in khaki shorts and a t-shirt, and he was wearing rubber sandals on his feet.

"Hi, sorry to intrude, but are you Adam?" Liam inquired.

"Yeah!" he exclaimed, "Are you the two guys looking for the dragon?" A few of the other patrons turned in their direction, and a young boy giggled as he squirmed in his seat.

"If you have some good information on where we might find him... then yes, that's definitely us," replied Liam. "Have you eaten yet? Let's get some lunch, our treat."

The three men shared a meal of simple sandwiches, hand-cut French fries, and some ice cold soda. It had been a hot and long day, and the cool, caffeinated liquid felt good going down Liam's throat. As the food was eaten and washed down by several refills from the waiter, Adam told the story of his encounter with the beast.

It happened two days after the attack on the airport, and fit perfectly with the sequence of other events that they had investigated, thus far. It seemed that the dragon was flying a fairly straight path towards something and had only deviated left or right in its flight by small degrees. Adam had been slowly thru-hiking the Appalachian Trail for the past summer, stopping at least once a month to work small jobs here and there to continue funding his expedition. After reaching Franconia Notch he planned to hike the Old Bridle Path trail that day. He had heard that the AMC Greenleaf Hut needed some help, and he was going up that morning to apply in person for a job as a temporary cook in the kitchen.

As Adam ascended the trail that morning, he found himself on the rockiest portion, where there was very little tree cover, and he had a clear view of the bright blue sky above him. Having just moved off the trail to sit down for a few minutes to catch his breath, he was eating a quick snack when he heard strange noises coming from down in the valley. He looked to the south across several of the lesser ridges going up the spine of Mount Lafayette and saw a flash of green swoop up the face of the mountain and fly past his head. He fell backwards over the rocks where he had been resting, and, after righting himself, watched the creature soar up into the sky, momentarily eclipse the sun, and dive back into the valley on the opposite side of the ridge beyond. The dragon glided down into a small marsh, where a moose was eating some of the marshy vegetation. With little effort, the creature bit the poor animal around the neck and grabbed it fast with all four sets of claws. Without slowing down, the dragon lifted the moose into the air and carried it away.

Pausing in his story, he pulled a trail map from his cargo pocket on his right leg of his shorts and unfolded it on the table. He pointed out an area on the eastern side of Cannon Mountain, which mostly consisted of rocky outcroppings and slides. He said that from the last sighting that he had of the dragon as it flew away, it was heading towards this rocky area. He explained that the area was littered with countless uncharted nooks and crannies and that a creature of its size could probably find a place to hide if it needed to do so.

Adam admitted, almost sheepishly, that he was pretty frightened by the whole situation, and didn't tell anyone about it until days later after seeing similar reports on the local news. He had figured that if he had told anyone what he had seen, that they would have laughed in his face and told him he was crazy. As he was rather low on funds, the last thing he wanted to do was jeopardize his chances of getting work. He only shared his story with a few friends at a bar later that week, which was how it was eventually passed along to Jim and Liam.

Furiously taking notes, Liam soaked up every detail of the story. He was unsure how much of it was the honest truth considering how recreationally altered this guy seemed to be, but he wasn't taking any chances in prematurely dismissing what could potentially be important information. As the story came to a close and the two men realized that they weren't getting anything else useful from Adam, they wrapped up the meeting and thanked him for his time and information.

When the check came for the lunch, Adam, as anticipated, didn't move for his wallet with any remarkable speed. Liam, looking over at his dad, sighed and grabbed the bill. Dropping down a few hard-earned dollars from his wallet, the teenager got up from the table, thanked their guest, and made his way out of the restaurant with his dad in tow.

As the doors to the truck clicked shut, the father and son looked at each other and smiled. While the hiker seemed high as a kite during their meeting, the information that he relayed to them was consistent with everything else they knew. Additionally, Adam's story gave them a crucial detail that they needed: the next place to look.

Driving north on I-93, the Tryggvisons did not have to travel far before reaching their destination. Shortly after passing by the

Flume Gorge and Mount Liberty, Mount Lafayette came up on their right with Cannon Mountain over on the left. Based on what Adam had described, the dragon was last seen somewhere in this very same area. Not really sure where and how to begin, Jim brought the vehicle to a dusty halt in one of the visitor parking lots. Putting the truck in park, he looked to his son for direction.

"Let's start here," Liam said. "We won't know where to go without more evidence, and this is just as good as anywhere else. I say we cross the road and hike up to the rocky side of Cannon. We'll see if we can find any large caves, footprints, or any other sign of the dragon over there."

In agreement with the loose plan, both men grabbed their gear and exited the truck. Liam proceeded to double check his pack for essential tools and survival gear, as well as tighten to up his boots. They tended to loosen during long drives and he wanted to make sure that he had solid footing during the upcoming hike. Additionally, he also pulled his knife out of his backpack and affixed it to his belt. Regardless of what they might encounter, he wanted to be prepared.

Apparently on the same train of thought, his dad was strapping a holster around his shoulders for his concealed carry. Liam had never known his dad to carry a firearm while hiking out in the woods, but they were hunting a dragon, after all. From what Liam had read in the police reports, the bullets from their service revolvers penetrate the dragon's scales, but their overall effectiveness was unknown. Watching him out of the corner of his eye, Liam saw his dad unlock his gun case under the seat of the truck and disengage the trigger lock on his 9mm semi-automatic pistol. He inspected the loaded magazine, and drove a cartridge home into the receiving slot. Jim also placed several extra pre-loaded magazines in his backpack, just in case.

With their gear ready, the two locked the truck, crossed the street, and headed over to the base of the adjacent mountain.

After several hours of careful searching, Liam was losing enthusiasm. While they had found plenty of deer prints and bear prints, not a single trace of the dragon was to be found. Jim, throughout it all, remained supportive of his son and his mission, even in the intense heat, which he hated. As the sun began to set over the backside of Cannon Mountain, they called it a day. Heading back to their motel, they went to bed early, planning to give it another go tomorrow.

And so, the duo repeated this process for several days more. Each morning, they would repack their gear, eat breakfast, get some coffee, and head out again. And each day, they found absolutely nothing of significance. If this dragon did not want to be found, it was obviously very good at it. It was as if the dragon had simply disappeared from existence.

Their lack of progress began to frustrate Liam tremendously. While rather mature for his age, he still had his limits and was beginning to approach his breaking point. It was a bittersweet comfort when Jim had to deliver some bad news to him one night while sitting in the motel room. After ending a phone call, Jim informed his son that he was just spoke with his boss back at the office. There was apparently a very important project coming down the pipeline and he was needed back in the office before the end of the week. Liam, although disappointed, tried to be realistic about it all and conceded that they had tried hard and given it their best shot. He was willing to move on, at least for now, and thanked his father for all he had done for him over the past two weeks.

"Well, we can stay for another day and drive home the following morning, if you like." offered his father, "In fact, why don't we have a relaxing day together, just you and me, and try to get our minds off the dragon."

"I don't know," replied Liam. "I don't really feel like doing much of anything right now. Let's just head home tomorrow."

Looking up, he saw the helplessness in Jim's eyes. He could see that his father didn't really know what to do, but just wanted to make his son happy and spend some more time with him. It was clear that they were having no luck finding the dragon, and that ultimately, they needed to go home soon anyways. Liam would be starting school back up in a few weeks as a senior, and his father didn't have much vacation time left after this little adventure. "Well, what did you have in mind?"

Smiling, his father pulled out a map and slid it across the coffee table. "Do you remember when you were younger and your mom and I took you down an alpine slide at one of the nearby ski resorts? Well, the resort is right over here, just an hour or so away."

"Dad! Come on," said Liam. "Those are for little kids."

"Yeah, and big kids who never grew up!" his father fired back. "How about this: We go ride the alpine slides tomorrow and then hike Washington the following day. We'll drive home after we descend and I'll still get to work on time the following morning. I'll be half-asleep at work, but at least we'll have a little more fun together."

Laughing, Liam agreed to the new itinerary for the next two days. After their long trek across Maine and New Hampshire in search of the dragon, this was exactly what they both needed right now. Jim pulled out his laptop and they inspected the website of the mountain to check times and pricing on the slides. It was a little pricey in comparison to the shoestring budget that this trip had operated on thus far, but it would be worth it.

Retiring to their individual beds, both Liam and his father pulled out the novels they had been reading and blissfully tried to shut out any thoughts of the dragon. After Jim said 'good night' and fell asleep, Liam simply stared at the pages of his open book. It occurred to him that he had been rereading the same page, his mind adrift and unable to focus on the story. Perhaps these next two days with his dad would help him get back to reality.

Over the next forty-eight hours, Jim and Liam lived each moment as happily as they could and tried to distance themselves from their previous mission. They rode the slides over and over again all day, stopping only to eat lunch. As soon as they got to the bottom of the slide, they picked up their sleds, walked back to the chair lift, rode to the top, and repeated the process once again.

They went up and down the slope of the mountain like this at least a dozen times before they decided to call it quits. The sun was getting low in the sky and they wanted to hit the road before it got too late. While Mount Washington wasn't far, they wanted to minimize their driving in the dark due to the area's large population of deer and moose, which often tried to cross the roads at night unaware of the dangers that the fast moving vehicles posed to them.

The next morning, they attacked the peak bright and early, and stayed for a while up top. Liam loved it up at the top of Mount Washington. It was always a bizarre experience, seeing one weather pattern at the bottom and a completely different one up top. It could be sunny and hot at the base, but cool and foggy at the peak with fifty-mile-per-hour winds battering you sideways.

Today, however, they were very fortunate. For only the second time in his life hiking this mountain, it was relatively calm and peaceful at the top. There weren't many clouds in the sky, it was comparatively warm, and everyone appeared to be having a great time. While eating their sandwiches, the two watched as other hikers made their way to the top. Several thru-hikers came along, carrying massive loads upon their backs and obviously in need of a good shower, based on the smell that wafted by as they passed. As Liam and Jim stretched their legs and prepared to descend through Tuckerman's Ravine, they could hear the sound of the old coal-fired locomotive coming up the railway. Visitors unable or unwilling to hike could still enjoy the mountain's beautiful views without busting their legs. Liam and his father, however, relished the experience of climbing the mountain.

Hopping from rock to rock, Liam succeeded in pushing thoughts of the dragon from his mind for at least two days now. Joyfully taking little risks here and there, he loved quickly descending trails like this. His dad had always referred to him as a mountain goat when hiking, and today was no exception. Bearing to the left, they headed for the Lion Head Trail and made their way down to Hermit Lake on their way back to the truck.

After several hours of blissful hiking, they settled into the cab of the vehicle and headed back south toward Manchester. While the trip wasn't a success by any means, Liam could at least say that he tried. And he did have a lot of fun with his dad. As the miles passed behind him and the day turned to night, Liam found himself leaning his head against the window. He hadn't spoken for a while and was lost in thought. Watching the reflectors on the side of the road whiz by, he couldn't shake the feeling that the dragon was still out there, somewhere, waiting for him. Would he find him again and end the violence for good, or would the attacks continue and condemn him to a lifetime of guilt?

PART FIVE
THE FINAL CUT

CHAPTER FOURTEEN
THE HUNT FOR NAUGHT

"Attention everyone!" proclaimed a young man from atop a stool at the bar. "Our friend Bobby here, with the successful ascent of Mount Willey this very afternoon, has bagged his final peak on the White Mountain Four Thousand Footer list!"

"Yaahh! Woohoo!" Many of the patrons cheered, and whistles rang out as glasses were raised in celebration to the stranger on his completion of a rigorous hiking challenge. After the hooting and hollering subsided, everyone resumed their prior conversations and consuming at the bar and its surrounding tables.

One of those patrons, sitting at table by himself in the far corner listening to the music on the jukebox, was Liam Tryggvison. Liam chuckled to himself as he listened in on the group's jubilant cries and congratulatory remarks about one of their friends completing, what was to him, a joke. Forty-eight fairly tame mountains was child's play for Liam at this point. At the fairly young age of twenty-seven, he had completed the list several times over without even trying. Heck, he had even bagged all one-hundred and fifteen of the Northeast 111. But he smiled and nodded at the guy as the group passed by at the end of the night.

For ten long years, Liam had hiked a mountain almost every day, sometimes two if they were easier to climb or close together. Ever since that summer of his junior year of high school, his life had been consumed with the search for any sign of that damn dragon. Ten years of his life, and he had almost nothing to show for it. Sure, he'd graduated high school and gone to college, but it was all pointless to him. When he should have been doing homework, he was poring over news articles, police reports, and maps of the mountains. When he should have been in the library studying, he was out hiking and searching. Always searching. Despite this, his natural intelligence and ability to remember odd facts was what had allowed him to barely graduate after five years. He netted Cs in most of his classes, putting in just enough time and effort to pass the class and move onward. His only real ambition was to earn a degree so that he could get a job that would pay for him to live in the mountains and continue his search. Everything else was secondary to him.

As it may sound, this meant a very solitary existence for the young man. He occasionally dated here and there, but rarely had any substantial money nor free time to devote to another human being. A young lady would latch onto his arm from time to time, but they were typically avid hikers themselves, and then would leave after realizing that hiking was all Liam had time for. He didn't hang out with many friends and spent all of his money on gas for his truck to drive from one mountain to another.

After graduation, he had spent the past few years drifting from one New Hampshire town to another. He had lived in Conway, Lincoln, and once along the shore of Lake Winnipesaukee for a few months after he had heard a good lead on a sighting of a large lizard over the water. Wherever rumors of sightings or available work took him, he went.

Currently, he was living and working in Jackson. He worked as a mechanic at a nearby ski resort, helping fix their chair lifts and snowmaking guns, and other necessary equipment for the operation of the mountain. He had picked up good mechanical skills at an early age from his father and the robotics programs that he had participated in, and found that they came in handy up here in this country. Most people came here on vacation, and very few natural residents wanted to stick around and do the dirty work. Plus, things were always breaking, and there was money to be found for those willing to fix them.

Still... it was a pretty lonely existence.

"NO!" Liam screamed in his sleep, waking himself up abruptly. It was very early in the morning by the look of the light coming in through the window. Glancing over at his bedside clock, he saw that it was just a little past two in the morning. Knowing how this would all play out, he gave up on trying to sleep, swung his legs over the edge of the bed and lightly padded his way to the bathroom to get ready for the day.

He had had another nightmare, an annoyingly consistent problem over the past ten years. Depending on what he had seen or heard previously that day, and how much he had been thinking about the past before falling asleep, he would often have one of several recurring dreams about dragons, hiking, and, sometimes, death.

His dream this night was the one he hated most, and sadly, the most frequent. It was slightly different each time, but it always started with him hiking with his dad in the mountains before reaching a rocky cave. He would freeze in terror as the mountain gave birth to a large, fire-breathing dragon, and watch as his father was immolated before his eyes. As always, he could neither move nor help his father in this dream sequence, but instead had to watch him die as the dragon poured fire upon his best friend. The dragon would then turn to him and let loose a bellowing roar. Even after waking up, the roar stayed ringing in his ears.

His father was alive and well, and he still lived down in Manchester with Liam's mother. But the nightmare felt so vivid that it was hard not to feel like it was somehow real. When the dreams first started, Liam would try to fall back asleep but would end up lying there, sometimes in tears. He had learned a long time ago to just get up, take a cold shower, and simply start the day a little early.

He didn't cry anymore. The passing years of enduring these repeated nightmares had emptied him of tears and left him feeling vacant inside. But the guilt of unleashing this tyrant upon the world had never left him after all of this time. Seven deaths. At least seven deaths. Who knew how many more lives had been ruined or destroyed because of him?

What followed was a typical day. Liam went to work very early in the morning to run the snow guns up on the popular black diamond trails. These were his machines, and he was responsible for keeping a good layer of snow on the ground. If it got too cold out, the snow would ice up and be not only difficult to ski, but downright dangerous to even consider traversing. After he got each machine up and running, he would do a few runs up and down the trails on his snowboard to see how the snow felt and reposition the guns wherever they seemed most appropriate. He would repeat this task several times until the crowds started to build up around eight o'clock, at which point he would head down to the shop for a break before tending to whatever needed fixing.

Sitting on the bench along the back wall of the repair shop, he watched the local news while eating some crunchy hash browns from the kitchen. He knew that they weren't the healthiest option, but he hiked and worked so much that he could eat pretty much whatever he wanted and just immediately burn off the fat build-up. Some weird things had happened to him over his lifetime, but he'd lucked out in the metabolism department.

A news alert suddenly appeared on the TV screen. "Earlier today along Route 2, just north of Mount Adams, a large section of trees was found to be on fire by a passing vehicle," explained a reporter standing before the charred remains of a small clearing. "As you can see, approximately two hundred trees were set ablaze randomly along the hillside with no clear evidence of what started it. Thankfully, the local fire crew resolved the issue before it could spread any further. The fire chief is investigating the matter and will not disclose any information pertaining to the case. An anonymous source within the fire department is telling us that arson by local teenagers is suspected. We'll follow up when we have more. Back to you in the studio, Dave."

Liam froze and just stared at the television for a moment. The image of the burnt trees, the pattern of the melted snow, and the charred remains of the vegetation on the ground looked all too familiar to him. He pulled out his phone, took a picture of the television screen, and switched over to a notes app to jot down pertinent details from what he had just heard. He would add this to his database later tonight. He couldn't miss a single scrap of data, no matter how insignificant it may seem.

After all that he had seen and experienced over these years, he couldn't take the chance that something was trivial. Over time, he had followed up on some leads that turned out to be bogus, but many turned out to be legitimate and fruitful to his investigation. He probably could have been an excellent police officer or detective if he didn't hate wearing uniforms or taking orders so much.

Finishing his hastily written notes, he slumped against the bench and sighed a little louder than he had intended to. A few coworkers cast subtle glances in his direction but said nothing. They knew that he had an odd past that he didn't elect to discuss, and they knew better than to press him. They looked at each other, gave questioning looks, and went back to their meals. Leaning his head against the wall, Liam looked up at the ceiling and closed his eyes. Another day had come and gone, and still the dragon was free.

Later that night, as he was unwinding before going to sleep for the night, Liam lay in bed and simply stared up at the ceiling. He may have had his eyes open and looking at the peeling white paint five feet above, but he wasn't registering anything in front of his eyes. He cycled through ten years' worth of memories, experiences, and thoughts. That first summer and all that had transpired. The attack. The aftermath. The deaths. The news anchors and their fabricated stories based on speculation. The trip with his father where they found no clues or traces of the damn beast.

He thought back to the summer afterwards in between his senior year of high school and freshmen year of college. After working the first month to earn enough money, he had travelled back north to the cave where he had first found the dragon and started his investigation from scratch. He had looked around for clues and evidence for several days before calling it quits. The trip had actually been rather productive, but ultimately didn't produce anything significant.

He had managed to pick his way inside after a solid day of manually excavating dirt and rocks from the blast zone of the pilot's rocket. The missile had weakened the cavern in various places, making it extremely dangerous. The alcove to the left where he had previously hid from the passing dragon's fire had caved in, sealing away those ancient weapons and armor. Carefully navigating around several boulders and avoiding an opened hole in the floor, he made his way back to the dragon's den. A large fissure had formed along the floor, sending the dragon's treasure hoard to the depths of the earth. All... except for one piece.

Liam touched the gold coin that hung from a chain around his neck. The feeling of its smooth edges and textured face was comforting to him. Not only was it historic and rather valuable, the coin was tangible proof of what had happened, a solid tether between his bizarre experience and reality.

Even after taking plaster molds of dragon prints and photographs of scrapes, burns, and bite marks in rock and wood, not a single person believed him. Everyone thought that he was crazy, despite the evidence and eyewitness accounts. The other witnesses to this atrocity were the saddest part of it all. Everyone else who he tried to contact were either denying that this ever happened, or under strict government orders to not speak of it. People who had previously discussed the matter with him openly the summer before were now no longer to be found or pretended that they didn't know who he was or what he was talking about. Somebody had gotten to them and forced them to remain silent... or disappear altogether.

This last aspect most of all made him nervous about continuing his search, and significantly slowed down his investigation during his time away at college. With his parents' advice and his own fears, he tried to literally forget about the dragon for several years and focus on his studies. It was impossible to do so, however, as the memories always crept back up to the forefront of his mind and pushed all other thoughts out of the way.

Once Liam had graduated and began working in the area, he once again dove headfirst into his research and continued to search the remote areas of New Hampshire and Maine for any clues that he could find. But after a five-year long wild goose chase, he was lonely and broke, with very little to show for his time and effort.

Both his mother and father had remained supportive, but even their patience had its limits. While they sent him some extra money in the beginning to keep him afloat, the money stopped flowing shortly after he finished his undergraduate degree. They tried to reinforce his need to establish himself professionally and wanted him to become self-sufficient. But it had been difficult for Liam to live on his own when his mind and budget were solely focused on this fool's errand. Now the topic simply wasn't discussed. Their conversations revolved around weather, hiking, politics, or whatever interesting project his dad was currently working on. The dragon and the attack from a decade ago became verboten topics in the Tryggvison household.

Unsure of what to do with his life and where to go from here, Liam began to think that this might have never happened, and perhaps he had made it all up in his head. With nothing to show for it all and nobody left to feign interest in the matter, he was contemplating giving up on it and starting fresh. Maybe he should go see a psychiatrist or a counselor, and get his head back on straight. Something needed to change.

CHAPTER FIFTEEN
MATERIALIZATION

Later that spring, after the winter had calmed down and the weather warmed back up again, Liam and his co-workers were going through their post ski-season rituals. The snow-making equipment was hooked up to ATVs and pulled back down to the base of the mountain for preventative maintenance work, cleaning, and storage. Basic landscaping was done to fix any areas damaged by mud flows as the snow and ice melted and pooled up around equipment and buildings. The chairs were pulled off of the lifts and the cables were inspected and tightened. From all outward appearances, it was just another spring as usual, and Liam was looking forward to a summer of hiking, kayaking, and enjoying the great outdoors, as always. He'd have to call his parents one of these nights to coordinate a good weekend sometime soon to meet up.

Liam was, for the first time in years, finally feeling free. He was gradually putting his life back together, and he had started meeting regularly with a counselor in Concord. She convinced him that the dragon attacks were not his fault, and that it was not his responsibility to give up his life and every fiber of his being to hunt this thing down. He started spending more time in social situations, and had made better friendships with some of the other workers at the mountain. He had even started going on occasional dates with girls that he met at the mountain and the local outfitter shops. He wasn't looking for anything serious, just yet, but it felt good to get out of the house and be around other people.

Stale air. Granite. Dirt. Decomposing life. Tryggvi tasted the air with his tongue as he opened his eyes for the first time in months. He looked around his current lair and detected no motion, nor any sign of disturbance since he had last laid down to hibernate for the colder months. The lack of any attackers or trespassers of significant bodily size was most likely due to his clever plan of blocking off his cave this time around. Previous encounters with inquisitive humans, bears, and other creatures enamored by the appeal of his domain had led him to value his privacy. When he had last gone to sleep in the fall, he had piled a number of boulders near the mouth of the cave, slipped by them, and then pulled them into place with his jaws to seal off the passage. He left just enough cracks in the walls to ensure the cave remained ventilated.

Stretching his neck and limbs, he felt several scales popping off and sections of his skin shed away. His body was slowly but surely replacing his outer protection to keep him rejuvenated and ready for the harsh New England environment. He shook his entire body, starting with his head all the way down to his tail, to fling off any remnants and further loosen his stiff body. Trudging forward, he approached the rocky door and nudged several of the boulders out of the way. Watching them fall forward and roll away, he carefully stuck his head out through the opening to see what was beyond.

It was nighttime, but the air was warmer on his face than he expected. It must be approaching summer, as the ground was mostly free of snow and the area in front of the cave was replenishing its plant life. Confident that it was safe to emerge, Tryggvi pushed the remainder of the rocks out of his way and walked out into the night. He lifted his head into the wind and smelled the cool, fresh air passing by and into his nostrils. He could smell animals in the vicinity, and if his memory served him correctly, it smelled like... whitetail deer. Feeling his stomach groan deep down in his torso, he decided that it was time to hunt.

Looking around at the hillside below him, he familiarized himself with the topography and decided on the best path forward.

Stretching his wings out to their full reach, he took several practice pumps to once again prepare his body for flight. Running down the grassy slope, he flapped his mighty wings, pushed off the earth below with all the strength that his legs would provide, and took to the air above.

The hunt had begun.

"Robert Grady?" inquired the stranger who just come through the door a few moments ago, after looking around the deserted bar and quickly finding its sole occupant.

Rob Grady, retired fighter pilot, continued to stare out the window next to his table. As he most often did these past few years, he was despondently patronizing his local watering hole and slowly but surely watching time tick by in front of him. Having just finished his shift at the air base for the White Mountain Rescue Crew, he was at his usual table, alone. It was a normal day, and he would drink away his paycheck until it was time to go home to sleep and do it all over again.

"Excuse me, are you Robert Grady, formerly of the United State Air Force?" the stranger asked.

"Yeah, who wants to know?" quipped the disgruntled pilot.

"That's classified, smart-ass," the man fired back. "And you should still have enough wits about you to show some respect when a colonel is speaking to you."

Triggered by years of experience and muscle memory, Rob nervously jumped out of the chair onto his feet and saluted. "Sir!" he shouted.

"As you were," said the man, identifying himself only by his rank. Watching Rob still standing nervously, he urged again, "Please, sit." He sat down in the chair opposite Rob, removed his cap and set it down in front of him. He also placed a folder on the table and kept his hands on top of it. "Officially speaking, I am not here, and this conversation never took place. Are you the Lt. Commander Robert Grady, who was honorably discharged eight years ago after a training accident which occurred in the woods of Maine?"

"I am," answered Rob, "but I can neither confirm nor deny my alleged involvement in any accident, sir."

"Good answer, and that's why I'm sharing this with you." The colonel pushed the folder across the table, spinning it around 180 degrees for Rob to read. "I have been tasked with following up on a number of recent sightings which correspond to the incident that took place ten years ago. The one that may or may not have ended with you ejecting from your fighter craft at two hundred miles per hour and stranding yourself in the middle of a forest."

Rob looked down at the folder in front of him and saw the words 'Classified' and 'Eyes Only' stamped on the cover. After glancing around the room for eavesdroppers, he opened the front cover and thumbed through the documents inside. There were eyewitness testimonies of encounters with a large creature, variously described as a snake, lizard, or dragon, as well as a number of photographs. Most of the photos were of footprints and markings on trees and rocks, but a few depicted the same creature he'd met in the air long ago...

What the hell was that?! Pulling back hard on the stick, Rob brought his jet around in as tight of an arc as this high-tech marvel would allow him to go. Streaking through the sky, he came around and lined himself up on the target once again. Squeeze. Squeeze. He pulled tight on the trigger, launching a stream of cannon fire upon the rock cluster where the creature was hiding. He couldn't believe that this thing shot fire at him. Dragons don't exist. Do they? Dodge. Swing around for another pass. This thing won't quit! Fire. Take the shot. Aim. Line up. Release missile. Missile away. How did he do that?

He blew the missile up in mid-shot . . . I need to get one through. One. Two. Go, go go! One down . . . one past. Agh, it hit the cave. Move, move, move. Getting hotter in here...oh God! The cockpit is on fire. Eject! Eject!

"Lt. Commander, are you in there?"

Rob jerked up from the photographs and realized that he had been day dreaming. Well, dreaming might not really be the correct term. He saw that the colonel was still sitting across from him, looking at him with a concerned look on his face. "Yes, sorry, sir," Rob said. "I was just . . . remembering."

"Yes, I can imagine," replied the colonel. "I was shot down a few times back in my day. It's not fun. But at least I had the luxury of knowing that my enemies were human, with predictable goals and actions. What you battled that day is unimaginable."

"Sorry about that, sir. I'm fine. What can I do to help?"

The two men spent the next few hours reviewing testimonies, photographs, maps, and other associated documents from the case. It brought back bad memories, but it was also cathartic for Rob to speak to someone who actually believed him. The colonel shared some off-the-record intel, but it was in piecemeal and barely gave Rob a larger glimpse of the situation. By the end of it, he didn't know much more about the case than he had earlier that day, but, he at least felt like he had helped it somehow.

As the colonel rose and gathered his belongings, Rob looked down at the folder and wondered if he was allowed to keep this information. Almost sensing what was going through his mind, the colonel quickly reached across the table, closed the cover, and tucked it under his arm. Giving Rob a stern look, he reiterated the fact that this meeting had never happened, and that he would be in a lot of trouble if he discussed any of it with anyone. With a crisp salute, the colonel left, and Rob slumped back down into his chair.

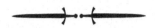

Later that same day, Liam came home from work and plopped himself down on the couch in his tiny living room. It had been a long day at the mountain, and he was glad to finally be back home. Popping the tab on the can of soda that he had just grabbed from the fridge, he took a long swig of the cool, sweet fluid as he swung his legs up onto the couch and stretched out. Grabbing his phone from the coffee table, he pulled up a browser window and accessed the website of the local news station to catch up on the happenings of the day. What he saw next made his heart skip a beat.

The homepage displayed a headline story with a large, vivid photograph of houses in flames. A small town just to the north had had ten homes set ablaze the night before. Police and volunteer fire crews responded from several nearby towns, but none of the homes could be saved. They primarily focused on rescuing the residents from the burning buildings and hosing down nearby houses to prevent them from catching aflame. At least two people were reported dead, but the officers were withholding further details. An eyewitness noted that at least one person was missing, possibly more. The fire chief suspected arson at this time, but they had yet to find any traces of an accelerant, how it was started or the motive behind the crime.

Liam spent the next twenty minutes rereading the article and absorbing the details. This felt all too familiar. He grabbed the remote and turned on the local cable news to see if there was anything else coming in to further explain the situation. He couldn't believe that this was all happening once again. Just when he'd put this dragon business behind him, he'd been thrown right back into the mix.

As the reporter was continuing his interview with one of the local volunteer firefighters, his phone screen switched from the article that he was reading to another view showing an incoming call. The number was unknown, but he recognized the area code and figured that it was somebody who he knew and just didn't have their number put into his contacts list. Hitting accept, he answered the call.

"Hello, this is Liam." he said.

"Is this Liam Tryggvison?" a voice asked.

"Yes..." Liam replied, but then paused. Who was this, and why the mystery act? "May I ask who's calling?"

"Not here, not now. It isn't safe," the caller said. "I'm assuming you just saw the news and have the same questions that I do. If you want to know more, meet me where it all began, two days from now, at noon. Come alone... and watch your back."

The call ended. Liam looked down at the phone for a few moments, his heart pounding. Curious, he grabbed his laptop and did a reverse search for the phone number. Sure enough, it was exactly as he had anticipated: a prepaid phone number with no way to trace it back to anyone in particular. Even if he tried to trace it back, the closest that he would get would be the place where the phone was sold. If this guy was smart, he would have paid in cash and left to trail to follow.

However, what the man had said lingered in Liam's brain. He called immediately as the news reported on the fire, a potential dragon attack, and then he said to meet where it all began. While Liam had never determined the dragon's true origins, for him it all had begun back in that cave in Maine. He just wasn't sure who knew that Liam had awoken the dragon, or how they would know where the cave was and his connection to it.

Then it hit him. He remembered the story about the jet fighter that was scrambled to the scene but failed to take the dragon out. He also remembered that the mouth of the cavern had been hit with a missile, mostly likely from that very same jet. While not a gambler, he would bet that this mystery caller was the surviving pilot. He saved the phone number as "P" for "Pilot" in his phone and pulled his laptop closer. He had work to do.

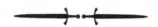

Two days later, Liam was bouncing down the same dusty road in Maine as on that fateful morning of his hike. He was a little nervous about this meeting. While he had a good guess, he was still unsure of whom he would be meeting.

He had, however, taken some precautions before heading out on this venture. He told his dad everything, including where he was going, and gave him the number of the man who called him. This way, at least, they could try to track its GPS signal if something happened. His dad, as always, wanted to be there with him, but Liam had assured him that he had a good feeling about this and wasn't worried. Somehow, he knew that the caller's intentions were sincere. He could hear and feel a familiar sound of guilt and regret in his voice when they talked. While he had only spoken a few words during the call, he had unknowingly communicated a lot more to Liam. He sensed that this man also blamed himself for everything that the dragon had done for the past ten years, and wanted to set right what had gone wrong.

Lost in thought, Liam was surprised to find himself at the trailhead. Bringing the pickup to a stop along the side of the road, he saw that another car was already here. It was unlikely to be a coincidence. There were no popular trails around here for miles. Liam had arrived an hour early, hoping to get a feel of the site before the mystery man showed up. Apparently, this guy had had the same idea.

Jumping out of the truck, Liam looked at the map and familiarized himself with the terrain. Not wanting anyone to get the jump on him, he spent the next hour blazing a trail through the forest in an unpredictable loop. It would take twice as long, and pass through more difficult ground, but he would come out from behind the bluff and see whether the man had set an ambush. Not wanting to waste any more time, he broke into a jog and made his way through the woods as quickly as his feet and the terrain would allow.

Thirty minutes later, he emerged from a cluster of trees just southeast of the entrance to the cave. Creeping through the low-hanging branches on his stomach, he got a clear view of the cavern entrance while minimally exposing himself to any onlookers. Sure enough, there was a lone man sitting on a rock near the mouth of the cave. He looked nervous and was glancing back and forth. He didn't appear armed or preparing for any kind of ambush on an unsuspecting visitor. Letting out a quiet sigh of relief, Liam felt better about this meeting already. However, he wasn't an idiot and decided to maintain his element of surprise in the situation.

Liam crept out from the cover, stayed low, and made his way around to the mouth of the cave while staying behind the man awaiting him. He wanted to get a good view of the man before announcing his arrival. Circling around, he was about thirty feet from the man, who was still sitting on the rock and holding his phone in his hand. He was about to call the stranger's phone, just to see if he'd honestly admit his location, when the man suddenly yelled out.

"I know that you're over there, Liam," the stranger said, mildly. "You can come out. If I were going to harm you, I would have done it long ago."

Liam froze in place. The gig was obviously up and the man somehow knew that he was here. But how? He had been so stealthy. He was like a hiking ninja. But he had no choice now but to face the situation head on. He double-checked that the knife was still clipped to his pocket and slowly poked his head above the rock. The man was looking down at the phone in his hand. He must have tracked Liam by his cell phone GPS signature.

Liam emerged from his hiding place and walked towards the man. "Sorry for the subterfuge, but I need to be cautious," Liam said. "Who are you, exactly?"

Relieved to see that it was just Liam alone, the man rose to his feet and put his phone away into his pocket. "My name is Rob Grady. I'm a former pilot with the Air Force."

"I knew it!" exclaimed Liam. "You fought him here, ten years ago, at this very mountain! I watched the aftermath on the news. But they've been very tight-lipped about it since."

"Yes, that was me. Although I wish that I'd been on leave that day," Rob said. "Nobody believes a word I say. But then again, I'm not allowed to say anything about it."

"Well, what can you tell me?" inquired the young man. "Or was this whole trip was for nothing?"

"Easy now," quipped the older man. "I didn't drag you out here for nothing. I couldn't say anything over the phone. They could be recording my calls. Ever since the first attacks, hidden forces have conspired to keep this quiet and out of the public eye. I'm surprised that you haven't been questioned more and eventually silenced, but it seems like you've done a good job so far of keeping a low profile. Others, sadly, have not been so lucky."

"What do you mean?" questioned the now very curious Liam. "What others?"

"Do you remember Mike, the guy from the airport?" Rob shook his head. "They got to him shortly after he handed information off to you at that cemetery. From what I have heard, he was a hard egg to crack and never gave you up. He hasn't been heard from in years. Same goes for his partner at the airstrip, and the farmers who got too mouthy on social media about their experiences. They pissed off a lot of high-ranking people by sharing photographs, video, and other so-called 'classified' information. As soon as people start talking... they just disappear. Your best bet is to keep your mouth shut and stay low until this all blows over."

"I can't," Liam replied strongly. "This is all my fault and I need to see this finished."

"I know how you feel, kid, but you can't take this thing on alone. Look, I tried to take it down with the military's most advanced fighter jet and it beat me without breaking a sweat. I shot fifty caliber bullets at it, even launched rockets to no avail. It's a giant, flying, fire-breathing lizard." Rob implored. "I came here to let you know that the Air Force is still investigating the case. Let them deal with it. Stay out of the way and you'll stay alive."

"I wish that I could," Liam muttered, "but that's not how I was raised. I will see this through, one way or the other."

The pilot quirked an eyebrow. "If you're really that committed, then let me help you," the pilot said. "I don't know how, just yet, but I've been brainstorming. This colonel is tailing me, and I believe that he's tapped my phone. Call me paranoid, but I think that they're keeping me on a short leash. For all that I know, they followed me here today. Keep your phone ready, and I'll call when I have more to offer. I'm going to head out now, taking a slightly different path back to my car. Hide under the trees over there, and wait ten minutes. Good luck."

And with that, he was gone. Liam stayed still for a while, deeply considering his options and trying to piece together some extra puzzle pieces that he had just picked up during his meeting with the Lt. Commander. Was this guy crazy, or did he just know more of the truth than Liam could fathom? The meeting had clarified some things while simultaneously adding even more confusion to the mix.

Checking his backpack and adjusting his boot laces, Liam gave a quick glance around, and up to the sky, before heading out. He made it back to the truck in good time, jumped in, and peeled off. It was going to be a long, nerve-wracking drive back home.

CHAPTER SIXTEEN
TUCKERMAN'S RAVINE

The next few months were uneventful. Liam saw nothing interesting on the news, and his connections in the hiking community offered no further clues. It was almost as if the dragon had emerged just to stretch its wings, eat a snack or two, and then disappear. But Liam knew in the back of his mind that this wasn't over yet.

Looking to fill his days with more hiking while helping out, Liam spent some time over the summer volunteering with the Appalachian Mountain Conservation. He purposely applied for a position that centered around Mount Washington and the other mountains within the Presidential Range. He loved hiking the region and spending time with other hikers and conservationists. Additionally, he could keep an eye out for evidence of dragon activity.

He spent his days hiking, cleaning up trails, kayaking nearby rivers and streams, and helping around the mountains and huts. All the while, he looked. He searched. He scanned the skies for any signs of impending doom. Light would hit the tree branches or leaves in a funny manner, and he would think that he had seen a shadow darting through his peripheral vision. It was a paranoid way to live, but he knew better than anyone that there was a killer out there, possibly just waiting around the corner. However, he had yet to see a single leaf out of place, stick burnt, or livestock kidnapped. Had the dragon just simply gone away?

Cold. Wet. The snowy winds whipped the mountainside with icy shrapnel and powerful gusts. It was winter in the White Mountains, and most living creatures were content to hide from the frigid climate.

There was one being, however, who still ventured into the hostile outdoors. Scanning the sky from the mouth of his cave, Tryggvi cautiously surveyed his new domain. While unafraid of the weather, he constantly watched the sky for flying intruders. The attack from that metallic craft years ago had left deep scars, both physical and mental on the dragon. He knew pain and was aware of his mortality. He had already died once as a human being. He knew that death could come for him in this form, as well.

Confident that no humans were nearby, Tryggvi took to the sky to hunt. It had been several weeks since his last meal, and his stomach ached for juicy meat. Watching the ground from high above, he swooped and soared back and forth over the nearby farmland in search of deer, moose, cattle, or horse. Even in this harsh environment, his prey would still need to wander out of their warm, protected habitats to find food. All of the above were delicious options and he would eat until his hunger was sated. Spotting motion on the side of a nearby ridge, Tryggvi dropped into a rapid dive and silently approached his next victim.

The next morning, Rob was working in the main hangar at the White Mountain Rescue Crew base. His job duties included coordinating flights with the other pilots and running rescue missions when needed. However, given his military background and extensive combat experience, he took on special assignments here and there. It also helped that he had a current special clearance level.

His job for this morning, and the next week probably, was receiving and decommissioning a donated helicopter from the New

Hampshire Air Force National Guard wing that was located a short distance away. They would often bring over equipment and vehicles that were no longer suitable for combat but still capable of helping with the rescue needs of the WMRC. This donation, however, was quite different than their normal deliveries. A flatbed truck waited outside of the hangar with a tired, but flightworthy, Apache attack helicopter loaded on the back.

Rob walked out into the bitter wind to meet the private driving the truck. After giving the helicopter a cursory inspection to ensure that the craft matched the description on the paperwork, he helped the driver guide the truck into the hangar and under the main rigging winch. Attaching the helicopter to the chain, they lifted it up from the flatbed and pulled the rigging materials out of the way. The truck then left the building, clearing room for the helicopter.

Closing the hangar doors as quickly as possible, he tried to preserve what little heat was still remaining in the cavernous space under the metal arch of the structure. Using the powered winch controls, Rob lowered the craft to the concrete floor. After removing the covers and extra gear put in place to protect it during shipping, he noticed something surprising. The helicopter had not been fully demilitarized. It was the correct helicopter, all right, but it still had three Stinger missiles mounted to the pylon under the left wing. This was highly against protocol. Somebody messed up big time, and it should have never been shipped in this manner. How this craft left the base like this was unimaginable and he was embarrassed for his former military branch over this breach of etiquette.

Picking up the landline phone receiver from its cradle, he started to dial the base commander when a thought crept from the back of his mind. This was exactly what he needed. If he were to take on the dragon someday, ordinance like this would be perfect. Granted, it was highly illegal. He'd go to jail if anyone from the military ever found out. But everyone there thought he was crazy and kept him under close watch anyways. He might as well see how far he could go on the way out.

Looking around to see if anyone else was here, he was relieved to see that he was alone. Casually walking over to his workbench, he grabbed his tools, walked over to the wing, and got to work removing the missiles. As he sat down on his rolling stool, and started in on removing the missiles, he looked around on the craft again and chuckled to himself. It was a shame that the person wasn't more careless and didn't also leave the rocket tubes and 30mm auto-cannon on the front.

Burying his hands deep in his pockets, Liam bounced from one foot to the other as he desperately tried to stay warm while he waited. Staring out into the vastness surrounding the mountain, which wasn't much given the roughly twenty foot visibility afforded in this weather, he started to regret volunteering for an extended stay at the Observatory on Mount Washington's peak. It was originally supposed to be just a summer gig, but he had a hard time saying no and liked his coworkers. Now, a few months later, he found himself part of the winter crew.

Hearing the crackle of a radio transmission coming through, Liam begrudgingly pulled his right hand from the protection of his jacket pocket, partially unzipped the front, and reached in to fish out the two-way radio clipped to his shirt. Zipping the jacket back up, he held the radio close to his ear. He could barely make out the words but heard something about a large creature by one of the huts and a fire breaking out in a storage shed. He glanced around the mountain to see if the hut in question was within visual range, but he still could see nothing through the snow and fog. Straining to hear anything else coming through the receiver against the sound of the roaring fifty mile per hour winds, he turned the volume up all the way.

Just as he was about to respond, Liam heard the distinctive rumble of a diesel-powered snowcat coming up the Auto Road.

This is why he was waiting out in the cold wind in the first place, so he was relieved to see the resupply vehicle arriving with their much needed food and wares. Given the elevation and weather conditions this time of year, the tracked vehicle was only way to get supplies up to the top of the mountain safely.

Staring off into the distance, he saw the outline of the vehicle approaching and jumped up and down a few times. A passerby might have thought that he was excited and jumping for joy, but really he was just making sure that his toes hadn't fallen off. Watching the vehicle finish its approach to the side of the observatory, Liam started to walk towards the cab to greet the two drivers seated inside the heated enclosure. He wanted to unload the gear quickly before calling back over the radio to see what was happening down below.

As he approached the driver's side door, he was suddenly engulfed by orange, yellow, and red light. Feeling his body leave the ground, Liam was thrown backwards ten feet and slammed into the wooden fence lining the edge of the road. Feeling something crunch in his left shoulder, he shielded his face with his right arm as bits of snowcat debris peppered his body and rained all around him. After a few seconds, he moved his hand from his face and looked up to take in the scene.

The snowcat was now a burning hulk of its former self. The frame, doors, and glass of the cab were gone, and the two drivers' bodies lay on the ground a short distance away. Whatever gear and provisions had formerly been inside of the vehicle were either vaporized or distributed around the epicenter of the blast. Still lying on the ground against his pained left shoulder, Liam glanced upward as a large shadow passed by overhead. He couldn't see much through the murky air, but he knew immediately what it was.

Appearing from thin air, a stream of fire blasted through the clouds and painted the side of the observatory in molten flames. The building, mostly steel and stone, dissipated the fire with ease. But some portions of the structure still burned after the dragon had flown away.

Realizing that he was a sitting duck out in the open, Liam quickly motivated himself to get up and move. But where should he go? There were only a few structures on top of the mountain, and unfortunately, the current target of the dragon's wrath was the place best suited to withstand the dragon's abuse. Going against his instincts, Liam ran towards the smoldering building while pressing the radio against his mouth.

"This is Liam Tryggvison, up on top of the Rock Pile," he shouted into the mouthpiece. "We're under attack from the dragon. Several are confirmed dead, and the Observatory is on fire. Send help now!" As he finished his sprint to the front door, he added, "And call Lt. Commander Rob Grady of the WMRC and get him through to me immediately!"

Soaring above the clouds, Tryggvi scanned the ground below in search of food. The winds buffeted him from side to side, making it difficult to keep a straight heading. He'd sometimes just let the wind take him where it may, but in weather like this, he could end up miles away if he failed to navigate effectively.

Over time, Tryggvi remembered more and more about his previous life. He could even understand things from the humans' perspective. However, he still was driven by his primitive instincts for eating, self-preservation, and survival. He wasn't sure what to make of it all, so he just tried to focus on staying alive in this harsh environment.

Staring through the foggy haze, Tryggvi noticed a four-legged animal walking along a rocky outcropping near a building down below. Banking to the right, he leaned into the wind and quickly dropped several hundred feet. He brought himself immediately behind the creature and just barely above the surface of the ground. Extending his wings to arrest his descent, he alighted gently on top of a large boulder.

Feeling that it was just within his reach, he opened his mouth and shot a few quick bursts of flame to roast his soon-to-be lunch. The first two blasts struck the animal in the side, but the third shot flew past the falling corpse and slammed into the building behind it. After vaporizing a section of the wooden wall, the fire continued to spread and scorch the hut. Unfazed by the collateral damage he had caused, Tryggvi jumped off of the boulder, landed onto the ground below, and proceeded to walk towards the dead animal to begin feeding.

Just as he bent down to begin consuming his latest kill, a human came running out of the building screaming and holding something black in its hand. A trio of loud bangs rang out as the dragon felt a succession of thuds against his torso. Wincing in pain, the dragon twisted his body and held an outstretched wing between his face and the attacker. Peeking past his wing, Tryggvi blasted dragonfire in the direction of the man.

Tryggvi watched in relief as the spray caught his body full on and threw him backwards into the side of the hut. The wall behind the dead man caught on fire as well, and proceeded to engulf the rest of the building. More people ran out of the hut as black smoke poured from the windows and doors. A group of brave humans approached the dragon with hiking sticks and knives.

Not wishing to fight any longer and simply looking to eat, Tryggvi let out a deafening roar at the tiny humans, grabbed the body of the deer with his claws, and took off into the air. Putting some distance between himself and the angry mob below, he rose higher to look for a quiet place to eat his meal. Flapping his wings harder as he ascended, he fought the thinning air for purchase in the thin atmosphere.

Swooping around an outcropping with his meal in tow, he was just ready to land in the fluffy snow and settle in when the loud roar of a mechanical engine startled him. Not seeing the vehicle in his way until it was almost too late, he practically barreled into the side of the snowcat and only managed to outmaneuver the roadblock thanks to releasing the deer into the foggy unknown below and pulling upwards as hard as he could. Soaring up and around too quickly, he proceeded to throw himself into a loop and found himself crashing back towards the ground and the vehicle all over again. Panicking from the forthcoming impact, he unleashed a fiery salvo of liquid destruction before him to remove the object from his path.

After flying through the smoky wreckage, Tryggvi again found his way blocked, this time by a large building. Reacting quickly, he let flow a gout of fire and soared upwards and away from the structure. Slipping just above the roofline, he circled around to get a better view of what had just happened.

Lying on his back, moving side to side across the span on the landing gear on his creeper, Rob was underneath the left side of the attack helicopter. He had moved it to one of the smaller bays about a month ago to keep it away from prying eyes, and had gone over almost every detail of the craft by now. He was currently doing some preventative maintenance work on the struts of the landing gear, lubricating the moving parts and checking for fatigue cracks in the support brackets. He was just about to roll over to the right side of the craft to inspect some rust spots on a steel mounting bracket when he heard the radio crackle in the background.

Pushing off of the underside of the helicopter with his hands, Rob slid out from underneath the craft and hustled over to the desk. He couldn't make out what the person on the other end was saying just yet, but, by the tone of her voice and the speed with which she was speaking, it was obviously important. Grabbing the two-way from the charging port on his desk, he brought it up to his mouth and said, "Rob Grady here. Shelley, is that you? Please repeat previous transmissions."

"Hi Rob, thank goodness. I didn't think that was going to be able to reach you," began Shelley, the communications coordinator for the AMC and liaison to the WMRC. "There's some kind of trouble brewing up on top of Washington. All I know is that a hut has been torched and the Observatory is partially on fire. Liam Tryggvison is barricaded inside with a few of the on-duty scientists. He says that they're under attack. He specifically asked for you to come and help."

Pausing before answering, Rob took a moment to let everything sink in and digest what he had just heard. *Liam was under attack, things were burning, and he requested my help. The dragon.* "Roger. Tell them that I'm on my way. I'll be there in less than ten minutes."

"Ten minutes?!" Shelley exclaimed, "You know that I said the top of the mountain, right?

"Yep, I've picked up a new toy that will get me there fast. I just need to top off the fuel tank and tighten a few things down," Rob said. "Give me a few, and I'll be off the ground in no time."

"Well, whatever you're doing, we appreciate the help. AMC Ground, out."

"Roger." Looking down at the radio, he couldn't believe that he was finally going to have the chance to take on the dragon once again. He could finally redeem himself for his mistakes ten years ago. He could finally make things right again. Taking a deep breath, he looked around the hangar bay to formulate his plan. It was time to get to work.

First, he needed to make sure that he had enough fuel in the tanks. He had kept the tanks mostly empty simply to aid in moving the helicopter around while working on it. Through his normal duties, he was taking it up into the air regularly enough that he wasn't worried about leaving the fuel in the tank for too long, but he also didn't want to blatantly horde valuable resources that the entire division needed for their daily tasks. After hooking up the fuel line, he ran across the floor to a nondescript section of the wall along the side of the prefab structure. To anyone not familiar with the way that these units were constructed, one might think that this was simply a wall panel with insulation behind it. However, in reality, it was a very slim section of empty space that was typically used as crawlspace storage for aviation packrats like him. Running his hands along the edge, he found the spring-loaded locking mechanism that he had previously installed, pushed in and up on it, and slid the section of metal out of the way.

Inside the space, he had stored what he hoped could turn the tide in this battle with the flying beast. Looking down at a blanket covered pile on the floor, he pulled the covering aside to reveal a rolling cart with the three Stinger missiles mounted onto its cradles. Grabbing the handles of the cart, he pulled it out of the storage area, wheeled it over to the helicopter, and prepared for combat.

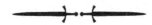

Bracing himself against the main load-bearing wall of the room that he was in, Liam scanned the windows across the building for signs of the enemy outside. From what he could tell, The Observatory was still on fire, and would probably remain so as long as the dragon continued to pour flames on it with each pass. Since he had taken shelter inside, the dragon had made at least six attack runs on the building with no apparent sign of letting up anytime soon.

While Liam was content to wait for an opening either to retaliate or escape, some of the scientists were getting a tad more unnerved about the situation than he appreciated. Just as he was about to get up to search the building for any weapons, the radio in his pocket began to crackle.

"This is Lt. Commander Rob Grady, incoming on an Apache helicopter from the west. Liam, do you copy?"

"Rob!" Liam exclaimed. "Thanks for coming up so quickly, we appreciate it. Stay on the lookout. The dragon has been making attacks passes across the roof here for the past twenty minutes. If he's not around here now, he will be soon."

"Copy, thanks for the heads up," Rob replied. "What's your status? Can you come out to meet me?"

"Uh, yeah, sure," Liam said. "But aren't you here to rescue us?"

"Not exactly, sorry, my friend," Rob started, "This helicopter only holds one extra person. I'm here for another reason. I'm going to try to touch down on the concrete outside in between the dragon's next attack. Come meet me, jump in, and I'll explain while we're in the air."

Although unsure of what Rob had in mind, Liam didn't really have any other options. After telling the scientists his plan, he zipped up his cold weather gear and prepared to run. He watched through the insulated window until he could see Rob's approach and then sprinted outside. Keeping his head low, he ran as hard as he could while scanning both sides and above, staying alert for the next attack. Thankfully, the dragon was nowhere to be seen.

Liam made it to the helicopter in a matter of seconds. Rob had mentioned acquiring a new craft, but Liam had no idea that it was this militarized. He expected some tiny used helicopter from a local news station. This thing, however, was ready to go to war. As he reached the cockpit, Rob raised the glass and yelled down for Liam to jump up inside. Rob was seated in the front position to pilot the craft, and had left the rear position open. Liam clamored up the side of the craft and quickly pulled himself into the cockpit.

Rob lowered the glass and rapidly shot the helicopter up and out at a 45-degree angle. Gaining altitude and putting distance between them and the burning building were Rob's primary objectives. Climbing high above the Observatory and fighting the near-continuous lateral winds slamming into the side of the helicopter, he turned 90 degrees to face the wind head on. This helped him to stay in position while minimizing the surface area of the craft affected by the wind. Peering out through the glass while keeping an eye on the radar output, the two men looked for any sign of the flying beast.

After a minute of hovering in place while trying to find the elusive attacker, they decided to keep moving so as not to become a sitting target for the dragon's next attack. Dropping into a slight dive, Rob took the helicopter through a wide arc around the summit of the mountain, scanning both sides of the glass for any sign of fire, flapping wings, or green scales. Over the roar of the engine behind his back and the chopping blades above, Liam spoke via the headset's microphone.

"Thanks for the rescue!" Liam cried out. "We were getting hammered in there. I don't see him anywhere around us. What's your plan if he comes back?"

"You're welcome! I'm happy to see that you're still alive," said Rob. "I was worried that I would not get up here quickly enough. My plan is simple: Shoot the bastard down. I tried to years ago and failed. I learned a little about his flight patterns and fighting style before, and I think that this time I'll be better prepared to predict and counter his moves now."

Too distracted by everything going on around the chopper, Liam hadn't even noticed the ordinance on the craft as he climbed up its side and jumped in moments ago. "What are you planning to shoot him with though? I didn't see an autocannon on the nose. Isn't this a rescue chopper?"

"Look out over the sides of the cockpit," Rob replied with a smile. "Those are Stinger missiles. They came with the chopper. I plan on firing these until I either run out or he's dead. I loaded one on the left and two on the right to spread out the weight."

Glancing around at the scene playing out before him, Liam started to ponder. There were still a lot of innocent people down there, not to mention the plants, animals, and natural wonders of the Presidential Range all around them. What happened if they missed? Where would the missiles go if they overshot the dragon? They could cause lot of collateral damage if something went wrong. These weren't just bullets. Stingers are highly explosive ordinance meant for taking down fighter jets. But coming to terms with the gravity of the situation, Liam conceded that this must be done.

"Awesome. Great work, Rob," Liam said. "These might just take him down. What do you need me to do?"

"Well, perhaps a dumb question, but have you ever fired a Stinger missile from an attack helicopter before?" Rob asked with a smirk, turning his head around in the cockpit to make eye contact with Liam. The younger man just stared back at him. "Yeah, I didn't think so. Well, you must have played video games when you were younger, right? Just grab the joystick and aim with the targeting computer on the display by your knees. Try your best to get a lock. I'll take care of the flying. We only have three missiles, so we won't get many chances at this. Hopefully you're good with on-the-job training."

Liam, despite the circumstances, kept his cool with the directions and orders coming from the Lt. Commander. As they flew, he played with the targeting reticle on the screen, practicing boxing in trees and rocks on the screen as Rob took them through some wide, sweeping passes of the mountains in their search for the creature. Would they ever see the dragon again? The monster had been gone for far too long. Something fishy was going on, and they were pretty sure that they weren't going to like it when they found out.

Perched atop the peak of nearby Mount Adams, Tryggvi watched the strange thing buzz around the top of the other mountain. It was unlike anything he had ever seen. Instead of big, long artificial wings like the other craft that he had seen, this mechanical creature flew with a whirling blur above it. It darted back and forth like a hummingbird, flying around the summit of the larger mountain. He was unsure what it was or where it came from, but he sensed that it was trying to hunt him down. Also, he felt that strange sensation again, like he knew it somehow. Something about that craft, or something in it, was familiar.

In any case, Tryggvi preferred to be the hunter, not the prey. The dragon leapt from the mountainside and rode a thermal updraft rising from the valley below. Pumping his wings lightly and infrequently to minimize drawing attention to himself, he banked to the left and swooped around to the right, trying to stay behind the craft and positioning himself outside of its field of view. He often enjoyed hunting with the sun up and behind him to help disguise his presence, but he wasn't afforded that luxury in this cloudy weather.

Coming up behind the craft, he still wasn't sure what to make of it as he approached. Deciding to move in closer for a better look, Tryggvi eased in beneath the craft and inspected it as he flew by. Allowing his body to drift left in the wind as he flew, he was able to look back and up over his right wing as he flew to check out the inside of the vehicle. He could see two humans inside the glass. Despite the fact that they were wearing helmets on their heads, he swore that he had seen them before.

Finished with his recon, Tryggvi dove to the left and disappeared into a cloud bank. Looping up and around, he stopped and hovered a quarter mile away and turned to look back. Surprisingly, he wasn't being followed. They must not have seen him.

"Did you see that?!" screamed Liam.

"I'm on it, I'm on it," Rob said. "And stop yelling so loudly into the microphone. I can hear you loud and clear."

Rob brought the helicopter to full throttle. He vectored them towards where the dragon had disappeared into the fog. While pushing through the thick, obscuring mist, Rob felt hesitant to keep this flying style up for long as he was going completely blind into an area that he knew to be deadly. While he was familiar with the topography of the Presidential Range, it was easy to crash or get momentarily lost while flying this quickly. Breaking through the cloud into an open pocket of sky, they found themselves alone with no sign of the dragon.

"Where'd he go?" Liam muttered from the back seat. Rob had no clue, and he didn't like that one bit.

Watching from high above, Tryggvi saw the humans break through the cloud formation below. They had followed him after all. "Why couldn't they just leave me alone?" he grumbled. All that Tryggvi had wanted to do that morning was to eat his fill of meat and go back to sleep. Battling some technological monstrosity had not been on the agenda. Still curious as to why they were following him, he decided to go investigate.

He tucked his wings close and flew in a tight loop to put himself just in front of the hovering craft. Stretching his wings out to their full length, he caught the air and brought himself to a rapid halt in front of the craft, about one hundred yards away. Flapping his wings just enough to stay in place, he stared through the glass of the cockpit and realized who these two humans were.

One was the boy that he had encountered several years ago, who had disturbed his hibernation. He seemed harmless enough. The other, however, was different. He remembered him. He remembered him very vividly. That man had flown in the fast craft that had tried to kill him with the exploding weapons. While Tryggvi had ultimately destroyed his plane, the human still managed to escape. Apparently, he was back to finish what he'd started.

While staring at the helicopter and remembering these events, Tryggvi noticed a cylinder on the side of the craft sparking to life. Without warning, it rocketed straight towards him. Instantly thinking back to those explosive objects that the pilot had last deployed against him, and how he had counteracted several of them, the dragon roared and expelled a billowing burst of fire.

Predicting what would come next, he entered a steep dive to get below the anticipated explosion. Sure enough, a moment later he felt and heard the shockwaves of a massive blast from above. "That was a little too close," he thought.

The rocket exploded closer than originally anticipated, and the two men felt the heat wash over the cockpit's glass. Thankfully, the helicopter appeared to have survived unscathed. However, they would need to play it safer in the future. Rob cursed their misfortune. First, they had just wasted one of their three missiles. Second, they had lost the element of surprise. Rob grinned darkly at his third thought. *Now the dragon will be hunting us.*

Gunning the throttle controls and banking around to the right, Rob put the craft into a long, arcing loop through the clouds and tried to spot their adversary. It was too cloudy to see much of anything, though, and the wind was hammering their craft. Without accurate radar, a visual line of sight, or thermal imaging, they were at a complete disadvantage. Rob wondered whether thermal imaging would even work, as the creature was more than likely cold blooded. They might only get a good thermal reading when he breathed fire, and at that point, it would already be too late.

Pushing the helicopter close to its maximum airspeed, he had almost circled the entire mountain but found no hints of the dragon's location. Starting a second orbit of the mountain, he noticed a faint hit on the radar screen. Watching the blips appear more frequently, Rob realized that it was coming right at them almost too late.

Banking the chopper hard to the left, he rolled sideways and dove towards the Lake in the Clouds hut. While doing so, the two men felt the temperature rise sharply in the metal below their feet. They didn't know it at the time, but the dragon had launched a stream of fire directly at the craft and only survived it because of Rob's quick thinking and swift maneuvering. They didn't get away completely unscathed, however. Unbeknownst to the pilot and gunner, the right landing gear had been melted away in the blast and the craft only had one leg to stand on.

Pulling back up while looking out the glass over his shoulder, Rob saw the dragon launch another salvo at them, and it appeared that he would hit the tail rotor. Adjusting the pitch of the main rotor blades, he allowed the craft to plummet several hundred feet in altitude. They dropped clear of the fireball, barely escaping a critical hit to their primary means of steering.

Changing back to a lifting configuration, Rob maxed out the throttle once again. They set off towards the northern side of Mount Eisenhower. Seeing the dragon following them in his rear camera, he maintained full power and put them into a tight loop around the peak. Swooping back around and putting them on a vector opposite of that from before, the helicopter continued onward to the Lake in the Clouds.

Looking behind, Rob noticed that the dragon had swung in far too wide of an arc around the mountain and was currently lost in the clouds. Not wanting to waste the slight advantage that they had gained, he brought the craft just up and over the hut and swiftly aligned the helicopter with the nook on the northwest side. Hovering just a foot or so above the rocky ground, Rob then gently lowered the helicopter to touch down on its landing gear. Feeling the slight crunch of stones underneath, he eased back on the angle of attack of the rotors to halt thrust and settle in. As soon as he reduced the vertical thrust, the entire body of the craft tilted to the right and crashed to the rocks and dirt.

"What was that?!" cried Liam from the rear seat, looking wildly left and right to see what had just happened.

"I'm not sure," said Rob, "but I'd bet my next paycheck that we lost the right landing strut when that jerk tried to fry us that last time. He probably melted the leg right off. It should be okay though. We didn't touch the building and the rotors still look good."

Completely cutting power to the engine, Rob tried to bring the helicopter to as silent of a state as possible to avoid further detection. While the building didn't completely block them from view, it would serve as a hiding spot while they formulated a plan. Rob hoped the dragon wouldn't realize that it was them behind the roofline.

They saw a radar blip of a large object coming northbound from where they last saw the dragon. They could just barely make it out through the glass cockpit over the ridge of the hut's roof. Unsure of what to do, Rob kept his hands on the engine controls, ready to bring the craft back to life. Liam waited at the weapons controls.

Flying towards the largest of the mountains once again, Tryggvi scolded himself for losing his prey so easily. How could he have lost that slow, lumbering craft? He knew he was so much faster. Following the smell of burning oil on the wind, he flew towards a building up on the spine of the mountain range. He couldn't see the craft or its human occupants anywhere.

Deciding to use the opportunity to catch his breath and recharge his body, he swooped low to the ground and alighted upon a pile of rocks down beside the larger of two frozen ponds. Crouching low to the rocky surface, he drank from a small break in the thin layer of ice. He then scooped a few fish with his lower jaw and swallowed his snack. Not exactly equal to the meal that he was missing several miles away thanks to the meddling humans, but it would tide him over for a while.

He raised his head and sniffed the cold mountain air for any trace of the humans. He could swear they were nearby. He just didn't know where.

The two men sat silently in the cockpit of the Apache. They were unsure of how much longer this could really go on for. There was nothing but a tiny hut standing between them and a centuries-old creature of unimaginable power. With only two missiles left, they were unsure if they would even get a chance to fire them. They watched the dragon drink some water, sniff the air, and even go fishing for a few minutes.

"This is getting ridiculous," Liam whispered. "I figured that he would have flown away by now to resume his search for us. He seems happy to just eat, drink, and relax by the pond. What kind of monster is this?"

"I'm not sure," Rob replied quietly, "but his actions, responses, and mannerisms seem almost human at times. It's wicked strange, I know that much at least." Thinking quietly for a moment, Rob decided that it was their turn to act and keep the initiative on their end. "Alright, here's what we're going to do. You keep yourself ready to fire. Arm the systems, keep your targeting computer ready to lock onto whatever kind of heat or motion signature that you can pick up, and I'll get you into a good position to fire. On my mark, I'm going to start the engine and bring this hunk of metal back to life. As soon as we clear the roofline, lock and launch the next missile. Once it's away, I'll put some distance between us and that thing. We might need to fire again or evade incoming return fire. Sound good?"

"Sounds as good as any plan that I'd come up with," Liam said. "Let's do it."

Looking down at their controls, both men flicked open all of the switch safety covers, got their hands into proper position, and mentally prepared themselves for whatever might come next. While their strategy was sound, a lot of their success hinged on their ability to take flight, climb at least ten feet vertically, and fire the missile before the dragon could respond in kind. While neither one said so out loud, neither man had a lot of confidence in this working out well for them. They would need a lot of luck, skill, and maybe some mistakes on the dragon's part to pull this off.

Looking out and around him, Tryggvi felt an odd sense of enjoyment being out here. He didn't know why and couldn't pinpoint exactly what it was about this place, but it felt comfortable and right. Something about the mountains, clean air, clear water, and a cool wind against his face felt good. He couldn't recall ever having this feeling before. Something in him felt different.

Bending his head down again to drink from the rippling water of the pond, he heard a loud, mechanical roar from behind. It sounded like that strange craft, but he couldn't see it anywhere. Whipping his head around, he scanned the cloudy, misty air for any sign of the craft. But it was nowhere to be found. It must be somewhere nearby. But where?

Just as Tryggvi was about to take to the sky to investigate, the noise grew louder and a black shape appeared above the adjacent building. As it rose into the air, Tryggvi realized two things. First, it was the helicopter that he was looking for. Second, another weapon was streaking towards him.

"On my mark," Rob said. "Three... two... one... Go, go, go!" The helicopter roared to life as the attack angle on the rotors changed pitch and suddenly provided upward thrust to the craft. The two men were planted down in their seats with the dramatic change in downward gee-forces. But they kept their cool and their hands on the controls.

As soon as they cleared the top of the hut's roof, Liam watched the targeting reticle lock on to whatever little heat signature was being produced by the dragon's body. While the beast was cold blooded, there must be some form of constant heat keeping the dragonfire ready to deploy. The helicopter's targeting computer successfully held onto the location of the dragon, which was uncharacteristically confused looking. In the past, the dragon would have tried to kill them immediately. Now, however, he seemed to stare right at Liam.

Liam thumbed the controls, finished the target lock, and announced the fire as he pressed the activation trigger. Looking out the side of the cockpit, he saw the back end of the missile housing shed off as fire erupted and propelled the missile towards their foe. The next few moments played out as if in slow motion in Liam's mind. The weapon cruised forward, leaving a trail of spent propellant and wispy smoke in its trail.

The target lock was perfect. The Stinger shot straight at the dragon with no apparent sign of deviating course. A smile crept upon Liam's face as he suddenly realized that a decade of his life may now come to a close and allow him to live normally again. Looking forward to that possible reality, he dreamed of someday putting this all behind him. He continued smiling as the missile headed straight for center mass of the dragon. There was no way he could miss this time.

As Tryggvi saw the expression on the human's face change, he knew that he was in trouble. The rocket was possibly too close to destroy with fire, and it moved too fast for him to fly away. But what could he do?

These thoughts transpired inside Tryggvi's mind within the blink of an eye. The dragon thought back to several centuries in the past when he'd first swam to catch fish in the stream outside of his first cave. He realized that the missiles only seemed to travel through the air. "Perhaps they cannot go under water," he thought.

Turning around and diving forward in one smooth motion, Tryggvi launched his massive body towards the pond and put his back towards the missile. Wrapping his wings around his torso and tucking his limbs in closely to his body, he dove towards the middle of the pond where the ice appeared the thinnest. In mid-dive, he rolled halfway over to have his back hit the water and ice first, and tucked his head up towards his chest to minimize injury upon impact. Completing the maneuver in the time that it took to reach the surface of the pond, he impacted on the ice, broke through with very little resistance, and plunged into the icy water below.

Feeling his chest constrict from the instantaneous change in temperature, he suddenly felt short of breath and instinctively sought to thrust his head above the water to breathe deeply from the mountain air. Fighting the urge to come up for breath, he looked up through the water at the scene above.

Watching the missile shoot through the space that he had previously occupied only a few heartbeats ago, he stared in amazement as the fire-trailing weapon scraped across the surface of the ice and deflected up into the air. While still over the surface of the pond, the weapon suddenly exploded several feet above his head. Although protected by the ice and water from the fiery explosion, he wasn't immune to the concussive shockwave of air that spontaneously expanded outward from the epicenter of the blast. In the blink of an eye, the shockwave travelled through several feet of air and slammed into the upper surface of the pond. The ice shattered into thousands of tiny shards and sliced through the water to the depths below. Tryggvi felt the wave ripple through the water and violently shove him to the rocky bottom of the pond. The ice shards peppered his scaly exterior, penetrating in multiple spots to the softer tissue below.

With pain shooting up and down his belly and limbs, and nearing the point of suffocation if he stayed underwater for much longer, Tryggvi flipped around and planted his feet into the rocky footing below. Standing up to his full height, he broke through the surface of the pond and filled his lungs with air. He would punish these humans for attacking him. He fired a long streak of blistering fire at the hut where they had hidden on the shore. The side of the building was quickly consumed in flames. While he continued his sustained salvo, he noticed in his peripheral vision that a group of humans had exited the building to inspect the commotion going on outside. At the sight of the dragon and the erupting fire, they scattered in all directions to escape the imminent doom that the dragon eagerly promised those who would cross him.

Ceasing the fire momentarily to catch his breath, Tryggvi looked up and around for any sight of the helicopter. He couldn't see it, but he could hear the distinctive sound of the engine echoing around the mountainsides through the clouds. Running through the water back onto dry land, he pumped his wings in rapid succession and took to the air in search of his attackers.

Watching the dragon dive into the water as the Stinger missile exploded over its head, the two men realized that the fight was far from over. "Get us out of here!" Liam yelled.

Agreeing entirely, Rob put some distance between them and the dragon while continuing to face it, watching for what might happen next. Slipping into a bank of clouds above and to the west of the now burning hut, the two men gave themselves a momentary respite as they thought through their next course of action.

"We need to get him away from these innocent people," Liam said. "I can't bear to watch more people die because of me." Looking at the radar in front of him, and conferring with his own mental image of the topography of the mountain range, Liam quickly formulated a plan. "Let's fly northeast and bring him into the ravine. Maybe we can box him in between the two bluffs and use our last missile there."

Seeing the merit in the idea, Rob nodded. They banked around towards the left to maximize their cloud coverage, and flew off towards Tuckerman's Ravine.

Tryggvi listened for the sound of the engine and could distinctly hear them travelling somewhere off to his right. Looking up, his keen eyes could just barely make out a shape moving through the clouds. Turning and lifting off in two powerful thrusts of his wings, he left the two ponds and flaming hut in the background and climbed in elevation. It was time to finish the hunt.

As Rob took the helicopter through the clouds and positioned himself for the next stage of the plan, Liam looked out the cockpit for any sign of the dragon. Not seeing anything, he checked the radar screen.

"He definitely took the bait. He's about a quarter mile behind us and gaining in altitude."

"I have an idea of how to get him into position," Rob said, gritting his teeth as he fought the controls to maintain some semblance of order in the high winds battering everything in their path. "Stand by on launch controls, and be ready for my signal."

The plan, while not guaranteed to any degree, was fairly straightforward. The two men would bring the helicopter through the natural features of the mountain range, try to gain some distance from the dragon during the maneuvers, hopefully tire it out in the pursuit, and then strike as soon as it entered the ravine. Rob would need to push the Apache to its absolute limits during this process if they hoped to survive. With only one Stinger missile left, no other forms of armament, and no hope of backup in the near future, this was their only viable option.

Pleading with the engine for additional output, Rob quickly banked to the right and rapidly dropped in elevation. His intent was twofold: throw the dragon off of their scent for a few seconds, if they were lucky, and pick up some extra airspeed during the drop. Holding on tight, the two men plunged down to the forest below near Glen Ellis Falls. Looking over his shoulder, Liam could see the outline of the dragon following behind them.

"He's still on us, but it looks like you bought us a little time," said Liam. "He's far enough behind that with a few of your aerial shenanigans, we should be in a good spot when we get to the ravine."

"If we're still alive by then..." Rob muttered. "Hold on!"

Skimming the treetops, Rob pulled back hard on the stick and brought them up and to the left through Pinkham Notch. Continuing the maneuver, he barreled straight up through the Gulf of Slides, only inches away from the branches below. He wanted to give the beast as little room to move back there and minimize their target profile. Hearing an abrupt roar from behind them, the men realized that their advantage over the beast was dwindling.

Liam watched as the dragon belched a flurry of fireballs at their tail. Acting as a spotter, he helped Rob dodge the ones that came too close. Wincing as he watched a few trees nearby catch the attacks intended for him, he saw many of them instantly catch fire and continue to burn. He hoped that it would die out quickly in the wind and not spread into the forest around them. It wouldn't be much of a victory if they set his favorite mountain on fire.

Another blast came rocketing towards the rear of the helicopter. Rob tried valiantly to juke to the side to let it slip by harmlessly, but Apaches were not designed for this level of fine handling. The fire grazed past the tail of the craft and licked the rear rotor with its deadly flames. Looking back, Liam couldn't see any immediate signs of damage to their vehicle aside from burns and peeling paint. They might just get through this after all.

These humans were unbearable! Tryggvi roared at the tiny, meddlesome creatures ahead of him in that aerial abomination. Letting off a near relentless bombardment of the air around the craft, the dragon poured on a lethal level of fire in their direction. He had never wanted to kill something so badly in his life. Hadn't this day merely begun with him just hunting for some food, and now he was fighting for his life?

Skimming the tree level trying to stay as close to the craft as possible, Tryggvi dodged several of the taller trees that were in his path. Watching the mountain come up in front of them, he pulled up on his body and pumped his wings harder than ever to gain some elevation as the ravine climbed up towards the spine of the mountain range. He watched the helicopter climb up the face of the ravine, shoot out into the open air, pass around Boott Spur, and nearly come to a complete stop. Twisting in midair, the craft banked sharply to the right and dove down into the next ravine. As the helicopter disappeared from view, he was rewarded with a promising sign: a trail of smoke was now erupting from the end of the craft.

Using his momentum, Tryggvi continued to climb and follow in the helicopter's path. Fighting the winds pounding him from the North, he overshot the turn and looped around the smaller peak. Shooting across the almost flat terrain between Boott Spur and the summit of Mount Washington, Tryggvi approached the lip of Tuckerman's Ravine and dove over the edge in pursuit.

"Woah! What is that?" exclaimed Rob from the front seat.

"What's wrong?" As soon as he asked the question, Liam suddenly felt a jolt come from the rear of the helicopter, followed by a muffled cyclical thumping sound reverberating through the frame of the craft. Looking back over his shoulder, he saw dark black smoke spitting out of the rear rotor assembly. "It looks like something exploded in the motor assembly back there. The rotor is still spinning, but something's definitely wrong."

As he gave Rob this update, the helicopter began to spin slightly around the axis of the main rotor. Without the rear rotor contributing its lateral thrust to counteract the resultant rotation from the main rotor, the helicopter would begin to spin uncontrollably.

"I'm losing full control of our orientation. I can still fly this thing, but it'll be tough to keep our bearing true." Rob explained. "I'll try to get you into a good position. But I can't promise much."

The attack helicopter raced past the icy face of Tuckerman's Ravine. Pouring extra power into the rear rotor, Rob kept his hands tight on the controls to try to keep their path as straight as possible. Diving towards the bottom of the ravine, he pulled back on the control stick and leveled the craft out with the snow at the base and shot forward.

"Get ready to shoot as soon as I spin us around!" Rob yelled into the helmet's microphone. Letting off the rear rotor control, he let the helicopter spin around 180 degrees so that they were facing back towards the wall of the ravine. He pulled hard on the control stick to point the nose of the helicopter back up towards the lip that they had just shot over. Looking up through the glass of the cockpit as the nose climbed higher, they saw the dragon soar over the lip and drop down towards them.

Its body was growing larger in their field of view as the milliseconds ticked by. As the complications of what was unfolding in front of them came to light, both men felt time slow down as their instincts and years of experience kicked in. Rob feathered the rotor controls to keep the helicopter in place and pointed upwards towards the dragon. As the targeting reticle on Liam's screen hovered into place and boxed in the dragon, he saw fire beginning to emerge from the black depths of the monster's throat.

Liam squeezed the firing trigger just as the roller bearings in the overheated rear rotor assembly finally gave way. Without proper support, the shaft spun off-center and created an unpredictable thrust vector for the pilot's controls. The minor change in axially orientation of the assembly was enough to kick the rear end of the craft a few degrees to the side and sent the missile a few inches off course.

As the Stinger streaked past and flew straight up the rock wall, the dragon had only a few seconds to react. A quick roll to his side brought him just barely out of the missile's path. Before it could loop around to reacquire its target, it slammed into the rock face just below top of the ravine wall.

Watching the missile streak upwards and miss, Rob grabbed the control stick and yanked back hard and to the right. Pulling the craft up and around, he got the helicopter moving as quickly as possible down the length of the ravine to escape the dragon.

Seeing the missile launch from the aircraft, the dragon swallowed his fire back down and twisted his body to try to dodge the oncoming impact. Tryggvi feared that he was dead on the spot, but then felt the weapon streak past his back. Unable to believe that he didn't just die, he puffed out his wings slightly to slow his descent and looked over his shoulder while still falling towards the floor of the ravine. Seeing the missile explode against the rock face, Tryggvi turned back towards his target and prepared to pull up before reaching the snow and rocks below.

High above him, the missile's detonation crumbled the rock face of the ravine and hurled a shower of rock, snow, and ice outward from the wall. Hundreds of tons of deadly debris tumbled down the rock face, quickly catching up with the speeding dragon. Unaware of the impending doom chasing him down, Tryggvi continued down on his intended path and prepared to launch another salvo of fiery death at the escaping helicopter. Opening his mouth to resume his attack on the two humans in their mechanical bird, hopefully for the last time, he let out a cry of pain as a thousand sharp objects pummeled his body from above.

Caught by surprise, the dragon was immediately winded and wracked with pain. He looked up over his shoulder to face a blizzard of falling rock and ice. Unable to react in time, he slammed into the snowy bottom of the ravine and crashed down amongst the raining boulders and ice that fell from high above.

On their rear monitors, the two men watched as the rubble fell upon the dragon. Almost at the bottom of the ravine, Rob struggled with the controls and managed to spin the helicopter around to face the rock wall once more. Rock and debris of varying compositions continued to rain down on the bottom of the gulley for almost another minute. Fighting to maintain a steady path, Rob brought the aircraft closer to the rubble and climbed twenty feet in elevation.

The two men could barely see any trace of the dragon below. Just its tail and the tip of a wing could be seen through the mess, and neither were moving. Where other people might have cheered in this situation, both men merely slumped into their seats and breathed a sigh of relief. As they sat and watched for any sign of movement coming from the rubble, the occasional rock would fall down the face of the ravine and bounce about. Dust continued to billow out from the site, but was instantly pushed away from the downward thrust of the helicopter's rotor wash. Looking up, the sky began to open up with a heavy snowfall, which quickly turned to sleet. The wind was picking up, and Rob had a hard time keeping the helicopter in one place.

"Let's head back to the hangar and call this in. There's nothing else we can do until the weather lets up. We can come back up tomorrow when things calm down."

Reluctant to leave just yet, Liam was having extremely mixed feelings over the outcome of this decade long adventure that this dragon had added to his life. While he had been fully prepared, and willing, to kill the creature, he was almost sad to see it end. Despite the death and destruction that the dragon had wrought upon countless people and animals, and the unknown collective destruction of personal and business property around New England, it was still a unique living creature. Silently agreeing to head back, Liam leaned forward over the seat and patted the pilot on the shoulder.

Rob spun the helicopter around and nursed the shaking aircraft back to the WMRC hangar below. As the whirl of the rotors faded into the distance, the snow continued to fall on Tuckerman's Ravine. Soon, all traces of the day's events were hidden from view.

AFTERWORD

As the moonlight fought to shine through the thick haze of the sleet pounding into the White Mountains that evening, a bright beam of light blasted through the air. It danced from side-to-side before settling on the pile of debris at the bottom of the ravine. Where the traditional 'snow arch' would eventually form in the spring, a large pile of detritus had inexplicably materialized in the past few hours.

Looking through the thermal imaging camera mounted on the tripod on the side of the Chinook helicopter, the Colonel scanned the area and found what he was looking for. Pressing the microphone button on the side of his helmet, he said to the pilot, "It's there, in that pile of snow. Take us down!"

ACKNOWLEDGEMENTS

I couldn't have written this without the love and support of my wife and best friend, Kristin. What started as a fun diversion quickly turned into a full-blown hobby. Thank you for the months of putting up with me while I wrote, bounced ideas off you, and kept you apprised of what sorts of adventures our son fictitiously was up to that day.

Thank you to Wilfried Voss for your advice and kind words as I ventured into the writing world. Your experience and help in pointing me in the right direction was invaluable. Thank you to Tom Willkens for keeping my words straight and making me sound like a seasoned author.

And to Liam, my best little buddy. It is for you that I wrote this story. I can't wait to read this together with you someday and take you on our own adventures around New England and beyond... especially if there are dragons to see.

About the Author

Tim Baird spends his days exploring the world of mechanical engineering through product development and industrial automation systems. Volunteering with children in several youth robotics programs, he is trying his hardest to avoid growing up, one robot at a time. Writing has been a life-long interest which has now turned into a full-blown addictive hobby. Please enjoy the fruits of that labor.

When he's not designing or writing, he enjoys time at home with his wife & son, watching/reading anything Star Wars related, and spending time out in the woods of New England.